HIDEOUS Beauty

"The UK finally has an answer to Adam Silvera." *@elfcouncillor*

"A touching tale of LGBTQ+ identity with an intense, emotional mystery...poignant and powerful." *@bradleybirkholz*

"Beautifully written and unpredictable." *@faridahlikestea*

"Had me completely hooked in a way that only the likes of Adam Silvera and Karen McManus have managed." *@LoofyJ*

"I love love love this book. Buy it, read it, support it. Brilliant, realistic characters; excellent queer representation; thrilling mystery; important themes; beautiful writing. Essential reading." *@nocaptainreuben*

"A mystery with same sex kissing. Lots of kissing. Heartbreakingly good." *@PewterWolf*

"A thriller like nothing I have ever read before... A beautiful, horrific, funny, sad, hilarious and tragic story. I implore everyone to read it." *@DMan1504*

"A brilliant reminder that regardless of our orientation, our race, our gender, our upbringing...we are all dealing with things, and we   hat

HIDEOUS Beauty

WILLIAM HUSSEY

USBORNE

In memory of Marilyn Hussey.
I think you'd have really liked this one, Mum

First published in the UK in 2020 by Usborne Publishing Ltd., Usborne House,
83-85 Saffron Hill, London EC1N 8RT, England. usborne.com
Usborne Verlag, Usborne Publishing Ltd., Prüfeninger Str. 20, 93049 Regensburg,
Deutschland, VK Nr. 17560

Text © William Hussey, 2020

The right of William Hussey to be identified as the author of this work has been asserted by
him in accordance with the Copyright, Designs and Patents Act, 1988.

Cover image © Getty Images / Mantas Kristijonas Kuliesis;
Type © Shutterstock / Epifantsev;
Back cover; Trees/lake © Shutterstock / PhotoVisions, Ripples © Shutterstock / BMJ
Couple © Shutterstock / Prazis Images

The name Usborne and the Balloon logo are Trade Marks of
Usborne Publishing Ltd.

A CIP catalogue record for this book is available from the British Library.

ISBN 9781474966177   05345/4 JF AMJJASOND/21

Printed and bound in Great Britain by CPI Group (UK) Ltd, Croydon, CR0 4YY.

MIX
Paper from
responsible sources
FSC® C020471

TRIGGER WARNING

Hideous Beauty is a work of fiction but it deals with many
real issues including grief, trauma, drug use, cancer,
physical and sexual abuse.

Links to advice and support can be found
at the back of the book.

NOW: Thursday 2nd April

1

El makes the suggestion and I bury my face in my hands.

"Are you seriously trying to kill me? Honestly, I'd like to know, just so I can decide who gets my stuff after I'm dead. To you, Ellis Bell, I leave my complete comics collection, plus this sweet middle finger, which I'm flipping you as we speak. I also hereby return all the drawings you've ever given me. You'll find the *really* filthy one taped under my desk drawer."

I pull my hands away and give El a sidelong smirk. He smirks back. And I know I've already lost the argument, because his smirks are in a different league and complemented by these huge brown eyes that compel you to surrender.

"C'mon." He rocks my shoulder. "Don't be a drama queen. It might be fun."

"Dude, I have had more than enough 'fun' for one day."

And that might be just about the greatest understatement in human history.

El sighs and turns his belching, beat-up old Nissan Micra out of my drive and onto Denvers Row. I watch his long dextrous fingers grip and slide and tube the steering wheel, and my stomach flips. Just a little.

"El," I say warningly, "this is the way to school."

"So anyway, I thought your parents took it pretty well," he says, deflecting like a pro. "Your mum laughed and clapped her hands like you'd just farted pixie dust out of your arse and your dad actually gave you a hug. Sort of. Honestly, was that a hug or was he burping you? I don't think I've ever seen anything so awkward. Oh, and by the way, I saw that brother of yours checking me out *again*. I'm not sure what creeps me out more, Chris lusting after me or that immense pube thing your mum keeps on the dining room table."

"First" – I raise a finger – "that is one of my mum's decorative sculptures. She made it at her art class last week, and she's very proud."

"Hey, I'm not judging. As far as immense pube things go, it's a keeper."

"Second," I say, forcing my lips into a straight line, "Chris is most definitely *not* into you. You embarrassed him fairly spectacularly at the Berringtons' barbecue, remember? And he has a girlfriend. Third girlfriend this year, in fact."

El shrugs and takes another turn towards school. "It's true," he says quickly, cutting off my latest protest, "that 'Chris' is the least gay name your parents could've come up with for their firstborn. But three girlfriends in twelve months? That's protesting way too much."

"And your gaydar is never wrong, I suppose?"

"Not where McKees are concerned. By the way, while we're talking names, with 'Dylan Lemuel Jasper' they were just asking for trouble. But I guess they're so hip and tolerant and everything, they actually wanted their second son to be at least a little flouncy."

"Flouncy?" I shake my head. "That's coming from *you*?"

And just like that the mood changes. It's the kind of jackknife switch around that might give anyone else whiplash, but after all these months of secret dating, I'm used to El's rhythms. He loses the adorable grin for a second and one of those strong, gentle hands reaches across the space between us, his fingers interlacing with mine. He draws my palm to his mouth and kisses it. I decide a millisecond beforehand that my stomach will *not* flip. Not this time. Not *every* time. Come on, it's getting ridiculous.

It flips.

"Dylan, I mean it. Your mum and dad? That was pretty awesome. I don't think you even realize how awesome. You told your parents who you were and you got to leave

9

the house with all your teeth. It's one up on my coming-out story, anyway."

I blink hard and cup the line of Ellis's jaw. He nestles his face into my palm. El very rarely cries, even when he has every reason.

"You know," I say, "I'm always here if you—"

"I know. But I've told you most of it anyway, and I had the dental work done the same day I moved into this cheesy little town. And, honestly, McKee D, a lot of rancid water has gone under that particular bridge; I don't really fancy wading back into it again."

He smiles. A strained grin so big that it reveals his pearly whites all the way to the back molars, like he's a living advertisement for the Ferrivale dental surgery. His teeth are perfect. Of course they are. He's Ellis Maximillian Bell. By the way, Maximillian? That's one of the few things about my boyfriend I haven't been able to figure out. From what I know of his parents, it seems unlikely they took *that* much trouble over his middle name. In fact, having to come up with a first name was probably a chore for which they never forgave him. My theory is El took Maximillian for himself, claimed it and owned it, and that it's as recent as last December, when Mr Morris introduced us to the main characters of the French Revolution and El became fascinated by the rebel leader Maximilien Robespierre. For all of a fortnight. El's passions are intense but fleeting.

Except, I'm happy to say, in my case.

My boyfriend. Weird how new that still sounds. I roll it around in my head for a bit. I like how it rolls, smooth and easy and natural. Okay, so he's been my boyfriend for quite a while, but as of tonight, it's official. My brother knows. My parents know. The world, or at least my tiny corner of it in Ferrivale, knows. It's thanks to some sweaty-palmed pervert at school who caught us unawares with his smartphone, then posted us all over Instagram. Honestly, I guess I should thank our friendly neighbourhood pornographer. His shonky camerawork gave me that final push when nothing else could. I had to bite the bullet and come out to my family.

El never understood what my problem was with telling the folks, and I guess to an outsider – especially one with El's family history – it must have looked unnecessarily cowardly. But you see, things aren't always as people make them out to be, and that look my parents exchanged when I told them, the look El didn't catch?

Well.

"Suh-*oooooo*," he prods, "can-we-can-we-can-we-can-we?"

I claw my fingers down my face and moan. If I really put my foot down he'll turn us around, I know he will, but here's the thing: scared as I am – freaking *petrified* as I am – I'm also kind of curious. So I admit defeat and give him the nod.

"Huzzah!" We've stopped at a junction and El paddles the steering wheel with his palms. Then, digging into the pocket of his perfectly contoured charity shop jacket, he takes out a lipstick and puckers. "Ellis *will* go to the ball!"

Less than a minute later we're screeching into the school car park. El's almost five months older than me and handles his Nissan with the air of a racing driver. He's even taken the "Unteachable Twonk" (yours truly) out for a few jittery lessons. In my defence, he's not exactly the most conscientious teacher. I still have no clue how to parallel park or even change gear smoothly, but he's done his utmost to pass on the über-important skills of handbrake turns and burning rubber. Among other things. I think back to our first driving lesson in the empty car park of the old MegaDeal supermarket at the edge of town, and a delicious heat prickles my cheeks. I learned a few things that night, none of them in the Highway Code.

El hurtles us through the gate and aces a ninety-degree handbrake turn before parking in front of Miss Harper, Grand High Dementor of the geography department. She gives him the kind of look that could suck the soul from a muggle at fifty paces. Then she sees who it is, and smiles like someone's just offered her a hamper full of kittens. I'm not sure whether she'd choose to pet them or eat them, but still.

"Looking fox-*haaaay*, Miss H!" El kind of dances around

her as we pass, and she giggles. Actually giggles. Jeeze. "You've done something with your hair. *Fssssst!* Hot as."

The fevered rat's nest atop Miss Harper's head has been a fixture ever since my arrival at Ferrivale High seven years ago. It probably predates even those long-ago days and has its roots way back in the dim and distant mists of her supervillain origin story.

We don't have tickets but such formalities are for mere mortals. Approaching the doors to the gymnasium, El beams a gigawatt grin that sets Katie Linton, Suzie Ford and the rest of the Easter Dance organizing committee swooning. Even Gemma Argyle gives him an indulgent smile. I roll my eyes as they usher us through. Jesus, are they just not getting the subtle signals El sends out? The ones that murmur, oh so softly, *GAAAAAAAAAAYYYYY!*

The bass hits us as we push through the swing doors. The usual stale funk of the gym is complemented tonight by some painfully perky pop. Ellis probably knows the name of the band, the members' ages and star signs, their favourite junk food and any scandalous rumours doing the rounds. I, meanwhile, have the musical tastes of a great-grandfather and anything post-80s Madonna might as well be ancient Sumerian as far as I'm concerned. Despite knowing this, and that I have all the co-ordination of a freshly ejected baby giraffe, El grabs the collar of my black T-shirt – always black, saves the headache of fashion

– and drags me through the crowd.

"Ellis, what the hell?" I seethe into the back of his neck.

"Stop it," he laughs, swatting my breath away, "tickles."

"I'll do more than tickle in a minute!"

He plunges us onto the sparsely populated dance floor, planting his hands on my hips, turning me to face him, drawing me close.

"Promise?"

And screw Ellis freaking Bell and his freaking gorgeous grin.

My stomach flips again.

Okay, Dylan, this is it. No going back. The closet door is firmly barred behind you, chained and bolted. No re-entry, no refunds. It's gay all the way from here on out. I'm guessing that at least fifty per cent of my classmates have now seen me doing the naked fandango with a guy anyway, so I can't pretend Catwoman does it for me any more, no matter how much she kicks ass. My heart feels light and fluttery, hardly there at all, but El's hands are strong and sure on my hips. I don't look around; I keep my eyes fixed on his.

Deep breath.

Here goes.

It's time to see what Ferrivale High makes of the new (improved?) Dylan McKee.

2

"You are, aren't you?" I whisper into his neck. "You are trying to kill me."

"Relax," he whispers back. "And know that, if you try to run, I *will* trip you."

The whole thing's happening so fast that I sort of forget to be petrified. Here we are at school, and I'm out, and El hasn't given me a moment to be scared. I suddenly realize this has been his plan all along. It's the last day before the Easter holidays. If he hadn't insisted on coming to the dance, storming us inside before I could catch my breath, I'd have had the whole break to worry myself stupid. This way, at least we'll get it over with. And so, yeah, I've got to hand it to my boyfriend: he is sort of a genius.

We dance on. Strobe lights from the disco heliograph across El's trademark pearls, picking them out in greens and blues and yellows. I don't think I've ever seen him without them. Those pearls are El's insistent, glorious flourish; his little wave to the world that says he is who he is, like it or not. They are also freaking cool! I love his pearls. I love his long graceful neck and the dark pixelation of stubble around his jaw and his sharp cheekbones and his sleek black curls and his strong hands in the small of my back and…

Him. I love him.

I love you, Ellis.

I love him so much that my fear vanishes. They know, all of them. Even if they didn't get to see the video on Instagram before the mods took it down this morning, it will have been downloaded and shared a hundred times by now. When the internet has got hold of your left nipple, a little of your right butt cheek, and your face screwed up in what is either full-on ecstasy or chronic constipation, it will never let you go.

But we dance, and I watch the faces that know go by, and I just don't care.

"Kill me now," I say, and don't mean it at all.

"Why would I kill you?" he murmurs. "I've only just found you."

The rhythm changes, the tempo ramps up, and he pushes us very gently apart. He's still dancing, but whatever I've been doing – it can't by any definition known to the human race be called "dancing" – stops. I just sort of stand there, swaying.

"What do you mean?" I mouth back. I can hear him perfectly but feel I have to mime because I'm now so lost against the music. "You found me ages ago. Last November. The bonfire. A Diet Pepsi and the school band and Alistair Pardue flat on his arse. Remember?"

"I'll always remember. But I really found you tonight, Frecks."

The tempo slows again and he pulls me in, tighter than before. El's a good head taller than me and I love it, how our bodies just kind of fit together, like they were made that way. And right then I think: *Screw every single evil knuckle-scraping bigot who screams "God hates fags!" If there is a God, then he made us to fit, El and me.*

His chin grazes softly against my cheek and the crest of freckles that earned me one of my El-brand nicknames. Frecks, the Unteachable Twonk, the Prof, and McKee D – the last because of my notorious (in El's eyes) love of all junk food.

"I found you tonight when you became you," he goes on. "When you told them."

He's right. I breathe. *I am me.* Totally me in a way I never thought possible before. And I don't care any more that I can't dance and that there are people lounging against the monkey bars whispering behind their hands and laughing at us, and that a single barked "QUEERS!" erupts when the song dies down. In fact the word's a prompt and I do something I would never have thought possible twenty-four hours ago.

I stretch up onto my tiptoes, throw my arms around his neck, and kiss Ellis.

Right there, in the gym of Ferrivale High, in front of our classmates and teachers, I snog the ever-loving face off my boyfriend. I'm still so new to kissing that I forget to close my eyes for the first few seconds, and I see El's lips hitch up at the corners. But then he gets lost in it too. He stops smiling and I shut my eyes and he cups the back of my head and I kiss him until my toes hurt. And yeah, I can still hear the giggles, but they're background music to the background music. They're tiny. Minuscule. Hate at the atomic level. They don't matter. And anyway, I also hear a voice call out: "Woooohooooooo! Go for it, McKeeeeee! Kiss that sexy centre-forward!"

A few whoops and a round of applause greet this encouragement, and then a hand falls on my shoulder.

"That'll do, gentlemen."

Mr Robarts, head teacher, looking ultra-stern. I blink up at him and he has this crappy *I'm certainly not approving of this kind of behaviour* face on. It's crappy because a second later it completely falls away and he hasn't a hope of suppressing a small smile. He pats us both on the back.

"Okay, lads, dance away, but try to keep it vaguely PG, will you? I would still like to have my job on Monday morning, and if some of the virgins get jealous, I'll be getting calls from the parents."

"Thanks, sir," I murmur, and even El knows not to pull me back into a snog when we've been treated this fairly. Instead he twirls me on the spot and we settle into some kind of ballroom pose, my head on his chest.

I still can't believe this is happening. Just yesterday I'd have thought it impossible. Us out and proud and dancing in front of the whole school. My heart gives this single deep grateful throb. Thank you, mysterious pervy porno poster, you did me a favour after all.

It suddenly occurs to me that El hasn't spoken for all of five minutes. This is worrying. It's like a politician forgetting to lie or Michael Bay making a movie that doesn't suck balls.

"What's the matter?" I ask.

"Nothing," he grumbles, and flicks his face away from me. "It's just…"

"Ellis?"

"All right." He looks back and gives this huge theatrical sigh. "I'd just like to know who taught you how to kiss like that."

I grin. "You really want to know?"

"Yes, I want to know."

"You might not like it."

"I'm man enough to deal."

"If you're absolutely sure…?"

"Frecks."

"Okay." I let him hang for a moment. "It was your aunt, Julia. We've been having this secret affair since the very beginning. The truth is, I'm coming out tonight as a straight guy who's really into aunts."

"The dirty old cow," he says, deadpan. "I'll be having words when I get home."

He gives me another spin and I take in the gym properly for the first time. And I have to admit, the dance committee girls (who are also the debate team girls, the history club girls, the community outreach girls, the freaking LGBTQ safe-space girls, even though the closest any of them has come to queer is when Katie slipped on a bit of quiche in the lunch hall and her head ended up in Gemma Argyle's lap) have outdone themselves. The walls are covered with sugary pink banners, while giant papier-mâché Easter eggs dangle from the ceiling like huge piñata turds.

And then I see their crowning glory and stop dead.

"Oh fuck, they haven't," I murmur.

"What is it?" El asks.

And as I stare at the display of unimaginable awfulness on the far side of the room, I feel this hot needle of guilt twist in my gut. Oh sure, it hasn't been the easiest of days, what with the manic chirruping of my phone at 7 a.m. this morning:

Dude, have you seen Instagram? Maybe take a look.
Nice ass, BTW

Dylan, my man! Didn't know you had it in you – but
now I see that's just where you like it!!!

Dear Dyls, I'm so sorry for what you're going through.
Just know, Gemma and Suze and me don't care at ALL
that you're gay now xxx

Etc. etc…

I almost broke my laptop in the rush to check out what
all these well-meaning friends were talking about. I sort of
guessed, of course, but even as I clicked the blurry freeze-
frame and the video started to play, I was whispering in my
head: *Please no, please no, please no, please no.* And then, as
if to mock me, my own voice came through the speakers,
tinny and mortifying: *"Please, yes. Yes, El, yes!"*

So yeah, it's been a hideous and then strangely glorious
day. It excuses nothing.

"Mike," I breathe. "Oh my God, Mike."

I pull back from El and weave my way through the
spectators who've assembled to watch our first public
dance. I'm not much good in crowds, but right now it's easy
to ignore the eyes that follow me across the gym. A few of
El's footie mates give me a brotherly pat as I pass. Moving

deeper, this seems to become some kind of meme, so that by the time I reach the huge blown-up picture of my best friend, my shoulder is actually aching.

Mike Berrington's big dopey handsome face grins down at me from the wall. There's the scar I gave him in nursery school when I accidentally elbowed him into the duck pond – a backward letter S that, inflated, looks like a brand across his chin. I feel El's hand slip into mine.

"What's the matter?"

I turn to him, hot tears scalding my eyes.

"Jesus, Ellis, I forgot. It's his fourth bloody session and I forgot." I see El's brow clear as he understands. "It's chemo day."

And I'm officially the worst best friend ever.

3

"Do you like it?" says Gemma Argyle, practically falling into us. She throws out her hand towards the big blown-up picture of Mike.

"What the hell is it supposed to be?" I mutter.

She looks at me as if I've just murdered her grandmother. Or worse, asked if I could borrow her Louis Vuitton ballpoint in English.

"The committee decided that this year's ball will be in honour of our brave, inspiring classmate Michael Berrington. All of tonight's ticket money will go towards buying Mike something really special, once he's finished his treatment."

"Right," El says, "lovely of you. But what the hell have you done to him?"

He gestures at the golden light that appears to be radiating out of Mike's head.

"It's the Easter Dance," Gemma explains.

"So he's…" El frowns. "Jesus?"

El has always liked Mike. He rates him highly because, as El puts it, "Mikey's smart, funny, nice to look at, and completely non-threatening to my love life." It's true. On a good day Mike could give Ansel Elgort a run for his money, but I've never once fancied him. It would be like lusting after my own brother.

"It's the season of renewal and new life and resurrection and miracles," Gemma says pertly. She ignores my groan. "And poor Mike needs all the help he can get."

Fuuuhhh-uk you! I want to say it, but don't. I think, deep down, part of all this is genuine and Gemma really does mean well. Anyway, she's not the villain in all this. I am.

I'm heading for the door when El catches up with me. I hold up my hand, palm out. "Give me a sec, okay?"

He nods, all understanding. "Tell the lazy sod I'll pop round tomorrow and we'll watch the match, if he's up for it."

I almost smile. Mike and Ellis and football. Ghosts of last autumn and the school bonfire and El's football petition and the first time I ever planted eyes on this beautiful boy run through my head. I give him a weird double-handed wave and push through the swing doors and out into the car park. It's cool and quiet outside. The tarmac shines blue-black in the moonlight. Kids are huddled in shadows, smoking, snogging, doing other things. I rest my back against El's car and bring up my contacts.

While the call connects, I glance up at the school roof: the scene of last night's surprise picnic, organized by my amazing boyfriend – and where we were secretly filmed mid-canoodle ("canoodle"? Jesus, Dylan!). I'm starting to wonder for the thousandth time who could have done such a thing when Mike picks up.

"Hey, porn star," he sighs.

He sounds tired. God, he sounds so bloody tired. I suddenly feel cold and almost as frightened as when he first told me his news.

"Please no," I groan. "Don't tell me you watched it!"

Mike chuckles like an old man. "Honestly? No. You guys are *so* not my type."

"Aw, c'mon. If you had to choose between me and Gemma Argyle?"

"If that was the choice?" he muses. "I guess in those *very* specific circumstances, you might just get lucky."

"I'm honoured," I laugh. "Bitch."

"Bumboy."

New nicknames, nothing nasty in them, coined around Christmas when I told him. He was the first to know, except for El, of course. He came out to me so I came out to him, quid pro quo: *I have leukaemia*; *I'm gay*. We hugged each other fierce under twinkly fairy lights.

25

"I tried calling. Sent you a couple of messages," he says.

"Yeah, I turned off my phone after the millionth *I'd get that mole on your butt checked out* text. Anyway, none of that matters. How are you doing, Mike?"

"We'll get to my woes in a minute, Dylan." He lets out a big breath. "So I guess you've had one fucked-up day. Do you know who posted it?"

"Not a clue. But El's determined to find out."

"I can't even imagine why anyone would do something like that," Mike mutters. "But I'm with El all the way. We *will* find out who it was, Dylan, I promise."

I smile despite myself. The two most important people in my life are El and Mike. They make me feel safe and wanted, and that's no small thing.

"I called your house," Mike goes on. "Your mum told me you'd gone to the dance. Dude, seriously? The actual Ferrivale High Easter Dance? You know I love El, but sometimes I think he's a bad influence on you, undoing all my years of hard work. Remember what we used to call that thing?"

"The Dipshits Ball," I laugh. "Yeah, and it's every bit as dipshitty as we imagined. There are these great big shiny turds hanging from the ceiling, and the gym's so pink it's like they sealed all the doors and gunned down a herd of flamingos. Seriously, Mike, did you know they've stuck a giant picture of you on the wall?"

He groans. "Yeah, one of the three witches sent me a screenshot, complete with hearts and crying emojis."

"Mate, they've photoshopped the crap out of you. It looks like someone's set fire to your farts and you're basking in the afterglow."

"It looks like I'm dead," he chuckles.

He meant it as a joke, but all I can do is stare at my hand, and yeah, I know it's ridiculous, but I swear I can see our two little hands held tight together. Mike and Dylan, walking buddies, trotting along in our supervised line from junior school to the council swimming pool. Mike and Dylan, karaoke buds, hand-in-hand at Tamsin Carlisle's fourteenth birthday party, belting out "I Got You Babe" and holding up our phones like lighters. Mike and Dylan, last Christmas, holding hands, coming out in our different ways.

"So do your family know?" Mike breaks into my thoughts. "How'd they take it?"

"Good." I nod though he can't see me. "Yeah. They were okay with it."

"Really?"

He lets it hang. Thing is, I sometimes forget Mike has known my folks for almost as long as I have.

"Uh huh."

"That's great then…" he says. "If you're sure?"

"Why wouldn't I be sure?"

"Dylan. It's me."

27

"Okay," I sigh. "So I guess Chris could've been a bit more vocal. I basically got a headlock and my skull knuckled, but as it's a miracle he ever learned to speak in the first place, I suppose that wasn't a bad reaction. And Mum and Dad? Pretty much how you'd expect."

"And they're cool with El?"

"How are you, Mike?" I blurt out.

"I'm fine, Dylan. Really, I am."

"And your chemo? You still at the hospital?"

"Oh, the wondrous world of chemo? Yeah, today was actually all kinds of mad. In the end they had to... Ah crap. Hold on." I can hear Mike's mum – not her words, but I'd know that distant mumble anywhere. Carol's like the Godzilla of mums – scary, but in a kind of awesome and iconic way, and if you're one of her scaly lizard babies she'll protect you with her life. Luckily, I've been counted as an honorary Berrington ever since I kissed Mike when he fell over and started bawling at his fourth birthday party. I actually can't wait to tell Carol my news, even though I'm pretty sure she's already guessed. Mike comes back on the line. "Sorry, buddy. So yeah, grim day. I'll tell you all about it later. Might make you smile or maybe burst a vessel. My dad nearly took someone's head off. But look, Dylan, I really have to go. Come over tomorrow, yeah? I haven't said a word to Mum or Dad, but I know they'll bake you a freaking cake or sign us all up for Pride or something."

"It's a date."

"Night, Bumboy."

"Night, Bitch."

He hangs up. He sounds okay. Really. Just a bit tired.

I head back into the dance.

And for a moment I just watch Ellis. My heart's still full of Mike, of all the fears we've never expressed since he told me his diagnosis, and it helps a little to watch El. Watch him and know that, whatever happens next with my oldest friend, this person will help us through it, just by being there.

More people are on the dance floor now. I can't help grinning as some of the football team start dancing with each other, mimicking my and El's moves. There's no sting in it. They're laughing and pretending to make out, and it feels like a kind of tribute. In a weird way, I'm sort of proud. It's something like progress, right? A little step for Ferrivale High. Maybe next year there'll be more out kids dancing together and there'll be no parody in it at all.

I switch from the boys whispering fake sweet nothings to each other to El. He's working the room in his usual easy way. It always amazes me how he can flit between these groups and be accepted by almost all of them. Now he's laughing and joking with Gemma and the committee witches. Now he's huddled up with the rugby lads, cackling over some sports reference I'd never get. Now he's with the library kids, probably talking the latest queer fiction and wondering whether Jane Austen was just a teeny bit bi. Then he's high-fiving this grinning parade of teachers – Dementor Harper, sweat-rings Robarts, little Miss Buchanan with her adorable moustache, Mr Morris, our history teacher, only skipping art teacher Mr Denman, just back from sick leave, who stood up too late. Sure he gets a couple of weird looks here and there, but he deals as El always deals – he makes them all silently ashamed with the hugeness of his heart.

I rock back against the monkey bars and think: *What now?* Everything in the past four months has been about me and El and making sure no one knows. Not gonna lie, it's been exhausting. But none of that effort is needed any more. I guess we can just *be*. We've got final exams coming up, then, if we get the grades (please God!) we'll be heading to Bristol in September. We decided way back we'd ditch halls and get a little student flat together. A cosy crib for two. Maybe we'll adopt a feral cat or try not to kill a goldfish for a month or two, and we'll be ultra-sociable with uni clubs and stuff, but it'll be our first real chance to exist properly together, as a couple. I get excited just thinking about it. But first there's summer, and all the possibilities of summer: El dragging me to gigs and galleries; me dragging him to comic book conventions and my favourite medieval castles and battlefields. Late nights, late mornings, breakfast in bed, reading, sketching, touching.

Me and El.

"Let's get out of here."

Another of El's whiplash moments. I'd been watching Mitchell Harrison and Joe Cotterill slow-waltzing to "Uptown Funk", laughing my head off, when suddenly he's there, right in front of me. And he's different. Ellis without at least a trace of a smile is always disconcerting. It's like you can finally see that darkness he trailed with him from Birmingham all those long months ago.

"What's the matter?" I say, catching at his sleeve.

"It's nothing. Just, let's go, okay?"

He looks over his shoulder, but I'm not sure where his eyes are focused: the committee girls; the footie lads; the library geeks; the teachers. All I know is that when he looks back at me, those perfect pink lips are trembling.

"Please can we go?" he repeats.

An unnamed fear, strange and yet horribly familiar, grips my heart. I've seen Ellis like this before – back in those dark days over Christmas when he inexplicably vanished on me. I won't go through the pain and fear of that miserable week again. I won't. We have to talk.

4

We're in the car, not moving. El sits silently in the driver's seat, his fingers plucking and twisting at his pearls. He looks...I don't know. The best I can come up with is lost. His eyes are huge and blank and it feels as if he isn't seeing me at all.

When I reach out to touch him he flinches, like I've scorched him with a cigarette. He looks down at my hand and swivels sideways in his seat, arching his back until his shoulders are almost touching the ceiling, as if being anywhere near me disgusts him in some way.

"El, Jesus, what the hell's going on?"

There's a weird sort of pleading in my voice, and I don't like it. It scares me that I've done something, today of all days, that has made him hate me. What the hell that could be, I've no idea. My mind flips back over the past thirty minutes or so. It can't be me heading off to talk with Mike, he can't be jealous of that. El has always understood the me-and-Mike thing. So has someone said something to him? Something awful about me? I'm now tearing through my entire school career, hunting for some deep dark secret that I've never confided to El. But that's impossible. The only secret I've ever had that's been a source of inner shame was exposed this morning, and, Jesus, it was El himself who taught me there was no shame in that at all.

Okay, so maybe it isn't a secret. Maybe it's a lie. Have I been kidding myself? All those pats on the back and the football team fake-smooching on the dance floor – maybe there *was* an edge to it after all, and I was just so caught up in the giddiness of this awful, wonderful day that I misinterpreted it. Has some nasty whisper been invented?

My brain vomits up a trove of poisonous gems:

You know McKee's a secret slut, don't you, Ellis? Sucked off half the footie lads before you rolled into town.

I heard he's been two-timing you with [insert name here] and they're gonna break it to you soon.

Ellis, man, wake up. He isn't even gay. He just tried it out for a laugh. You know, like a phase?

Funny how the brain works. I know deep down that

it's all complete bullshit, but each of these imaginary conversations seems more plausible than the last. I even start thinking up ways to counter them:

Holy Christ, Ellis, a slut? Was there anyone on the planet who could've out-virgined me back when we met?

Two-timing? Like I'd be able to fit in a secret affair between homework, history club, uni applications and snogging your face off every break period?

Not gay? Seriously? Not gay? The only thing about me that isn't gay is my dance moves.

But all I can say is: "Ellis. Please, talk to me."

My heart is like a bird smashing itself against the cage of my ribs. But I decide I have to be brave. I reach for him again.

His reaction terrifies me. He pushes out the flat of his hand to meet mine, and I think, *This is it. There's no going back from this. I don't know what's happened, don't know what's been said, but if he thrusts me away physically my heart will break and I'll go right back to being the Dylan of six months ago. Screw that, it'll be worse, because once you're out there's no going back, and now I'll be out alone. Not just alone either. I was alone for seventeen years, but at least then I didn't know what the alternative could feel like. I didn't have this…this fullness in my life* – it's a crappy description, but it's the best I can do – *so what will be left of me, when he goes?*

Empty people don't know they're empty. It's a kind of blissful ignorance, I guess. We can try to imagine something different – romantic movies, mushy love songs, other kids holding hands and smiling in that totally alien way – we can make believe we understand all of that. But we don't. Not really. Not until it happens to us.

Suddenly the pressure of his fingers pushes my hand up to meet his, palm to palm. We stay like that for seconds that roll like oceans. Then he looks at me, finally, from under those endless lashes, and the pain in those tea-dark eyes is unbearable. Pain but no anger, no disgust. I rotate my wrist and feed my fingers between his.

"El, you scared me. You *are* scaring me."

"I'm sorry."

His voice is normal, or at least really well controlled. That's what no one gets about El: they think he's this impetuous, outrageous guy who says and does whatever he likes, and I guess that's partly true. But we're all contradictions, right? My boyfriend has been through stuff that would break the spirit of any so-called hero I've ever idolized in a comic book, but you'd never know it. Not unless you know *him*. Really know him. That's why I'm not fooled by his voice.

"So…" He twists back around to sit square in the driver's seat again. "How was Mike? Did you give him my message? He should really just shave his head completely. It would be like Professor X meets Jack Wills."

Even after all this time, I can't help but be impressed. I have no idea how he does this Control Alt Delete thing with his emotions. But I'm not having it. Not tonight.

"El, just stop."

"Stop what?"

"Deflecting."

"Hon, if you can't take me complimenting your best mate then that's your issue, not mine."

"Jesus!" I throw my head back against the rest. "Will you cut the comedy routine for just one minute? Mike's fine, okay? And I know you genuinely care, and you'd have asked anyway, but it's still kind of disrespectful, you know?"

He blinks, again like I've scorched him. "Dylan, I'm sorry. I didn't mean—"

"I know you didn't, but it isn't right, using Mike to wheedle your way out of this. But okay, let's get it out of the way and then we can get back to whatever the hell is up with you." I close my eyes. "So Mike's having his chemo, and he's tired, and he's being brave and funny and caring, and he's worried about us. And Carol's gonna bake us a cake and march with us in Pride, and *fuck!*"

I burst into tears. Real, full-on waterworks with heaving

and snot and hiccups, the complete melodrama. Unlike El, I *do* cry. It's completely freaking ridiculous. Pixar movies, Oscar speeches, adverts with meerkats – I'm in almost constant danger of serious dehydration. But this feels different.

"Honey." His long fingers comb through my curls. He cups the back of my neck, pulls me in, and I get the strong, sweet scent of him under his deodorant.

"Just tell me what happened," I say. "This time, *tell* me."

"It's nothing."

"El…"

He fixes me with his eyes. "All right then. It's something. But I don't want you mixed up in it. And anyway, it's over."

Okay, I've avoided it long enough – basically because even thinking about that time makes me sick to my stomach – but I have to say something now.

"Has this got anything to do with what happened in December?"

El disappeared on me over the Christmas break. Disappeared completely. No phone calls, no texts, nothing. We'd only properly got together the week before, and without him I tortured myself trying to figure out what I'd done wrong. When he came back to me in the new year, I accepted all his feeble excuses because I was just so relieved to have him back in my life. But honestly, I never believed his reasons for vanishing.

I don't want to revisit that time – I can't think of anything worse – but the fear I've seen in him tonight? It all feels like a horrible echo of Christmas.

El shakes his head determinedly. "No, Dylan. It's nothing to do with what happened back then."

I don't want to push this but I have to. "You promised you'd never shut me out like that again. El, you *promised*."

"And I'm not shutting you out," he insists. "This thing, it's different."

"Well then…" My head's reeling. I take a breath. "Is it someone else?"

"*No*, Dylan." And when I try to look away he takes my chin and guides me back to him. "There is no one else. There won't *ever* be anyone else. You dope." He grins that crooked Ellis grin, brighter than Broadway neon, and the pain in his eyes becomes a memory. "Don't you know by now? Right, here goes…I can't believe I'm actually going to say this." He laughs and makes a grab for my ribs with tickling fingers. "You're the one, Dylan. You and your gorgeous freckles and your gingery hair and your moley bum and your geeky history stuff and your comic-book crap and your so-cute-it's-actually-annoying shyness and your eternal klutziness and your passion for Starburst sweets and *YOU*."

He releases me and I fall back into my seat, laughing, glowing.

El's laughing too, and then his predictable switch kicks in.

"It's you, Dylan," he says, his voice almost cracking. "And I know you think for some insane reason you don't deserve to be loved by me, but that makes you just about the most intelligent idiot I've ever met. I love you, Frecks. And it's fairy-tale bullshit, I know, but I've sort of loved you ever since the first time I saw you."

I sit there, stunned.

"You can't have," I say quietly. "All I was doing was standing gawping at you."

El shakes his head. "You couldn't see yourself. Your gawps are one of the best things about you. You know how everyone stared at me that first night at the bonfire? In I flounced, the new kid, all self-righteous and up for a row, and I got these looks of shock and laughter and instant hatred and weird admiration – the usual glorious rainbow. But you? You looked at me without any judgement or expectation at all. You just looked as if you'd like to say hello."

"And I did."

"And you did."

Shadows pass the steamed-up windows. Kids lurching, giving each other piggybacks, seventeen-year-olds playing tag.

"You saved me that night. You have no idea, but that's exactly what you did. The way it ended with my family.

39

The screams and swearing and unholy shit they threw at me after I told them. 'It's okay,' I said, 'I'm still me. I'm still Ellis. Still your son.' And then Dad knocked me to the floor and my mum stepped right over me and started packing my clothes. And I was just lying there, watching my little sister in her playpen. She didn't cry or anything. She just squatted down in her nappy and reached through the bars with her chubby little arms and she picked up my tooth off the carpet and she..." He takes a huge swallow. "She held it out for me. 'Ellis's,' she said. And then I was in the street and Dad was throwing tenners in my face and Mum was behind him shouting, 'Don't you ever come back!'" El looks at me, his expression so desolate it breaks my heart. "You know how you cope with that, Dylan? You either become more you than you've ever been before, or you curl up and die. But it's a hard act, you know? Straining all the time to be who you need to be. And then I came here and I got up that stupid petition—"

"It wasn't stupid," I tell him.

"And I see this cute comic-book geek," he continues, "his face glowing in the bonfire light. I ask him to sign my petition. And he does. And while he's signing, I can see he just wants to say hello. Because he really would like to know me... Ha! You scared the crap of me, you know?"

"Wait. *I* scared *you*?"

He laughs and presses his forefinger to my nose. "Yes,

Frecks. Because I thought, what if he gets to know me and I disappoint him?"

"You're an idiot," I laugh.

"I don't know." He turns and draws a perfect circle on the driver window. "I'm pretty good at disappointing people."

"You won't." I grab his shoulder, but he keeps his back turned. "It's us now. Just us. You and me, El, forever."

He sighs. "No such thing as forever, Frecks."

5

We've been driving for five minutes or so when I circle us back round to the fear that still gnaws inside me. When I start questioning him again, El cuts me short.

"Please, Dylan," he sighs, "I swear I will be your servant for an entire week. You can ask me to do your homework, walk the dog, give you massages without me getting pouty and expecting one in return, *if* you just agree to drop it."

"Ellis, I don't have a dog for you to walk, I wouldn't let you within a mile of my homework, and…well, okay, the massage thing might have swung it for you, but you matter more to me than scented oils and erections."

He flaps a hand over his heart. "That is the single sweetest thing anyone has ever said to me."

But it's my turn to jackknife the tone. "I want to know what happened. Listen, if some bastard upset you back there—"

"Enough." He doesn't shout but there's a definite finality to the word. "Dylan, I don't ask you for much. In fact, apart from the odd shoulder rub, I don't really ask you for anything, but I'd just like this one thing: let it be. It's done. Over. It doesn't affect us."

"Of course it bloody affects us," I shoot back. "Do you even remember what state you were in ten minutes ago? You are fearless, El, I mean it, but right then it was like you were trapped inside a nightmare or something."

"Come on. Don't be so melodramatic."

He's serious, I can tell. He hasn't called me Frecks or Prof or McKee D for all of five minutes.

"It's just, I never want to see you like that again," I tell him. "And if I know why you shut down, why you pulled away from me, why you didn't even seem to know who I was, well, then—"

"Then what? Then you'll be able to protect me forever? My knight in shining armour?"

There's nothing snide in what he says. It actually sounds kind of hopeful.

"If you like," I say. "Look, I know I'm not Daredevil or The Punisher or anything. In fact, I'm more like Steve Rogers *before* he took the super-soldier serum and became Captain America. But I would fight for you, El."

"And I believe you," he says simply. And for some reason this infuriates me.

"It is, isn't it?" I stare at him. "Whatever's gone down tonight, it's all to do with your vanishing act back in December. Why won't you just *tell me*? Whatever it is, I'd understand."

He nods. "I know you'd understand, Frecks. Of course you would. But here's the thing: you don't have to prove *anything* to me and I don't have to tell you everything either. Despite what you read in your *Teen Vogue* magazine, relationships aren't always about absolute disclosure. What matters is trust. So trust me – that thing back there was a moment of madness. A bit of stupidity and, what with everything else today, I had a kind of weird meltdown. Remember what I said about all that murky sewer water that flowed under my bridge before I hit Ferrivale? Well, maybe some of it is still swirling around my ankles after all. It won't happen again."

"You've promised that before," I mutter.

We drive on in silence. For the second time in our relationship, it seems that whatever I say, El won't open up. It's then that I realize something awful: I don't know my boyfriend. Not completely. Maybe I never will.

I crack my window. A slipstream of forest air. Trees billow in the early darkness, bursting with the smell of new life. Our school sits in the middle of town, just where Ferrivale's quaint cobbled streets and picture-postcard shops give way to the crescent of lake and forest that divides houses like mine and Mike's from the estate where El lives with his Aunt Julia.

While the trees flash by, I have a word with myself. So I'm reading a lot right now; this book on the Ottoman Empire, one on Japanese isolationism, and then this one on the American War of Independence, all in my spare time. Yeah, because I have *so* much of that at the minute, what with final exams and essays looming. Mr Morris says my "commendable but unfocused" love of history might result in me failing the subject altogether, just because I have this irresistible need to satisfy my curiosity. El made a face when I told him. He says education should be about just that – feeding irresistible curiosity. He has a point, but if I want to teach the subject myself one day, I have to pass these exams.

Anyway, the American Revolution, the Battle of Monmouth, 1778 (I'm kind of anal about dates): this guy, Major General Charles Lee, has the British in retreat. Everything's going great for him, more or less, and then for no reason anyone can really understand, Lee orders *his* men to retreat. He's turned victory into disaster and General George Washington basically bitch-slaps the hell out of him, right in front of Lee's own troops. All this strikes a chord. *I'm Lee.* All through my relationship with El I've been advancing a bit and then retreating. I'm not sure why. Maybe El's right, maybe it's because I think I'm unworthy of him. Screw that, I *am* unworthy. Jesus, just look at him. But I'm done with acting out my own personal Battle of Monmouth.

I'm done retreating.

"Okay." I nod. "I'll let it go."

El turns to look at me, his smile full of relief.

"*But*," I add, "this is the last time. You never told me what went on with you at Christmas, not really, and you're holding back again now. So promise me: no more secrets."

"All right," he says quietly. "I promise."

El's headlights splash along the forest road, and I give his promise a moment to bed in.

"So," I sigh, unkinking the stress in my neck, "where are we going?"

"Home, of course."

"Oh. Yours or mine?" I can't hide my disappointment. It's a warm night, full of the kind of possibilities that home won't allow.

"Neither," he says. "Ours."

I grin. "Hideous Beauty?"

He nods. "Check the back seat."

I glance over the headrest. There's the wicker hamper from yesterday's surprise rooftop picnic, one of the sides pushed up, a bottle of red wine poking out. And so the weirdest, but also the most *amazing* night of my life is about to get a lot more amazing! I can picture it already.

Moonlight in the belfry, the bottle empty, our lips plummy with the aftertaste. The tartan blanket on the groaning wooden planks, rolling and twisting under us. Kisses, caresses, firmness, softness, teasing and tender promises, all under the watch of the gargoyle that El has sketched over and over since I first took him to the ruined country church. Stanley, El's nickname for our stone protector, will stand watch, keeping us safe from any darkness that might threaten us.

I turn back to El, grinning. "You planned all this? When?"

He shrugs. "However it went today, I thought you might need this."

God, he *is* a genius. First the school dance and now this.

"Where'd you get the wine?"

"I have my contacts." He winks. "And I learned my lesson, by the way. All the food I've brought is the most God-awful crap. Pizza slices, crisps, bottles of Coke, chocolate cake. Not a single piece of fruit for the junk-food junkie."

He smiles. Then, taking a hand from the steering wheel, starts tracing images with his swift expressive fingers. He tells me what will happen tonight. He paints aching pictures with words, with the heavy silences between words, with the sudden flares and then the slow rolling of his fingers. It's then I realize just how pitiful my imagination is by comparison. The images of us in the belfry become vivid, the voices keener, the promises sweeter, the touching a thousand times more varied. I listen and I watch and my throat runs salty. I hope I can live up to all this.

I can see Ellis is turned on by his own words. His finger flicks to the stereo and he silences George Ezra, something he never does. His tongue moistens his lips. I swallow hard. And now his hand is on my headrest. It's in my hair. I roll with his touch, my eyes closed, my breath catching. His knuckles trace the contours of my face. His palm presses my chest. I arch my back to meet him and his hand slips under my T-shirt, and all he has to do is brush my nipple and I moan.

His hand is gone. *No, you bloody tease!* But then it's back. My right knee…Ellis's fingers crabbed there and fanning out. It's a spot that makes me go weak; a place I had no idea about until El found it a month ago. He moves on, slowly, slowly, inside my thigh, a warm hand, pressing and pushing upwards.

"Ellis," I whisper. "El, I—"

And then his hand whips away, and he screams, and the car screams, and the trees race towards us.

6

Something had flashed into the road – white on black – a comet streaking across the dark strip of tarmac. People, animals? No idea. Their blur was all I could make out before El wrenched the steering wheel and the car spun ninety degrees, its back wheels shrieking.

The g-force slams me sideways and I bump shoulders with El. He's straight as an arrow in the driver's seat, hands cemented to the wheel, foot ramming the brake. His shirtsleeves have hitched up and I can see his beautiful, self-designed tattoos spiralling down his arm.

He grabs the handbrake and wrenches it up. Hey, he's the master of the handbrake turn, right? But this is too much for the old Nissan. El has ridden his luck with it once too often, maybe, and if it's heading for the scrapyard, it's not going alone. A split second later we're facing the opposite direction, half in the road, half on the forest verge, and my passenger-side wheels are leaving the ground.

What starts as an almost tender motion picks up momentum. All at once, the Nissan hurls itself onto its roof, leaving the road completely and tossing us into the forest. I thrust my hands against the ceiling just as the windscreen buckles and breaks. Glass pixelates, frosts over. My passenger window shatters too, the impact knocking the safety glass into the car. It's a weirdly soft sort of implosion, a bit like a sudden gale of snow, and I don't know if it's the pieces of window or a bit of random junk – loose CDs, pens, books, the little snow globe I gave El the first night we ever spent together, everything's flying around in this insane vortex – but somehow I'm cut and a flash of blood strikes across my eyes.

The world spins downwards. My body shuttles away from El and hits the passenger door with a dull crack. In the hard flashes that come to me then, I realize I've been lucky. If my arm had flailed out of the broken window it would have been crushed as the Nissan tipped over. A rectangle of dewy spring grass fills the window and I crane my neck sideways as we continue to roll. I catch a glimpse of El hanging face down in his seatbelt, cradled there like a fly in a web.

I try to reach for him. He looks so scared. El is hardly ever scared. He reaches out. Then the car is upright again and gravity drops our arms to our sides. Misty through the fractured windscreen, I see the bonnet sheared into something like a mountain range. Smoke hisses from jagged peaks. But the car seems to have stopped moving. *This is it*, I think. *Thank God, it's over.* A few cuts and bruises, maybe a broken bone or two, but in a couple of hours we'll be sitting up in our adjoining hospital beds, reliving this close call, laughing at mortality. Adjoining beds. I wonder if we can get away with pushing them together when no one's looking? I almost smile.

I see El take a breath. He's hurt. But not badly.

Don't say badly.

And then it's like that moment when the washing machine fools you. When it's finished what seems to be the final super-mad spin cycle and starts to whir down, only for it to start up again the second you reach for the door release. I begin to call his name, my blood surging, when El is suddenly thrust against the driver door.

We're rolling again, picking up speed, going faster if anything. As my seatbelt cuts into my shoulder and my head smacks the ceiling, I see the path we've cut through the tall grass, the trail of rubbish and broken belongings we've left in our wake. The wine bottle has been thrown clear and is now rolling down the hillside. Except it isn't quite a hill. We left the road at that part of the forest where the trees are sparsest and the land drifts downwards, sloping its way through a clearing until it reaches a shingled shore.

Hunter's Lake.

"No!" I scream as this new reality hits me. "NO!"

Because I'm looking over at El and his eyes are shut. Not screwed tight in terror, but loosely lidded, like he's drifted off to sleep. He is hurt. Badly. Half his face is awash with blood, like a red-lit Phantom of the Opera mask.

"El!" I try to reach him, but the cyclone continues and he's twisted and dangled in his seatbelt web. "EL, WAKE UP!"

Through my window, then through his as we roll, I see the dark shimmer of the lake. They have punting and pedalos here in the summer. El and I haven't spent a summer together yet. Messing about on Hunter's Lake was a tiny part of the plan we made at last night's picnic. The lake is bigger than I remember. They say a toddler drowned here once. She was chasing a butterfly and her parents weren't watching. She flew with it right to the end of the diving pier, and then beyond.

I don't know when we hit the water. Maybe it's the blood loss, but I pass out for a minute or two. It can't be much longer than that, because when I come round we've finally stopped and we're upright and the black water is only just beginning to slosh around my ankles. It seeps and gushes through a thousand different openings in the car, big and small, seen and unseen, and I swear it's laughing at me.

So you thought this was forever? it chuckles. *There is no forever, Dylan. Not for you and him. There never was.*

It's a warm night but the water's cold and murky and stinks. My skin freezes as it oils its way slowly up my leg, across my knee and along my thigh, moving like an anti-Ellis, its touch intimate and disgusting. I try to free myself but the belt holds me fast. It's jammed and for some reason I don't have the strength to unclip it. It's like my fingers are being worked by some drunk puppeteer. I watch them fumble and paw at the fastening, and all the while I switch my gaze from the creeping water to El and back again.

Ironically, his seatbelt has snapped at the buckle. He's free, slumped forward over the wheel, unmoving. For twenty heart-stopping seconds I think he's not breathing. Then he takes a shallow, stuttering inhalation. I shout and plead with him, try to grab something random to throw at him, but my hands won't do as they're told and he won't wake up. Gouts of red that make me shriek drop from his chin into the water. They billow around his waist and send out tentacles towards me.

I turn to the broken window and the shore. We're within a few breaststrokes of land but Hunter's Lake is notorious for its deep and sudden plunges, and just as I'm about to cry out for help, the Nissan lurches sideways. The lake bed is a kind of loose black peat that squelches through your toes like sinking sand, clinging to you, trying to claim you. It's a jealous lake and it wants me and Ellis.

We begin to slide deeper and deeper. El's side of the car is soon underwater but his window is intact. Fresh springs hiss through the cracks and shower his motionless face, washing it clean of blood. We're drifting downwards, forty degrees maybe, and the lapping waterline bubbles up to El's chin. My heart thunders. I thrash the water, rip my hand raw against the belt clip. Still my fingers won't work properly. I glance right. Black, filthy, frothing water touches that beautiful bottom lip – the lip I used to catch between my teeth, teasing him. The lake quivers there for a moment and then begins to dribble into Ellis's unresisting mouth.

"No! Please, NO!"

I can't watch him drown. I want to die first. *Please, God, let me die first.*

And then a miracle. The rear end of the car starts to pivot in the sludge, edging us around until, at last, we're facing shoreward with the crumpled bonnet tipping up. Still unconscious, El gasps as the water slides from his face and flows backwards, over his shoulder, into the rear seats. I laugh through chattering teeth.

"We'll be okay," I promise him. "We'll be okay."

But the lake won't give us up. Maybe it's toying with us, I don't know.

The rear of the Nissan groans like some prehistoric animal caught in a tar pit and we begin to sink again. My T-shirt billows out as the water reinvades the front of the car.

It chuckles as it creeps forward, like some bratty little kid that won't stay strapped into its booster seat. Still harnessed by the belt, I manage to free my leg from the footwell and, straining, lurch sideways, kicking across the gear column. My trainer hits El in the ribs.

"Wake up! El, please, if you love me, WAKE UP!"

But he won't. I kick until a spasm of cramp shoots down my frozen calf and makes me roar. Reluctantly, I draw my leg back. I've probably broken one of his ribs. I look at him through a haze of tears.

"Please, El. Please. Please, I love you. I love you so much…" I whisper the words. Then scream: "Fuck you, Ellis! Don't you dare die! Don't you even dare do that to me! PLEASE! PLEASE, PLEASE, PLEASE! You're killing me. You're *killing* me!"

I bellow against this new feeling. I hate him. Why won't he wake up? He would if he really loved me.

The car lunges backwards. The water laps at my throat. At his lips. My head swims. I shake myself. I'm so cold. Inside the car it's getting darker. My anger starts to ebb. It doesn't matter. Not really. I withdraw my torn-to-pieces hand from its futile battle with the belt and push it through the lake. It's very hard and takes all my concentration. It's just a slab of useless meat now; hardly any sensation at all. But I pray there's a little feeling left. Just so I can touch him, one last time.

My hand surfaces and I move it as gently as I can towards him. The lake is trying to make him drink again. I ignore it. *I can't save you from it, El. All I can do is this.* I brush my icy fingers against his face; his wonderful light brown skin, his strong jaw, his perfect cheeks. There isn't a millimetre of this face I haven't kissed. *Thank you, Ellis. Thank you for being my first. Thank you for being my friend. Thank you for showing me who I am.*

Who I was.

Movement behind the shattered windscreen. A lurching, splashing darkness. My eyes flicker. I don't want to stop touching El but I have nothing left. My fingers drift on the current as I feel my thoughts float with the lake. If there's an afterlife, let me be with El. If there's nothingness, that's okay too. But don't part us…

Then an arm, warm, incredibly warm, reaches across my face and body. It presses against me and I breathe in its heat, like oxygen. There's a moment of fumbling, and I'm released. The belt flashes past my eyes and I can't believe this incredible sense of freedom. It feels like that moment after I told my family who I was. I'm giddy with possibility again.

I turn, ready to make a grab for El, but my freedom vanishes. The same arm that saved me now destroys me. It takes hold of me somehow and, within a few seconds, I'm being dragged backwards through the broken window.

I kick and fight but I've already used every morsel of strength. I scream, gag, try to reason with my rescuer. I don't know what I say, maybe it's just noise; I'm ignored anyhow. It's lucky I'm skinny, I guess, because getting me out through the window seems easy enough. I drift back, back, back, and all I see before the darkness takes me is…

El.

I love you, I tell him. His face floats just above the waterline and seems to turn to me, like a child listening. *You hear me, Ellis? I love you. My El. My heart. My reason. My future.*

My past.

7

Darkness there and nothing more.

It's a line from an Edgar Allan Poe poem we studied in English. "The Raven". It's about this guy driven mad by grief when he loses the girl he loves. Everything he sees and hears reminds him of this one amazing person, and he's so obsessed with her memory that he'd rather go mad than say goodbye forever.

Poe knew his shit.

I sit up in my hospital bed and stare at the empty bed across the aisle. That's Ellis's. No bastard had better take it. A nurse is gluing my head together – at least I think that's what she's doing. She did tell me. I forget. Anyway, she's really nice and very gentle and keeps asking if what she's doing hurts. I tell her no, but honestly? I couldn't say. I tell her thank you when she's finished. Maybe I don't say it right. All I know is she gives me this long look and when

I look back she does this little sniffy thing, like she's embarrassed that her eyes are damp. I don't know, are damp eyes considered unprofessional?

Before she goes, she tells me I'm really lucky, I have the ward all to myself. It's a sort of post-surgery ward, you see, and there was this really annoying cyberattack on the NHS today and the computers went down, so all non-emergency treatment was cancelled. She hopes there's a special place reserved in hell for this particular hacker.

"There's no such place," I say, and she nods and kind of bows and leaves.

Jeeze, I think I totally freaked her out. And after she made my boo-boo all better too. Not much of a human being, am I? Practically a monster, really. Yeah. A snivelling little monster, up and breathing and dressed in his nice new jim-jams brought straight from home. Remember what El said he slept in when he was a kid? His underwear. Same filthy underwear, night after night after night, until he was so raw with rashes even his dad said maybe someone should wash those pants.

But Dylan McKee? Well, I've always had everything I ever wanted, and I still ended up a whiny little bitch. If El had been given even a fraction of what I took for granted, just imagine what he could have achieved. But the universe doesn't work for people like Ellis Bell, does it? Just as his life was turning around, he gets this card dealt to him. And all because he was making me feel better after I'd hassled him with my stupid questions and suspicions. If only he'd been watching the road, he'd have seen that bastard thing – whatever it was – darting out of the trees. But no. Because needy little Dylan needed reassuring again, Ellis Bell is dead.

"I'm sorry to have to tell you this, Dylan, but your friend was found dead at the scene. Now, the police want to question you—"

I look down at my empty left hand. The hand my mum held because my right is taped up and bandaged. I can see her hand there now as clearly as I can see the doctor who was standing at the end of the bed, even though Mum's popped out for a coffee and the doc's probably writing up his notes somewhere. He had these thick glasses, the doc, and this big bald head that made him look a bit like a nerdy Lex Luthor.

"Oh, darling," my mum said, squeezing my hand. "Thank goodness you're all right."

"He's going to be just fine," said Dad from across the room.

My brother just stood there, looking tired and confused. I glanced at him and thought: *Was he right about you? Three girlfriends, yeah, but El's gaydar is pretty spectacular. Was. No, is. I don't care what Dr Luthor says.*

"Now, before my son answers any questions I want to

make one thing absolutely clear," said Dad in his pompous lawyer's voice, even though he only ever really draws up people's wills. I'd imagined him drawing up mine after I decided to leave all my worldly goods to El. When did that conversation happen, anyway? A week ago? A month? Dad butted into my thoughts: "Dylan will *not* be interviewed without legal representation."

"Well," said the doctor, blinking, "that's not really my department, but I believe the police only want a preliminary word. He won't be interviewed tonight as such."

"Oh. Well then," Dad huffed. "I suppose that's all right."

"Poor Ellis," said Mum, giving my hand another squeeze. "We all really liked him. Didn't we, love?"

"Eh?" Dad grunted.

"Ellis. He was a nice boy, wasn't he?"

"Oh. Yes. Interesting. Interesting boy. Very..."

"Interesting," I agreed, and my dad relaxed so much I wondered if Dr Luthor had given him an enema.

"And very funny. Wasn't he funny, Chris?"

My brother dragged himself into semi-consciousness. "What? Oh, yeah. Funny. He was really funny." I could practically hear the gears grinding into reverse. "I mean, funny ha-ha. Not weird-funny. You guys weren't weird. Being gay isn't weird at all. In fact, Hannah only just said tonight she thought you were really nice together. Cute." He grasped at the word like a life jacket. "Really cute."

Hannah's his old girlfriend. Number two since Christmas. The current one is Izzy.

It was then that I noticed the doctor looking at me, and I couldn't be sure – those lenses were so thick – but I thought I saw pity in his eyes. He consulted my chart and sighed.

"Ellis was your boyfriend, Dylan?"

"Yeah. He's…he's my boyfriend."

Dr Luthor nodded his great dome of a head. "Then you've lost someone very special. All right, once we've got your head fixed up, I think I'm going to allow the constable outside to have a few minutes with you, but then I'm going to prescribe a sedative, okay? It's just something to help you sleep."

The doc checked my pulse, asked if I was warm enough, took my temperature, listened to my chest, grunted, made a note. While all this was going on, Mum said Dad and Chris were heading home; she would just go grab herself a coffee from the canteen and be right back. Dad said he was leaving his mobile for me and that he'd call first thing in the morning. Chris seemed at a loss. Then he gave me a thumbs up and appeared delighted with himself.

I was left with Dr Luthor. He waved a pen light in front of my eyes.

"Dylan, do you know you're in shock?" He tutted at himself. "I'm sorry, stupid question. Now look, I can't sugar-coat this for you, I wish I could. What you've experienced tonight…" He shot a glance at the door and then gave me the saddest smile I've ever seen. And suddenly I knew who this man was. It woke me up, just a little. "It's better for your generation than it was for mine," he confided. "When we lost someone we loved it wasn't always easy to show our grief. Not that any of that matters tonight, or at all, really. The grief's exactly the same. But, Dylan, it is important that you *do* grieve. Do you understand?"

"Yeah," I told him. "Course."

He looked uncertain. "All right," he said finally. "Now I'm going to attend to a bit of paperwork while the nurse takes a look at your head, and then I'll let this police officer in to see you."

Right about then my brain went into free fall. Time got confused somehow. I have my head glued by the nice nurse, and I freak her out, and now the police officer is coming in just as I'm remembering my chat with the doc. Honestly, I have no idea what the officer looks like or what he's saying to me.

"Well, that's enough for now," he murmurs as I resurface. "A horrible accident. I'm really sorry about your friend."

My friend? Does he mean El? I shake my head. "So what about the guy who rescued me?" I wonder why I haven't asked this before. Shock, I guess, just like the doc said.

"I'm sorry?"

"The person who pulled me out of the car? Didn't he help Ellis too?"

The officer's frown deepens. It's weird because even now that I'm concentrating, I still can't really see what he looks like.

"I don't understand."

Jesus. Why is this man so dense? I'm not asking him the socio-economic causes of the French Revolution. It's a simple bloody question.

"Who," I say slowly, "saved me?"

And as I say it, the hideous extension of the question plays out in my mind: *Who saved me…and why did they leave El to die?* Because there was time. There had to be. The car wasn't all that far from the shore. Whoever dragged me out of the window only had to wade back a little way and drop me on the bank, then return for El. In fact it's simpler even than that. El wasn't trapped by his seatbelt. It would have been just as easy – no, *easier* – to pull him free first, then try to unharness me.

But they didn't do that. Which means it must have been a choice.

Ellis, they deliberately *left you to drown.*

"Who was it?" I shout.

Because I want to find them and then I want to kill them. I don't care that they saved my life. I don't want *this* life. Ellis is dead, I believe that now, and it's just like the poem says: *Darkness there and nothing more.* So who showed me mercy and condemned him? Who stood by and let the lake claim my El? I rise and fall with these questions as I tear the bed sheets from my body. I'm throwing things, I don't know what, pushing, wrenching, scratching at my own face until the glue that holds my cheek together breaks apart.

"WHO WAS IT? WHO SAVED ME? BECAUSE THEY KILLED HIM! THEY MURDERED *HIIIIIIIIM!*"

And then I see Dr Luthor swim into view. I'm on the floor. Has the officer knocked me down? Did I fall? I don't know. I just don't. The doc kneels over me, cradles my shoulders, smooths the blood from my face. His voice switches: softness for me, sharp orders for the nurse. He names drugs that sound like characters in a comic book.

"He was mine," I sob, and he nods and says:

"I know, Dylan. I know."

"I miss him."

"I know. You will."

And I feel the tiniest scratch.

The world becomes distant again. Edges blur. It's like drowning, I think.

"I loved him. He was mine. I miss him, I love him."

"All right. All right."

I'm lifted; sheets are straightened around me.

"They saved me. They left him. Why?"

Luthor shakes his head. He's a very long way away now. His glasses gleam like car headlights failing in the blackness of the lake.

"But there wasn't anyone," says the officer. "A passing motorist saw some of the debris in the road and called it in. The kid was alone on the shore when we found him. No one rescued him, doctor. He got himself out of that car. So why…?"

"Guilt," whispers the doctor. "Survivor's guilt maybe. He'll realize the truth, in time…"

THEN: Tuesday 5th November

The Bonfire

Mr Morris treats me to a half-hearted disapproving stare, then sighs and drops into the chair behind his desk.

"Your grades are good, Dylan, no one's disputing that. In fact, I've never had a better student in all my years of teaching... Oh, no offence, Mr Berrington."

Mike looks up from his desk where he's been role playing strategies for the footie team, crumbs of rubber eraser standing in for players.

"Huh? Oh, no offence taken, Mr M. Please, continue finding faults in the amazing McKee."

I shoot Mike the stink-eye. We're having our appraisal together simply because we're Dylan and Mike. It's understood we come as a pair, like Caesar and Brutus, Batman and Robin, social media and low self-esteem.

"You're doing pretty well in your other subjects too," Morris continues, as images of Mike's Batcave flash through my head. Mike would clearly be the Dark Knight in this combo, me his accident-prone Dick Grayson. The Boy Blunder. "*But*" – clearly my favourite teacher can tell I'm daydreaming – "as I say, there is this one weakness."

"Is it his ankles?" Mike asks. "Because that's not really his fault, sir. He's always had weak ankles. It's pitiful, really. You should've seen him as a baby fawn emerging from his mummy deer's gunk and trying to stand up. He was all trembly and cute and then some hunter went and shot his mum and... No, wait, that's *Bambi*. Sorry, I'll shut up."

"If there's a God, you will." Morris leans back and uses thumb and forefinger to smooth his nicotine-stained moustache. "Now, you must understand, I do have *some* sympathy with this whole 'school community spirit' thing, and the plain fact is, McKee, it's been noted that you show absolutely no interest in any extracurricular activities."

I look at him as if he's just told us that he secretly hates history.

"I'm sorry, sir?"

"No clubs, no societies, nothing. You too, Mr Berrington. Although in your case the accusation is softened due to your excellent performances on the football field."

"Oh God." Mike's head hits the desk, scattering his rubbery teammates. "C'mon, Mr Morris, you hate this bullshit as much as we do."

"Language."

"But, sir, Mike's right," I say. "This is all Gemma Argyle. Branded sweatshirts, school dances, charity bike rides, hero-worshipping the football team—"

"Hey," Mike interjects, "she has the occasional good idea."

I ignore him. "She's been watching too many bad American teen movies. Now she's like this ruthless social engineer, determined to make Ferrivale High into her own personal Hollywood high school nightmare. C'mon, Mr Morris, don't I contribute enough by getting good grades? Me and Mike alone are carrying half our class."

Mr Morris slaps his hands on the desk. "It is bullshit, boys, you're right. But you will find out pretty soon that ninety-nine per cent of your entire adult existence will be spent wading through other people's bullshit, and you'll have no choice but to smile and nod like it's the most fragrant summer stream. So. The Guy Fawkes Bonfire. Be there."

"Can you honestly believe this crap?" Mike says as we head down the hall. Posters for tonight's entertainment are splashed everywhere – they're basically this drawing of a scarecrow figure wreathed in flame. It looks like a human sacrifice; kind of feels like one too. "I guess I should be grateful. All the profits are going towards new strips for the footie team. But 'A Guy for the Guys'? Woooohoooo! Who came up with that title?"

Mike makes a limp-wrist gesture and skips around me as we walk.

"Yeah." I force a smile. "Lame."

Why can't I just tell him? Mike would be cool, I know he would. Cooler than my parents anyway, although they pride themselves on being *painfully* liberal. I think my mum would actually be okay with it, but maybe only because she already has this alpha male firstborn. If Chris didn't exist and I was her only kid? I don't know. It makes me nervous to think about it, so I try not to. But Mike? I'm pretty sure my own personal Batman would grin this huge Bat-grin and pull me into a massive Bat-hug and parade me around on his Bat-shoulders telling the world how Bat-proud he is of me. One thing I do know – he'd be mortified about all the gay jokes. To be fair, they are few and far between, yet every time he lets one slip it kind of kills me a little inside.

Death by a thousand Bat-cuts.

The school's quiet; we're probably the last students still here. I grab my bag from the sixth-form common room and we head for the exit. We're pushing through the main doors when Mike takes this sudden deep breath and reaches for the wall to steady himself.

"Hey." I grab his elbow. "You okay?"

"Yeah. I'm good." He looks at me. I know his face better than my own. I see it more regularly anyway. He can't hide stuff from me. "It's nothing."

"Mate, I've told you before: go – to – the – freaking – doctor. This is, what, the third time this has happened? I'm sure it's nothing, but if you don't go I will take you the hell down and haul your gorgeous arse there myself. Understood?"

"You think my arse is gorgeous? What would you give it out of ten?"

I roll my eyes. This is an old routine. "I'd give you a seriously hard ONE and you'd love it."

He titters, tells me I'm the worst, and skips off towards the bike sheds.

So this is the weird thing: I am *not* attracted to Mike. I never have been. But we have this stupid gay banter and it kind of blinds him to the reality of what's really going on with me. It's a technique I trialled and developed when we were twelve and it's worked beautifully for six years.

Right, and how many times have I wished he'd call me on it, just once?

"Hey! What about the Bullshit Bonfire tonight?" I shout after him.

"See you there, Sweet Cheeks!"

He blows me a kiss, which I catch one-handed.

Back at home I can hear my brother slaughtering zombies in his room. This is Chris's daily routine: breakfast around noon, followed by an hour in the tub, followed by an undead apocalypse. He's twenty-one, doesn't study, doesn't work. My dad's vaguely irritated but Mum likes having him around as her own personal chimp butler. He drives her to the shops, carries bags, compliments her latest night-class creations. She's lonely, I guess.

I dump my stuff on my bed and lock the door. I do *not* fancy Mike, but that stupid air-kiss? I don't know. I scoot onto my beanbag, flip open my laptop and bring up a couple of my favourite porn comics. I'm not really into "proper" porn; I can't see how anyone is. Two impossibly built dudes humping away? It makes me feel both pervy and inadequate. But comic book-style ridiculousness? Now, that's my world. And so, as Deadpool and the Joker and Mister Fantastic look down at me from my wall, I beat one off to this really well-drawn pirate porn comic. Despite the horrible historical inaccuracies (I'm pretty sure hot pants were *not* all the rage on the high seas in the seventeenth century), the story of Captain Colossus and his lusty crew does the job.

When I'm done I delete my browser history and use a wet wipe to mop up any spillage. TMI? Sorry. My mum's a snoop and my dad sometimes borrows my computer without asking. I'm just pulling up my trousers when the lady herself shoulder-barges the door. I know it's locked but still my penis shrivels immediately.

"What's going on?" she calls.

"Door's locked!"

"Why?"

"Um. Because I'm seventeen?"

"Oh." It takes a moment to compute. "Right. Sorry, love. Laundry?"

An hour later, I'm sitting on a stool in our stupidly immense kitchen spooning chilli into my mouth and checking my watch. I'm going to be late. I get up, throw my dish in the sink, and start towards the door.

"So this bonfire jamboree thing sounds exciting!" Mum calls after me.

"It's not a jamboree." I frown. "I don't know what a jamboree is exactly, but this isn't one."

"Will there be any girls there?" She smiles like she thinks there's some food stuck in her teeth and she wants me to check.

"I think that's very likely," I say.

She pouts. "When will you get a girlfriend, Dylan?"

"When he grows pubes," says Chris, then glances around like he's the reincarnation of Oscar Wilde. My dad doesn't look up from his laptop and Mum ignores him, for once. "You should just get yourself out there," Chris advises. "I've started dating this total babe called Hannah. Bit out of your league, bro, but—"

"Don't make your brother feel inadequate," Mum scolds.

"It will be a cold afternoon in waster hell when that twat makes me feel inadequate."

I flash them a grin and head for the door. I think Chris is probably still working out the insult. Anyway, I can't hear the rumble of a heavy primate advancing on all fours, so he's not following me.

There's a pinch in the air as I cycle down my drive onto Denvers Row. Already I can smell that smoky autumn bite, and above the trees and rooftops the sky glows here and there with the orange thumbmark of bonfires. It takes less than ten minutes to reach the football pitch, where I screech to a halt, turning a few heads in the queue for the entrance. Their vaguely hostile gaze makes me nervous as I wheel my bike to the stands.

I hate the idea of queueing up without Mike, but maybe he's already inside. I try his mobile. No answer. Crap. Taking a deep breath, I shuffle forward. Some people I don't know pile in behind me and, lost among them, my nerves finally start to settle. Being at the end of a queue always makes me feel horribly exposed.

Up ahead, I can see Gemma and the committee girls taking money and handing out tickets. Bloody Gemma Argyle. I was even thinking of discreetly checking out the LGBTQ safe-space group before she added it to her fiefdom.

"Hello there." She frowns at me as I reach the head of the line. "I want to say…David."

"You can say David," I tell her. "That is your right. But my name's Dylan."

"Of *course* it is," she beams, as if my first name had been her idea all along. "Are you alone tonight, Dylan?"

"Seems so."

"Oh, but you are just the most *terrible* date! Disowning me the first chance you get? Two tickets please."

I smile up at Mike as he elbows me aside and hands over a few quid to Gemma.

And so, the "Guy for the Guys" Bullshit Bonfire... It hurts my Gemma-loathing heart to admit it, but the committee has done a pretty good job. We wander around the field, grinning at the spectacles. Terrifying Miss Harper is behind a shooting gallery, snagging any passers-by with a hooked stick and basically bullying the cash out of their pockets. Mr Robarts is doing a roaring trade standing in the stocks while eager students pay fortunes to pelt him with wet sponges. Under a string of fairground lights, Mr Denman, the obscenely young new art teacher, is also raking it in drawing caricatures. Just about every girl in our year waits in line. Denman gives us a wave as we pass. He's pretty cool, and, if I'm honest, the subject of quite a few daydreams.

"Well." Mike grimaces as we reach the huge unlit bonfire at the centre of the field. "This kind of *doesn't* suck."

"I know. Maybe our school isn't the lamest place in the cosmos."

"Well, let's not go crazy."

Mike's laugh hasn't changed since Year Six. It's still a bit high and jittery and totally doesn't go with his footballer's physique. I sort of love that about him.

A random firework goes off from one of the houses neighbouring the school and Mike's grin is lit in blue and red flashes. I should just tell him. Worst case scenario: I spill my secret, he looks at me like I'm a bit of dog shit on the toe-end of his shoe and walks off, never to talk to me again. That would kill me, of course, but there's no way it would *ever* happen. Because he's Mike, and he's awesome.

Okay. So I'm telling him.

Here goes.

"Mikey boy! Bro, what was your deal today?"

Ollie Reynolds marches up to us, fist-bumping Mike. I don't dislike Ollie, but right at that moment I picture him strapped to a chair, the helpless victim of Slaughter Master, this comic-book villain Mike and I made up in primary school. Denzel Dreyfuss, aka Slaughter Master, is a mild-mannered candyfloss seller by day, but at night he captures superheroes in his sticky pink webs and tortures them in all kinds of inventive ways: pulling fingernails out, branding with hot irons, taking selfies with stupid candyfloss moustaches. Ollie would get the full treatment.

"Oh, hey, Dylan," he says, noticing me at last. "Now

listen, Mike, I know you're captain and everything, but I have to be honest, you are starting to suck out there. I mean, *majorly* suck. You barely made it through the first fifteen minutes this afternoon."

Mike shoots me a glance and, in another firework flare, I notice how exhausted he looks. There are these deep purple bruises under his eyes. Shit. What is going on with him? I need to get him alone, and I'm about to make up some excuse so we can take a walk, when Gemma and half the committee girls roll up. We all give her the compliments she's clearly expecting and she smiles and loops her arm through Ollie's. I had no idea they were dating. Weirdly, Ollie looks surprised too.

"So what are we all discussing, as if I can't guess!"

"It's a really amazing night, Gemma," one of her handmaidens trills.

"Not that." Gemma shoots her the stink-eye. "I mean our new arrival."

Ollie grins. "Yeah, he made quite an impression at training today."

I have no idea what they're talking about. Some new kid? Big deal. I just want to go somewhere I can talk privately to Mike.

"He's a little... Well, don't get me wrong, I am in no way prejudiced," says Ollie.

"You'd better not be," Gemma puts in. "As head of the

LGBTQ safe-space group, I will not tolerate intolerance in our school."

I drag my gaze back to Gemma.

"Right." Ollie nods. "But don't you think people can take it a bit far? I mean, turning up like that to practice, and then expecting Mr Highfield to let him on the team? Come on!"

"The question should be, was he any good?" Gemma says.

"Well, I really liked him." Mike shrugs. "And he *was* good. You can't deny it, Ollie, he placed that corner like a pro. I don't care if he was wearing pearls."

"Pearls?" I say.

"No one in our team could've taken that corner as sweetly, and you know it," Mike continues. "I argued with Highfield after the game. It's a disgrace Ellis wasn't selected."

Ellis? He wears pearls to footie try-outs? I have to know this kid.

Ollie holds up his hands. "I'm with you, but what you gonna do? You know Highfield. He's a pig-headed old bastard. He won't back down."

"Oh, please, that bitch is going to back down all right. Trust me."

It's a sweet, strong, musical voice. Our little huddle turns and there's this kid standing behind us, tall and smiling and beautiful and just…overwhelming. I take a sidestep behind Mike, not because I'm scared or shy – something about this guy tells me he'd never want to inspire those emotions – but because I want a moment just to take him in. While I'm watching, he waves about a hundred sheets of paper in the air.

"So, students of Ferrivale, who's going to be first to sign my petition?"

NOW: Monday 27th April

8

Mumzilla's brake lights flash in the rain like two angry eyes. I blink, sneeze, and swipe the downpour from my face with the sleeve of my jacket. Carol Berrington gets out of the car just a second or two after Mike bursts from the passenger door. I stand stock-still and watch him splash his way up the gleaming lane. He's moving fast, no stumble, and for the first time in almost a month I feel my heart beat in a way that isn't just mechanical. When Mike reaches me his breathing is strong and steady and the bruises under his eyes seem to have faded a little. I want to smile, but don't. Even for Mike, a smile would be a betrayal.

"Jesus, Dylan, you're drenched!"

I look down at myself. My black school shoes feel squelchy and my funeral suit is starting to bobble.

"Yeah." I squint up at him. "I am a bit."

Carol reaches us and draws up short, hands on her

hips as she takes me in.

"Oh, honey, what were you thinking?" She shakes her head, but not in the condescending way that has recently earned my parents a pretty spectacular *Fuck you!* Behind the rain I can see her eyes fill with tears. "Michael," she says gently, "get him into the car."

Mike puts an arm around my shoulder and guides me to the grumbling Volkswagen estate. Exhaust fumes coil, smoky and dragonish around my ankles. I want to kick the fumes away but that would be crazy, and I'm trying my best not to show the crazy today.

So I've learned recently that I'm a pretty good actor. I performed my heart out to our GP anyway, and he never once saw through me. He just gave me a bottle of diaze-something and told me to come back if I ever felt like lying down in front of a train. For that whole seven-minute appointment, I kept everything beautifully under control. I did this by imagining I was standing in front of a huge computer workstation, like Homer's in *The Simpsons*. If I sensed a danger signal, I'd vent a little toxic gas and the dials would flick back into the green.

Did I learn this from you, El? The ability to keep everything running smoothly while underneath all you want to do is scream and shout and tear down the world? Were you at your own safety station that night of the dance, adjusting your switches and dials? You were so scared…

Suddenly I realize I'm in the back of the Volkswagen, my body half-turned towards Mike. Carol has put on the heater full blast and Mike's dug out a blanket and is towelling my hair. We always joke that Mumzilla's car is like Mary Poppins' handbag – whatever is required can be found, you only have to *believe*.

"Hey, Bitch," I say as Mike unveils me.

He gives me this watery smile. "Hey, Bumboy."

I hear snuffling from the boot and Beckham appears at the guard. I reach through the cage and Becks licks my fingers. I used to have this weird dream a while back that the actual David Beckham would take the place of the Berringtons' family pet and lick my digits. Weird, I know. The still-sprightly ten-year-old collie gives me this dewy-eyed look.

"I love you too, Becks," I tell him.

"Here," says Mike. He holds out his black suit jacket. "Take yours off. Mum'll get it dry-cleaned."

"Mum will," Carol confirms.

"I can't, what will you wear?"

"I've got my coat."

I thank him and pull on the jacket. It's too big but Mike manages to arrange it somehow on my skinny shoulders, and I guess it looks okay. Better than my sopping jacket anyway. If I'd walked in like that, the congregation might have thought I'd stopped off for a dip in Hunter's Lake –

you know, for old times' sake. I shiver. It's like I can still feel the water's touch creeping along the inside of my thigh, still hear the jealous lake whispering:

So you thought this was forever?

Mike sees my hand trembling. He takes it and cups it in his own. It's my bad hand; the one I damaged trying to free myself from the seatbelt. My shoulder still aches occasionally – bruised bone – and the cuts on my scalp continue to itch, but the scar on my cheek doesn't cause me any trouble, and Chris says it looks pretty badass. But my hand won't do everything it's told, basically because of nerve damage. It hurts like hell most of the time too. The doctor gave me these painkillers, told me to use them sparingly, but he needn't have bothered. Soon as I got home they were flushed.

I deserve the pain. I deserve the crazy. I deserve a messed-up hand. No one's taking these things away from me.

The windscreen wipers whump. The heater chunters. Mike angles his body back into his seat, keeping hold of my hand the whole time. We've sat like this a lot over the past three-and-a-half weeks, comfortable as we can be in this endless silence.

"Dylan," says Carol from the front, "where's your mum and dad?"

Hey, it would've been weird if she hadn't asked.

84

"They didn't think it was appropriate to come today."

"What?" Mike glares. "Why the hell not?"

"Michael," says Mumzilla. "I'm sure Barbara and Gordon have their reasons."

A nerve jumps in Mike's throat.

So it's a short story. It went like this:

I knew your Aunt Julia would struggle with the funeral, El. You lived in a rented flat in Mount Pleasant and, although Julia worked herself ragged managing the bakery, there was never quite enough money. And, El, you were a miracle-worker. You put together the most delicious meals and you looked freaking awesome every single day of your life, accessorizing your uniform in such a stylish way that Mr Robarts could never quite bring himself to enforce the school dress code. But the truth was, you and Julia were only just about getting by. And you were my boyfriend. You were amazing. All I wanted was for your send-off to be amazing too.

"I'm just saying we could host the wake here," I said. "It only needs to be a small tea for family and friends."

"But, Dylan, it's not really our place," my dad objected.

"His aunt might think it presumptuous." Mum nodded.

"I'll ask her," I said. "No problem. I'll go over there right now and if she says she's cool with it, then—"

"You don't understand, Dylan. These people can be very proud."

My mum's mouth clamped shut but the words were out. No way I wasn't calling her on that.

"*These* people? What exactly do you mean by that, Mum?"

"Dylan, I think your mother—"

"Dad." I stopped him mid-excuse. "I'm asking for a few pots of tea, a couple of sandwiches, maybe some biscuits – what's the big deal? We can give El a really nice…" My throat thickened over the word, but I forced it out. "…send-off. And you won't have to pay. Not really. It'll be a loan to me. Whatever it costs, I'll give you back every penny, I promise."

"Son, it isn't about the money."

"Good, then—"

"It's the principle. Hosting a stranger's wake?" He shook his head. "It's just not the done thing."

That was when I sent Mum's pube sculpture flying. It smashed against the wall and bits of reed or whatever the hell it was made of ended up just about everywhere.

"El wasn't a stranger! I loved him. He was my boyfriend. We laughed and told each other stories and held hands and went to the movies and argued and… And he was my partner, Dad, just the same as Mum is your partner, and I want to give him a final party, that's all."

"Dylan, it isn't the same."

I stared at both of them. "If you don't know that it's *exactly* the same then you never understood us at all."

Hunching down, I tried to pick a few of the reeds from the carpet, but my stupid hand wouldn't work. "Look," I said, getting up, "I know you've saved for my uni stuff. Well, I don't want it. I'm not going. So just give me a few fucking quid so I can say goodbye to my dead boyfriend."

Mum ran out of the room crying; Dad hung his head and said nothing. So I told him he had a pube in his hair and went to my room.

I would've left home that night, except where would I have gone? To Mike's maybe. Mumzilla would take me in, no question, but I didn't want to bring all my crap to their door. Anyway, Mike was really sick all of last week, throwing up practically every time he took a breath. That last round of chemo really took it out of him.

But the simple fact is, I'm not as brave as you, Ellis. I'm too much of a pussy to leave home properly.

"Here we are," says Carol gently.

We glide into a parking space at a proper funereal pace and all get out. It looks like we're running late. There's no one outside the crematorium chapel. Carol turns me to face her, brushes some fluff from my shoulders, and gives me a smile that's all raised chin.

"You look very handsome, Dylan." And she just can't help it. She bursts into tears. "You'll do him proud today, I know you will."

"Mum." Mike puts an arm around her shoulder and

starts to guide her into the chapel, then glances back. "You coming, mate?"

"I will," I promise. "Just give me a minute."

He nods and they disappear.

The rain has stopped. It pisses me off. The world should weep its heart out today. I walk under the crematorium awning where the hearses pull up.

Yours is there, El. There's a name card in the window, but it's empty. I look over the cream-coloured building, built to resemble some peaceful country chapel. It's all wrong. You should be taken to Hideous Beauty. To *our* church. To our home. I'd carry you up those winding steps to the belfry and lay your body on the bare boards that used to groan and sing under us. I'd bring you handfuls of snowdrops, the ones that grow around the unreadable gravestones, and make a halo for your head. And then, once I've answered the questions that need to be answered – once I've found out who scared you so much and who left you to die – I'll make a place for you in that tangled churchyard and place a marker that reads *Ellis Maximillian Bell* and nothing else. Because there is no lifetime to fill up the rest of the stone, no special dates and memories and achievements. All we have left ahead of us is ash and dirt.

I wander into the vestibule. There's a half-open door with an easel beside it that states: *Funeral of Ellis Bell.* There's a book of condolence on the opposite side of the room with a pen on a chain. I snap the chain and use the pen to insert an arrow symbol between *Ellis* and *Bell* and write above it *Maximillian*.

Then I take a huge breath and enter the chapel.

9

George Ezra fills the chapel. That deep, soulful voice that hums in your chest. It's a bluesy, country tune with soul and twang and, most people would think, completely inappropriate for a funeral. I think it's perfect.

Except it tries to force me back into the car: *your finger reaching for the off-switch, killing the music before you start touching me.*

No. I won't go back there. Not yet.

So the tragic death of a schoolboy is clearly a draw. The place is packed. Carol and Mike have saved a space for me at the back and I start moving towards them. A few kids from school give me a couple of shy waves, which I automatically return. If they weren't hanging around in the halls when I told Mr Morris I was quitting, or in that assembly where I made the mother of all scenes, then they haven't seen me since the Easter dance. Mr Morris didn't say much when I told him, just advised me to take whatever time I needed. I will. Because I'm not "commendable but unfocused" now, sir. I'm very focused indeed. I *will* find out who pulled me out of that car and why they left Ellis to drown.

Morris himself is there with Mr Robarts and most of the other teachers – so many teachers that they must have shut down the entire school for the afternoon. Even El's art teacher Mr Denman, who's only recently back from sick leave, has shown up. He sits next to Miss Harper, who blows her nose and waves a very un-Harperish handkerchief at me.

A row or two from the front sits Gemma and the committee witches and at the end of their line is Ollie Reynolds. I note in passing that Ollie isn't the boy clutching Gemma's shoulder and handing her Kleenex after Kleenex. I think it's Paul Donovan, but I can't be sure. All those square-backed rugby boys look alike. Is that prejudice? Am I ruggerist? I'm pondering this question when a hand touches my arm.

"Dylan, would you like to come see him?"

It takes all my willpower to look up into that old-before-its-time face. El's Aunt Julia is in her fifties, and is always pretty glamorous, but today she looks seventy. Her make-up and mascara have already run into deep lines and canyons.

In the weeks since you died, El, I've sat down a hundred times to call her, and each time I've cancelled the call before it could connect. What could I possibly tell her apart from that it's all my fault? If you hadn't been distracted by the need to comfort and reassure me, then the accident would never have happened.

I feel Mike's hand pat my back as Julia guides me gently out of the row and down the central aisle. Eyes are on me; there are murmurs. I daren't look up. Not because I'm afraid of the stares – I would have been, back in the days before the bonfire, before you – but because I know you're waiting for me, like always, somewhere up ahead.

I'm fighting flashes of memory as we go. The ones that have haunted me these past weeks and won't let me sleep, but also flashes of Julia herself: the bathroom floor at your flat, blood on the lino, you comforting and cursing her at the same time. I mount two shallow steps and, head still down, see the side of your coffin and the sawhorse things that hold it up. My eyes drift. I see puffy satin; the sleeve of a smart suit I don't recognize. Maybe it's not you in there. Maybe this is all a joke.

Let it be a joke.

"I'm sorry, Dylan. I didn't know if you'd want him like this, but I had no way of contacting you and I had to make a decision. It had to be an open casket, didn't it? Because we don't want our boy shut away in the dark."

I shake my head. "It's fine. Whatever you want. It was your decision."

I can't move beyond the suit. Not yet.

"No, sweet boy," she says. "He wasn't just mine. He was *ours*."

I nod, though I know she wouldn't think this if she knew the truth. She'd hate me then, maybe almost as much as I hate myself.

"I'm sorry, Julia. I should've come to see you." I fight the lump in my throat. Surely we have to move. Surely they have to start the service. But Julia isn't the kind of person anyone can move before she's ready. "I wasn't..."

I see her hands reach out and straighten something in the coffin.

"Now listen," she says. "None of this is your fault. Are you hearing me, Dylan? *None* of it."

But you don't know, Julia, I think. *You have no idea...* I reach into the back pocket of my trousers and take out a crumpled, rain-stained envelope. Unfolding it, I pull back the flap and thumb through a few damp notes, then try to pass it to her.

Is this appropriate? Who the hell knows? I don't think there's an etiquette for losing you.

Julia sees what I'm trying to do and waves her hand. "What is this, Dylan?"

"A hundred pounds. I'm not sure if that's even close to

93

being enough, but… It's some of my uni savings. I'm not going. Please take it, Julia. I know you've probably already paid for all this, but I'd like to make a contribution, maybe towards the wake."

"Put that back in your pocket before we fall out," she tells me. She isn't offended, she just sounds tired. "If I took that, Ellis would never forgive me. He was so excited about you going to Bristol. It's all he ever bloody talked about." And suddenly she's laughing and straightening something else I can't – won't – look at. "Morning, noon and night. You know he had your whole student flat decorated in his mind."

I nod. "It would've been spectacular."

"Course it would. Now listen, don't you give up on that dream. If you do, you'll have me to answer to, understand?" She laughs again, and there's a stir behind us as if everyone's super-curious about this endless coffin-side conference. "I'm just fine with the expenses. I stopped taking that junk the day you and Ellis found me, so I've saved a bit. And it's a simple coffin…"

I twine my fingers together. George Ezra has stopped singing about his "Saviour" and there's a shuffling quiet in the chapel. Someone whispers in Julia's ear and she hisses back, "*Wait. Give him time.*

"Look at him, Dylan," she says softly.

I can't. I ball up my fists. I can't.

"It's okay, sweetheart. Just look."

And I do.

You have a halo, but it isn't snowdrops. It's even more perfect. Pillowing your head and fanning out all around you are your drawings. Dozens of them, big and small, scribbled into life on napkins and carefully worked out on foolscap. Quick, breathless sketches, some barely more than a scratch or two on the paper, others spellbindingly intricate studies. People, animals, still life, cityscapes and country lanes, abstract shapes and honest portraits, every style mastered, every subject echoing your force and energy. Your work is your shroud, Ellis, and it's the saddest, most wonderful thing I've ever seen.

I grasp the edge of your coffin when I see it. I'm here, right with you. A simple portrait you must have sketched of me when I had no idea you were working. This seems impossible, because surely I was *always* watching you. But here I am, looking off into the distance, the side of my lip caught between my teeth, my eyes brimming with happiness. Where were we that day? A rooftop picnic? Cross-legged under our favourite tree in the park? High up in our bell tower? The thing is, Julia has placed me so that I am nestled right beside you on the pillow, and those joyful eyes seem focused on one thing only – you.

I gather up the last shreds of my courage and let my eyes move inwards from this perfect halo. I remember hating you when you wouldn't wake up in the car. How could I ever hate this face? Those eyes, closed now, that saw some worth in me. That chin and jaw and those sharp cheekbones that rested against my own poor face when we held each other. Those lips that gifted me my first real kiss, and my last.

"El," I murmur.

I reach for your hands, folded across your chest like you're trying to protect your heart. When I touch you, I realize something. There is no cold like this – not anywhere in the world. It isn't the cold of stone or wind or ice.

It's emptiness.

And suddenly this sound rises up from someplace I've never felt before. It's not my stomach or my lungs, it's a deeper, secret place that perhaps you only get to reach into once or twice in a lifetime. Some of the people behind us give this little surprised cry when they hear it. El, I can't describe this sound. It's all our tossed and torn and battered hopes, all our stolen future and our darkened past rolled into one. It comes without tears. It's too huge for them.

Mike. Mike is here and holding me like I'm his own child.

"It's okay, Dylan," he whispers, and cradles my head to his shoulder. "Jesus, if I could just... It's okay."

Julia squeezes his arm. "Take him outside. El never liked these places anyway. Let him do his grieving in the open air."

But you did like churches, I want to tell her. Not fake clinical pretend places like this. Not factories for processing the dead. You told me once you never believed in God, not even when you were little, but you loved the houses worshippers had built for Him. *People say Art is about truth, you told me, but that's bullshit. Truth is dull and frightening and soul-destroying. Art is about the wonderful lies we tell ourselves so that we can bear to live with the truth. Churches are like that. Beautiful, hideous lies.*

I don't know how Mike gets us out of the chapel. One minute I'm making this inhuman sound over your body and the next we're under the awning where the hearses wait. I go limp. Mike has to catch me and hold me up. Because I've just understood something and it's taken the last of my strength away.

I am never ever going to see you again.

You're gone, El. Officially gone. And it's about time I started.

I turn to Mike. "Will you do something for me?"

He nods without hesitation. "Anything. You know that."

"Then help me find the person who rescued me," I say. "Because I need to ask them one important question."

"What question?"

I shake my head. "Why did they leave him to die?"

10

Mike removes his black baseball cap and rubs a hand across a smooth, hairless scalp. I'm an idiot. I should have realized what he'd done as soon as I saw the cap. Mike has hated hats ever since World Book Day in Year Seven when Jessie Atkins laughed at the diamanté-studded cowboy hat Carol had bought him. Mike had come as this hard-as-nails gunslinger from these old Wild West novels he read with his dad. He was so proud, and then Jessie started laughing and pointing and calling him "Brokeback Berrington". The name stuck for a whole term and that was the end of Mike's love affair with both hats and reading.

"I know." He shrugs. "How hard am I rocking this look?"

"Pretty frickin' hard." I nod.

"So I finally took El's advice," he says. "Shaved off the lot. It was getting really patchy and gross-looking anyway. Do you think he'd approve?"

Mike had the most amazing hair before this fuckstorm of horribleness hit him. Honestly, girls used to ogle those thick curly locks from the other side of the canteen.

"I think El would love it," I say. "It makes your eyes really stand out somehow. I never realized before how blue they are."

He seems pleased with this. We're sitting on a bench in an area of the crematorium called The Garden of Tranquillity. I guess it lives up to its name. There are these long avenues with arches of trailing flowers, pink and purple and white trumpets, and the air smells of honeysuckle.

"All right," he says, "so do you want to tell me what's going on?"

But suddenly I'm not ready. Saying what I need to say to Mike might reveal things about me that I'm not sure I want revealed. It has to be done, I know, but I need a moment. I press my hands between my knees and lower my gaze. "How're you doing, Mike?"

"Well, apparently I have these incredibly sexy eyes now." He bats his eyelids and I notice his lashes, like the rest of his hair, are gone. He catches my look and shrugs. "It's been a week, bit more, since my last chemo, and I no longer feel like hurling my guts up every five seconds. I've started jogging again too, and Ollie comes round for a kickabout every now and then."

"You were at the hospital that day," I murmur.

He nods and looks away. "Hooked up to my favourite drip and then wheeled home. Sorry I wasn't still there when…" He makes this wet coughing sound. "When they brought you in."

"Dude, don't be ridiculous."

"But we are ridiculous, mate." He sucks his forefinger and waggles it in my ear until I laugh and slap him away.

I *laugh*. I'm sorry, El.

"Berrington and McKee, the Incredible Twat Brothers. Remember?"

I do. Our escapology act, Year Seven. We'd seen this documentary about how magician Harry Houdini had escaped from a water tank while suspended upside down, and decided, in our stupidity, that before the summer was over we'd thrill the town with our own death-defying feat. We borrowed books from the library, built our own props, secretly printed a million tickets on my dad's printer, and invited the whole neighbourhood to the show. The result: Mike nearly suffocated inside a sack and my mum had to call the fire brigade to cut me out of my chains. Ollie Reynolds pissed his pants laughing and came up with the name of our extinct double act: the Incredible Twat Brothers.

"Okay," Mike says, "no more beating about the bush. Let's hear it."

And so I take a huge breath, and tell him everything. Some he already knows – the pervy Instagram video and me and El showing up at the Dipshits Ball, but then I describe El's mood switch after the dance and Mike looks troubled.

"Maybe someone said something to him or he saw something, I don't know, but for those few minutes he was frightened. I mean, genuinely terrified. But El had this amazing self-control, and when I tried to question him about it, he turned the conversation around. I know that sounds weak – I guess you had to be there."

"I knew Ellis," Mike assures me. "I can see how that could happen. So you left the dance… What next?"

"We're driving by the lake. El seems okay again, and then…" I hesitate.

A little omission I can't bring myself to confess: how you were touching me before the accident; how my stupid insecurities distracted you.

"Something flashed into the road," I go on. "I don't know what it was. An animal, probably. El loses control and the car flips."

Weird, this bullet-point summary. No terror, no grief, nothing between the lines. It's the only way I can tell it.

"We're in the lake, and I'm about to pass out when someone wades into the water and drags me out of the car. And this is the whole point: he saves *me* and leaves El."

I explain my reasoning as to why it would have been easier to rescue El first, and that anyway there had to have been time to save us both.

"Why didn't you tell me all this before?" Mike asks, his voice heavy.

"It's something El said. When I kept asking about what had frightened him at the dance, he said he didn't want me mixed up in it. Like maybe it was dangerous. And if it *is* dangerous, Mike, I'm not sure I want you involved. But, look, I've been turning it all over and over in my mind, night after night, and it seems impossible. How do I even start to find out what really happened?"

Mike holds up his hand. "First, you're an idiot. You *always* come to me when you need help, Dylan. And if you think something's dangerous? You come running."

"I know, but—"

"No buts. Now, what exactly do you want to know?"

"For starters, who made that video of us? Because maybe it's all connected. The video started this chain of events that led to El's death. No video, no me coming out, no dance, no distracted El driving. But I also want to know what upset him that night. You should've seen him, Mike, I don't think you'd have recognized him. Last, and most important, I want to know who saved me and why they left El to die."

Mike takes a breath. "Dylan, I don't know…"

I look up at him. "What do you mean, you don't know?"

"This whole thing." He hesitates. "This investigation – whatever you want to call it – are you sure it's what you really want?"

"What I *want*? Jesus, Mike, we're talking about someone who scared the shit out of my boyfriend. Someone who left him to drown."

"Okay." Mike holds up his hands. "But didn't your doctor say all of this could be survivor's guilt? You acted on instinct, you got yourself out of the car. No one would ever blame you for that, mate. But this person you imagined saving you? Maybe it's just your way of dealing with that reality."

My hands curl into fists and I have to take a moment. "Mike," I say at last, "I tore my hand to pieces on the belt buckle trying to free myself. It was jammed. I couldn't do it. I had to be rescued. But here's the thing: El's belt had snapped. Saving him would have been *much* easier than saving me. But he wasn't saved. He was left. Now, do you believe me when I tell you that's what happened?"

"Dylan, I just—"

"*Do you believe me?* Because if you don't then you're saying that *I* abandoned Ellis. Is that what you think?"

"No." He looks away. "No, Dylan, of course I don't think that."

"Then are you going to help me? Because believe me,

Mike, with or without you, I'm going to find out the answers to these questions. I owe Ellis that much."

We sit in silence for a long time. Eventually Mike stirs.

"Okay, so let's think this through. Logically, I don't think these three things are connected. It would be too much of a coincidence that the video perv also happened to be at the lake when you crashed. And I can't see how the video thing would frighten El at the dance. He knew about it already."

"And it sort of served his purpose," I say. "He thought I should come out to my folks and the video was the prompt to do it. Don't get me wrong, he was angry, but, yeah, that wasn't what scared him."

"And again, it would be too much of a coincidence if the person that scared El at the dance was also at the lake. So we're talking about three separate things: 1. Who is video perv? 2. What scared El at the dance? 3. Who was your rescuer, and what was his deal with El?"

"So you do believe me," I ask, "about the rescuer?"

He leans back, looking skyward. "Yes, I believe you."

"Good. Because no one else does. You heard about the Year Seven assembly?"

He nods. "I heard."

It happened the same day I told Mr Morris I was putting my A levels on hold. I was heading down the corridor, keeping my gaze fixed on the floor, because everywhere I looked reminded me of El: El chasing a squealing Gemma

104

out of biology, an imaginary frog cupped in his hand; El joshing with the footie lads, messing up Ollie's perfectly waxed hair; El and me, out of sight in the little alcove under the stairs, brushing fingertips.

Passing the main hall, a familiar voice drew my gaze from the floor and through the glass doors. The same police officer who had interviewed me at the hospital was standing at the podium, lecturing Year Sevens about bike safety. He was sweating, like pushing the clicker on his PowerPoint was such hard work. I threw open the doors and started stalking towards him.

"Hey, Shit-for-Brains!" I called out. "Any chance you could fit in a murder investigation between cycle safety and doughnut hour? Yeah, that's right, my boyfriend's still dead, in case you were wondering."

Mr Denman tried to get in my way. I elbowed him aside and he made this surprised, ragged grunt. I feel bad about that. It's pretty obvious his arm's never going to be the same after that car hit him over the Christmas break, and I've got a sick feeling that exact weak spot was where I shoved him. Right then, however, I didn't give Denman a second thought. Instead, I went toe-to-toe with PC Asshat. He said something gently threatening and put a hand on my shoulder.

"Why're you touching me?" I said. "All I'm doing is asking a question."

He told me, very quietly and firmly, that there was no evidence of another person at the scene of the accident, then advised me to leave before I was arrested. I called him a lying bastard and headed for the door.

"Not my finest hour," I mutter to Mike.

"Oh, I don't know. Pretty standard for one of the Twat Brothers, I'd say."

"You see, the police *do* think it's survivor's guilt," I continue. "But, Mike, I swear, I relive that night every minute of every day, and I *know* there was someone else. So that means El must have had enemies. Someone who would leave him to die. Except who could ever hate him that much?"

Mike shakes his head. "I don't know."

I look over to the chapel. People are starting to file out into the watery spring daylight, chatting, sharing a joke, folding service cards into their pockets.

"There's something else too," I say. "I think that whatever scared El at the dance is connected to his disappearing act at Christmas. Remember I told you how strange that whole week was? Well, something about his fear at the dance reminded me of how he was back in December. It was like—"

Suddenly Mike stands up, his gaze flitting along the avenue.

"What's wrong?" I ask, joining him.

"Nothing." He shakes his head. "No, it's nothing. It was just for a minute I thought I saw someone standing there, watching us." Then he loops an arm around my shoulder and we start back towards the chapel. "It's going be all right, Dylan," he tells me. "I swear it will."

THEN: Saturday 23rd November

The Bookshop

I'm nesting in my usual corner in Hug-A-Book, hiding behind my copy of *The French Revolution 1789-1799*, eating Starbursts and daydreaming about the boy who sits across from me in history. It's been almost three weeks since the bonfire, and I can't get him out of my head. Okay, so I've had crushes before – *High School Musical*-era Zac Efron, early-Wolverine Hugh Jackman, and some real-life studs too, like Alex Dayus, who was in Year Eleven when we were in Year Nine – but this Ellis kid is different. Whenever the bell rings and he packs up his stuff and heads off for a lesson I won't be in, it just kind of kills me.

Arrrggghhhhhhhh! Why am I so bloody shy? It's not like he hasn't given me opportunities to talk to him. Even that first night, he was flirting with me. I think. I'm not exactly a world expert on flirting. I rock back in my favourite squidgy Hug-A-Book chair and replay the bonfire in my mind, occasionally tenting the *The French Revolution* over my jeans. Yeah, I am honestly that ridiculous…

"So, students of Ferrivale, who's going to be first to sign my petition?"

He's wearing this amazing sand-coloured coat that reaches down to his ankles, like those duster jackets cowboys wore in old movies. The skinniest of skinny jeans, a purple T-shirt with Cookin' picked out in diamantés, and black leather boots complete the outfit. A string of pearls around his neck runs red in the bonfire that has just ignited behind us, and his smooth skin seems to hold the light. His smile is kind and gently mocking at the same time.

He doesn't ask permission but hands us each a petition sheet and a ballpoint. I notice he gives everyone a sentence or two and they grin, as if he only has words for them. This kid's a born politician.

He stops in front of me. And I think he pauses longer with me than anyone else. Or am I delusional? All I know is my mouth is like a desert, and I'm gawping.

"Well," says the boy in the pearls, "will you help a brother out?"

I have this awkward liberal-white-guy moment. Does he mean "brother" in a black brotherhood kind of way, in which case it would be totally inappropriate for me to respond. Or…

My mouth is now a desert on Mars. Does he know? Just by looking at me, does he have this ultra-sensitive gaydar that can penetrate the civilian disguise of the most lame-brained, straight-acting, doofussy gay guy and identify him as a "brother" just by looking at him? My brain is jellifying and I keep glancing up from the petition to find him looking at me with this crooked sideways smile.

I sign and hand back the petition.

"Thank you, Frecks," he says.

Then he touches me. Or not quite. The pads of his fingers hover over the bridge of freckles that span my nose, and it's like electricity moving across my face. I smell the sweetness of his fingers. Starburst. My junk food connoisseur senses would know that smell anywhere. He likes Starburst. I file that fact away for future reference.

"Hello," I say. "I'm, uh, Dylan."

He shakes his head and, because I'm an idiot, I shake mine. "No?"

"No," he says. "You're Frecks. And now I'm going to scold you, Frecks."

"Okay."

"You just signed something without reading it. Do you know what that piece of paper actually says?"

"I don't."

"It says that you must be my friend and live only to please me until your dying day. This is a legally binding document,

Mr Frecks." He brandishes it like the Magna Carta. "Will you honour your commitments?"

"I will," I say, and I take a knee, as if I'm about to be knighted.

He laughs and swats me with the petition. "Get up, you adorable moron. See, it says here that Mr Highfield, the protoplasmic bigot who runs Ferrivale High football, must give me a place on the team. Doubtless you've heard about my stellar try-out today? And anyway, just look at these thighs! Don't they deserve to be seen in very short shorts?"

He pushes out his right leg and cups a bulging thigh muscle between his big hands. Is there a place drier than the deserts of Mars? My mouth is now that place.

"You make a strong argument…"

"Ellis," he tells me.

"Ellis."

He stands up again and looks at me for a long time. I drop my gaze. Jesus, I want to look at his thigh again. I want to look at his dancing fingers and his swimmer's body and his coal-black curls and his eyes. Maybe just his eyes. For an hour or two.

But then I hear Gemma's piercing voice and hers and Ollie's and Mike's petitions are thrust into Ellis's hand.

"Welcome to Ferrivale, new boy! I'm Gemma and I run the LGBTQ safe space at school, and I want you to know that you're welcome any time. Our meetings are—"

He arches an eyebrow. "What makes you think I'm gay?"

"Well. I just assu—"

"Assumptions are at the root of all prejudice," he tells her, and flashes me a sidelong smile. I have to bite the inside of my cheek. "What kind of school is this anyway?"

Behind Gemma both Ollie and Mike are grinning like hyenas. Ellis lets her hang for a minute, then catches her in a hug. I'm immediately jealous.

"I'm only playing with you, honey. I'm sorry."

Gemma cracks up in that high-pitched way of hers. I swear it sets off car alarms five streets over. Ellis is still hugging her and assuring her of his gay credentials when this hand comes out of nowhere and shoves him in the back. We're all stunned as Gemma stumbles a bit, but Ellis trots gently forward as though he's been expecting it all evening.

"What do you think you're doing, you little homo?"

I turn to see Alistair Pardue, followed by a couple of his fellow knuckle-draggers. Honestly, these guys make the Incredible Hulk look witty and sophisticated.

Alistair's knocked Ellis pretty close to the bonfire, but he just brushes himself down and saunters back into our huddle.

"Homo?" he muses. "Okay, but I assure you, in no department can I be described as 'little'."

"Are you guys just gonna stand here and let this queer make a laughing stock of the team?" Alistair spits at Mike and Ollie.

Mike groans and Ollie pinches the bridge between his eyes.

They've both wanted Alistair off the team for ages but Mr Highfield is drinking buddies with Al's dad. Mike tells me he'd rather have me in defence than Pardue, which is a pretty harsh indictment of Alistair's skills.

"Get lost, Al," Mike says. "You wear me out."

"It's okay," Ellis holds up his hand. "Let the man speak."

Alistair rolls his head, shoulder to shoulder, and fronts up to Ellis. I should do something. I'm no fighter, never have been, but this crap makes me feel ashamed of our school. And anyway, I'd rather Alistair rearrange my imperfect face than Ellis's perfect one. I'm about to say something – Christ knows what – when Alistair says:

"You try out for the team again, I will personally fuck you up."

Ellis shrugs. "You can try."

Alistair roars and starts to swing his fist. And Ellis is like Barry Allen, aka the Flash. I'm not even kidding. That long, lithe body stoops and draws back, then he throws his hand behind his shoulder and uses those huge (breathtaking!) thigh muscles to power his punch right the way through his body. Four knuckles strike Alistair in the sweet spot under his jaw and his head snaps back. And then he's flying, almost somersaulting, and the knuckle-draggers are quickly making room for a very awkward landing. Al hits the deck just as Ellis shakes loose his fingers.

Then, from the other side of the field, and right on cue, the school band trills –

Ta-dah!

"That. Was. Awe. Some!" Mike shouts.

Ollie just stands there, mouth open. Gemma squeaks. Meanwhile Ellis sidles over.

"Hey, Frecks."

"Um. Hey?"

"Do me a favour?"

"Um. Yeah?"

"Could you buy me a cold drink?"

"Um. Okay."

We walk in silence over to this little kiosk selling food and drink. From behind, I hear Mike telling Al he's off the team, and screw Mr Highfield because if Al isn't off the team Mike will walk. And so will Ollie. And they're Ferrivale's only decent strikers.

I buy Ellis a can of diet Pepsi and he rolls it against his fist. "Better?"

He gives me this smile that honestly takes my breath away. What the hell is going on tonight? Doesn't this sort of thing only happen in books and movies? Ellis cracks the tab and takes a swig.

"Wet your whistle?"

He offers me the can. Jesus, I want to put my lips right where his lips have been…but I can't. Because this isn't a movie and he's just teasing and I'm not ready. It makes me feel awful. If I'm not ready for him who will I ever be ready for? Take a chance, my brain screams, so what if he laughs? But that would kill me, and so I shake my head. He shrugs and finishes the can.

"Better get a move on," he says, "petitions to hand out."

I nod. Suddenly it's like someone's busted up the most amazing party and the music's been killed and the lights are all on and everyone's heading home.

"Yeah," I say. "Of course. Good luck."

He's moving off, the crowds about to swallow him, when he turns back and grins.

"Don't forget, you are legally my friend now. No get out of jail, no turn around touch the ground, no going backsies. Friends until our dying day. Be seeing you, adorable Frecks."

And we *have* seen each other. All around school and at every history lesson and whenever I head out to the field to watch Mike and the team. Somehow Mike wangled it with Mr Highfield and a be-pearled Ellis is on the left wing. He's amazing, too; Quicksilver and The Flash rolled into one. Meanwhile, a bruised and dumped Alistair Pardue stalks the corridors, looking murderous in this limp-dicked kind of way. Even the Year Sevens tease him.

But Ellis and me? We seem sort of stuck. It's my fault. Weeks go by and he gives me all these openings and I keep cock-blocking myself, if that's even possible. He'll come up with clichéd stuff like, "Can I borrow a pen?" Or intriguing gambits, like telling me his middle name is Maximillian, like that French revolutionary dude we're studying in history. And me? I hand over the biro and beat a hasty retreat.

I'm going to be closeted and single forever.

The bell jangles above the bookshop door and the memory of bonfire smoke evaporates. I sigh and start to pack up my stuff. And then stop. It's him. Ellis Maximillian Bell! He's just walked into Hug-A-Book, Gemma Argyle hanging off his arm. I sink back into my chair and mask my face with the French Revolution.

Shit shit shit.

But why *shit shit shit*?

What the hell is wrong with me?

I keep glancing around the corner of my book. I watch them take a seat in the cafe area and order some complicated coffee creations. Gemma is yammering away...

"Oh God, Ellis, you *must* help me pick a dress for the Easter dance. Yes, I know it's *eons* away, but I want something really spectac this year, and I would ask Kates or Suzie but they've got all the fashion sense of a colour-blind horse. Ha! I don't even know what that means. Anyway, they're always telling me they're busy at weekends, which is total bullshit because I saw them out together at Nando's last Saturday..." Her eyes flicker and she takes a long sip of her coffee. "Anyway, my mum's *promised* she'll take me shopping, but she's mega busy with my big sister right now. Did I tell you my sister's going to be a model? Not that I care. I've got *so* much of my own stuff going on. But the thing is, I really, really, *really* need you right now, Ellis. So please say you'll be my shopping buddy?"

Draped over the table, Ellis has been using his little finger to make swirls in his drink. Then all of a sudden he bolts upright, licks the coffee from his pinkie, and zeroes in on me. I literally leap back behind my book.

My face is burning. My lips are parched. I want him to find me. Crap, no, I don't want him to find me. I'll just wait here, forever if needs be. A chair and a book, what else does a boy need to survive…?

Long elegant fingers grasp the top of my book and slide it out of my hands. I look up into an overpowering smile.

"Oh. Hey, Ellis."

"Hello, Frecks."

He holds the book above me, almost daring me to make a grab for it.

"So, Frecks, I have a serious question. Will you promise to answer it honestly?"

This is it. He's going to ask if I'm gay. And I'm going to tell him. If I don't, I think I'll explode and take half of Ferrivale with me, just like Jean Grey when she becomes Dark Phoenix in— Oh shut up, nerd brain!

117

"I will answer honestly, yes," I tell him.

"Okay." He takes a breath. "So here's the thing: were you always this rubbish at hide-and-seek?"

NOW: Tuesday 28th April

11

I know I'm in my bedroom, sitting at my desk, staring into space – a bit like Professor X in his Cerebro mind machine – but mostly I'm with you, El. In the car. In the lake.

"Hands at nine and three on the steering wheel," you tell me in your best driving instructor's voice. "Then mirror, signal…"

My elbows splosh in the freezing water as I take a grip on the wheel. I angle the rear-view mirror and see our picnic hamper floating above the back seats, reeds dancing outside the windows like mermaid hair.

"Manoeuvre."

Your hand creeps across my lap and dips into that sweet spot of my inner thigh. I close my eyes and you giggle. It's a horrible, burbling sound, not a bit like your usual laughter. I turn and look at you. You've taken back your hand and you're twirling your pearls, except when I look closer they aren't pearls at all. They're all exact copies of the tooth you lost the night you came out to your parents.

"Are you enjoying your latest episode, Mr Frecks?" *A dribble of black lake water escapes your lips when you speak. It makes me want to scream.* "You know what's happening right now, don't you? Course you do. I know my Prof. You'll have done all your post-traumatic stress disorder research." *He reels off my symptoms on his fingers.* "Flashbacks. Nightmares. Visual and auditory hallucinations. Avoiding places that remind you of me. Giving up on school and uni and everything that made you you. Anger, aggression, guilt, shame—"

"Stop it." *I want to take my hands from the wheel but I can't. It wouldn't be safe.*

"A sense that you have no future."

I notice the cheery snow globe on the dashboard, the cheeky little elf clutching his sack of presents. Remember the story we made up about him? Gangsta elf on the run? The water picks him up and he starts to float, just as the radio crackles into life. George Ezra. That deep, soulful voice singing about his own personal paradise...

And suddenly I'm back in my bedroom. April sunshine beats at the closed curtains. Dust motes spiral like atoms in a crematorium furnace. It's been twenty-four hours since your funeral. Are you gone yet, El? Last night I was tempted to google how long it takes to burn a body, but just like when I thought about leaving home, I didn't have the guts.

I twist on my swivel chair. I have nothing to do. No homework, no revision, no PowerPoint-illustrated argument to convince you that the doner kebab is among the finest of mankind's achievements. What was my go-to activity in my pre-El days? Well, it's worth a try. I drag my laptop across the desk, type a couple of gay porn comic sites into the address bar and unzip my jeans. I click and stare, click and stare. My gaze drifts from the computer to my desk and I picture the drawing you gave me at the Berringtons' barbecue, currently taped on the underside of the drawer. Maybe it would inspire a burst of hardness, maybe it would leave me in a curled-up ball on the floor, heaving for air.

I snap my laptop shut, zip up my jeans, and head for the door. At the top of the stairs, I stop and listen. I still can't look at my parents. Was I being unreasonable, expecting them to host your wake? Was that actually insane? I really don't know any more. When I got home yesterday they gave me these shy smiles and asked how it had gone.

"They shoved him inside a cardboard coffin and put him in an oven," I told them, and immediately hated myself. It was cruel, not only to my folks but to Julia. Your coffin was perfect, El.

Later Mum tried bringing me up a sandwich but I kept the door locked. I think you'd tear me a new one over that, but hey, you were always a better human being than I am. So I should just apologize, right? Yes, okay, El, do you ever get tired of always being the bigger person?

I start down the stairs, holding out my hand for yours as I go, because that's how we rolled the night we told them. Final tactical mission briefing in my room, then I kissed you and we set out together, hand in hand, sallying forth to do battle with Barbara and Gordon. Except there was no battle. It worked out fine. Or at least you thought so. But between Mum bouncing up and down and Dad's awkward hug, there was that look you didn't catch, and I never told you because next to broken teeth and homelessness it seemed so small.

I'm almost at the kitchen door when Chris's voice stops me in my tracks.

"Look, I don't want to be mean, but Dylan is, what, seventeen?"

"Eighteen," Mum corrects him. "His birthday was just before Christmas, remember? Really, Christopher."

"Okay, okay," Chris mutters. "My point is, Ellis was his first boyfriend, so of course he thinks the world's coming to an end. Remember when I split up with Vicki Clarkson? I cried my eyes out for a whole afternoon."

"You were thirteen and Vicki didn't die in front of you,"

Mum says. My heart thaws for her a little.

"Right, but what I'm saying is, your first love is always this really melodramatic thing. And what with Dylan being the way he is…well, of course he's gonna make a song and dance out of it."

"Chris, I really think you should show more understanding. And I don't know what you mean by 'Dylan being the way he is'."

"I *mean*," Chris persists, "that Dylan has always made a big deal out of things. I'm not saying he does it because he's gay, he's just that way inclined. And anyway…"

"What?"

"Well…it could be a phase."

"Oh, I don't think—"

"Just hear me out. Ellis was a good kid, I'm not saying he wasn't. But did you ever notice Dylan being…*you know*, before *he* turned up?"

"Dylan is a very intelligent young man," Mum counters. "He knows his own mind."

"Mum, come on. Dylan's always been a follower. Bloody hell, he couldn't even walk through the centre of town a few months ago because it made him antsy. People like that need strong figures to latch onto. Look, I'm just saying, if El had been a tightrope walker then Dylan would have joined the freaking circus. So of course he's gonna be acting a bit mental right now, but I honestly think he'll come round.

As soon as the memory of Ellis fades a bit, we'll get the old Dylan back."

My heart is pounding. I want to go in there and smash the bastard's head right through the marble tabletop. There's a pause, and then Mum says:

"You could be right. Even if Dylan is gay, or maybe bi, Ellis wasn't good for him. Your father said so that day at the Berringtons' barbecue. Now, Dad's got this new intern at his firm, a boy from the community college, but really nice, and *he's* gay. But you'd never know it. Not like… Well. Anyway. Maybe we could introduce him to Dyls one day and…"

I slam the front door loud enough so they know I've heard. Yeah, it's childish but it's important they get the message: first, I wouldn't trust Numbnuts Chris to psychoanalyse the teddy bear he still sleeps with. Second, Mum: I. Am. *Gay*. Jesus, I've been gay ever since I first started paddling around in your womb, and I've known it ever since a two-page spread of a shirtless Hal Jordan (aka Green Lantern) gave me my first ever boner. And Dad? No, I do not want to meet your straight-acting twink intern.

So do you get it now, El? Do you understand why I wasn't jumping for joy at my parents' reaction that night? Because I know just how far their tolerance goes.

I'm halfway down the drive, heading I don't know where, when the postman calls my name. Letter for me.

If it's another bunch of cards from Gemma and the LGBTQ safe-space guys, I swear… I ask him to leave it with my mum, but then I suddenly notice *URGENT* printed across the top. I've never received an urgent letter in my life, and that handwriting, ultra-careful and characterless, makes me stop.

"Second thoughts, I'll take it."

I weigh it in my hand. Nothing to it, maybe just a single sheet inside. Perhaps it's a poison pen letter. I haven't received any homophobic hate mail since you died, El, but sick minds might bide their time, and maybe Mum has filtered my post without me knowing. I wander over to my bike, hands shaking a little. What if there's a razor blade inside, or a needle? I've read about nasty crap like that.

Pulling my bike from the fence, I angle it so I can rest my bum on the seat. This is ridiculous. I can't keep staring at the thing like it might be a home-made bomb or a phial of anthrax about to go off in my face. I tear open the flap and pull out the sheet inside.

And my stomach flips.

Jesus, that's my first stomach somersault in weeks. Because this is from *you*. I know it as soon as I see the distinctive yellow paper, torn from the journal you carried about everywhere. Your "Moodles and Doodles" book. I once asked if I could take a proper look inside and you shook your head: "*Everyone needs a secret corner all to* themselves, Frecks." I remember frowning at that: "Even from me?" A pause, a moment to collect your thoughts, then: "Even from you, sweetheart. You'll have that corner too. It might not be a book, but there's some place you keep all to yourself and I won't be there."

Oh, I have that place now, El. It's called the world.

I unfold the page like it's a sacred object. It is. The sun glitters in your pencil strokes, ebony in a yellow sea, and for the first time since I lost you, I feel silent tears. I hold the drawing up so they don't spoil this beauty. Is that arrogant? Because this picture is me. Dylan McKee, shy and prettier than I could ever really be, peeping out from behind a book. Carefully, oh so carefully, I place a trembling finger along the pencil line of my arm. My skin tingles like I've bridged some strange psychic connection across time and space. I'm both there, hiding away in Hug-A-Book, and I'm with you later when you take out your journal and recapture me. With you when you write these words in a circle around me:

Frecks. Dream-haunter. Frecks of the EXTRAORDINARY green eyes and the LOVELIEST smile. Do I haunt your dreams too?

I wipe my eyes ferociously, making sure there are no more tears, then hold the page to my chest. What an idiot I was. I wasted so much time because I thought time didn't matter. I'm so sorry, El.

After a while I manage to stop looking at the drawing of me and check out the reverse side. Maybe there are more sketches to warm and hurt my heart. There is a drawing here, but it has none of the sweetness of mine. I frown at the page, and all at once I know it wasn't you who sent this treasure. Of course it wasn't. Even if you posted it the day you died, it wouldn't have taken three weeks to arrive.

Gemma Argyle stares back at me. You've captured her perfectly, the pouting, preening princess and her other face creeping beneath. She's dressed in a cloak and hood, something like the Evil Queen's from Disney's *Snow White*. Crooked talons are emerging from her hooped sleeves, twisting in the air as she conjures some dark spell.

Straight away a memory clicks: it's the Hug-A-Book day, and suddenly I'm thinking about what happened after you left her in the cafe. And I think I know why you might have drawn her like this…

Questions burn inside my head: who sent this and why? A friend, an enemy? How did they even get hold of the drawing? All I know is that we now have something concrete to go on. We were looking for someone who might hate you, El, and with this we could have our first clue. I slide the page carefully back into its envelope, mount my bike, and set off towards Mike's.

THEN: Saturday 23rd November

The Library

"I wasn't hiding," I tell him.

El gives me a wink. "I believe you."

He hands back my book, and immediately I drop it. Course I do. Shooting to my feet just as he's bending down to help, I smash my head into his and all at once seven kinds of crap fall out of my pockets and scatter across the floor of the Hug-A-Book bookshop. El snorts with laughter and scoots down onto his haunches. We squat there like little kids fishing in a rock pool, and he's talking but all I can do is look at his thighs. I thought they were impressive at the bonfire, but tensed up like this? Sheesh.

"What? Pardon?" I fluster.

He grins and hands me a well-gnawed biro.

"I said, freckles *and* a complete klutz. Is this an act, Dylan?"

"Dylan? I thought my name was Frecks?"

"Frecks so soon after 'freckles' in that sentence would've sounded weird, no? Hey, maybe I should call you Prof! Your hand is never down in history and your hair's always a bit Einsteiny. Yeeeeee…" He seesaws his hand. "It's all right, but I prefer Frecks. And anyway, you've not answered my question. Have you worked out this entire routine?"

"I'm sorry?"

"Freckles meets klutz? It's an irresistible combo." His eyes suddenly light up and he snatches a packet from the floor. "Hey, Starburst!"

Does he know his fingers smell of Starburst? Will he deduce that this is why I've been carrying around multipacks of them ever since the bonfire? He pops an orange one into his mouth and rolls it around. His tongue is very red and wet, I notice. Oh God, I'm such a perv.

"Did you know these are my absolute favourite sweets of all time?"

"No," I say quickly, "I had no idea."

He gives me a hooded look. I feel like a convict under a floodlight.

"Um, I think your friend needs you," I tell him.

Gemma Argyle is throwing us both the stink-eye and beckoning to Ellis like he's a primary-school kid who's lost his buddy on an outing.

"The only thing that young lady needs is a sense of perspective, and perhaps a more stereotypical gay BFF.

129

I think I've been a disappointment to her. I tend to disappoint people, Frecks, this is something you will learn in time. To be fair, I was kind of lonely when I first got here and walked right into the GBFF role without understanding what I was getting myself into. She adores my wardrobe but hates that I play footie and that I've been known to crack a sly beer with the boys after a match. I also hate her little dog. It craps in her handbag and she calls the turds 'chocolate treasure drops'."

"Okay." I nod. "So can I ask? Why are you even friends with her?"

El's grin falters and he looks away. "I think because she doesn't have any."

"What?" I almost laugh. "But Gemma Argyle's the most popular girl in school."

"Being popular and having friends aren't always the same thing." He shakes his head and his smile returns. "But I've done my duty for today. Rescue me, Frecks!"

"Oh, I…no," I say, edging around him. "I have to be somewhere."

He falls to one knee, hands clasped together. "Somewhere sounds wonderful."

"Yeah. Okay, but… Sorry, I, uh, really can't. I… You see, it's this restricted, um, place and I just couldn't…"

DYLAN! my brain screams. *HE WANTS TO BE WITH YOU! SAY YES! GRAB HIS HAND AND JUST GO!*

Yeah, but what if he doesn't? What if I'm misreading this?
HE'S ON HIS KNEES, NUMBNUTS!

"Right," I fumble. "So, I'm sorry about the head-bump thing… Okay. Bye."

Still kneeling, he gives me this stunned sort of wave as I crash out of the shop.

Crap crap crap. I try to keep my brain out of my head as I walk. I know that sounds mad, but you get what I mean. I walk fast, thumbs pulling at my backpack straps until they cut into my armpits. I haven't been this bad since puberty, but hey, it seems that old anxieties never die.

Head down all the way, I end up at Ferrivale Library. My own personal Fortress of Solitude. Mrs Jackson says "hi" as I pass the issues desk. She's around fifty, just about the nicest person you could meet, and has this titanic bosom that holds a particular fascination for Mike. I don't think he actually fancies Mrs J, it's more a sort of scientific aerodynamic interest. Anyway, I'm pretty sure my favourite librarian knows I'm gay. She's like the most discreet person ever, but every so often her book suggestions give her away. Don't get me wrong, Adam Silvera is an amazing writer, but Mrs J needs to subtle up her hints. Once she gave me the Tom Daley autobiography, the one with Daley on the cover, snug in his budgie smugglers, because, and I quote, "I know you like diving, dear." Honestly, I have never once discussed diving with her.

I start in the history section, subconsciously hunting for something that might annoy Mr Morris by confirming he's right about me being unfocused. We're not studying anything about nineteenth century American inventors, so I grab a biography of Thomas Edison. Next, I head into *Graphic Novels*. I still call them "comics", because it's a grown-up word in its own right, goddamn it. I'm just taking down a bound omnibus edition of *The Walking Dead* when a hand snakes through the shelf and grabs my wrist. Because I'm already thinking *zombies*, I yelp, and someone on the other side of the shelf giggles.

My stomach flips. It's a weird, fluttery, fairground kind of sensation.

"Sorry, Frecks, I couldn't resist."

Immediately, my mouth's back building sandcastles on planet Mars. El saunters around the corner and plants his elbow on the bookshelf, chin in his hand.

"I like your ultra-secret, strictly-restricted special place," he tells me. "I had to give the lady at the desk a weird handshake just to get in."

He looks me up and down, and I'm not sure if he's amused or annoyed.

"Where's Gemma?" I ask.

"Do you care?"

"Um. No."

"Hey, Frecks?"

"Yeah?"

"Can I have another Starburst?"

"Oh. Okay."

I drop my bag and fish in my jacket pocket. Then I realize it's my old jacket with the hole in the pocket and the sweets have fallen into the lining.

"Just a minute."

I dig my hand deeper, almost up to the elbow, but the bloody things keep slipping between my fingers and sliding further around the back, so now it looks like I'm a vet with my arm halfway up a cow's anus. Ellis's nonchalant expression cracks. Yeah, yeah, it's freaking hilarious. In the end I drag out my hand and shrug.

"No," I tell him, "I'm sorry, but you can't have a Starburst."

He's now practically on the floor in hysterics. Between giggles, he holds out a hand to me, palm up, as if in surrender. I want to put my palm against his. I want to twine my fingers through his. I actually lift my hand, and I'm going to do it. My heart is raging. I can hear the blood pounding in my ears. I step forward and he grabs my sleeve and pulls me down to the floor with him.

I don't know how it happens, but suddenly I'm lying on my back and he's on all fours, his arms planted either side of my head. His face is centimetres from mine and he's hiccupping with laughter. I'm laughing too, but quietly, because it's the library and I'm Dylan. It takes hours (seconds really, but time's elastic in moments like this) for him to stop laughing and just settle into a smile. Down in the children's section I can hear a librarian reading aloud to the little kids: "*Will you, won't you, will you, won't you, will you join the dance?*"

Yes, I think. *Yes, please. I'd like to join the dance now.*

El catches his bottom lip between his teeth and touches me. It's like at the bonfire, but different too. Not the shock of electricity this time but a slow, wonderfully excruciating warmth. Three fingers, tracing my freckles and my jaw and my cheek. I take a shuddery breath. The whites of his eyes are *so* white, his skin *so* flawless, and yet he seems fascinated with *my* face, with my blemishes and imperfections. It's crazy.

"Do you mind?" he asks, his little finger edging closer to my mouth.

I shake my head, though I have no idea what he means.

Gently, very gently, he traces my lips with his fingertip.

And I'm lost. The library, Ferrivale, all of it, falls away from me. And then suddenly an old man shouts something random and clumps towards our half-hidden section. Panicked, I snake my way between Ellis's arms and drag myself onto a small reading couch. I can't stand up. Not yet. El, still on all fours, gives me this wolfish grin and crawls over to the couch, sliding into the seat next to mine

134

just as the Grinch rounds the bend. He glares at us for a second.

Ellis, who's picked up a volume of *Hellboy*, gives him the arched eyebrow treatment.

"Do you mind, sir? This is an ultra-secret restricted area. Isn't that right, Frecks?"

"That's correct." I nod to the geezer. "Super-restricted."

The old guy looks at us like we might be deviants. If we are, I don't care. Anyway, he grunts and trundles off. I laugh and bury my head in El's shoulder. I don't even think about how easy that feels until later.

"I love your tattoos," I say suddenly, emerging from his sweet, football-field scent.

"Random." He nods. "But thanks." He spreads out his arms. His sleeves are rolled up and he flexes, making the jags and swirls of each intricate design appear like running ink.

"Did you design them yourself?" I ask, and he nods again. "So what do they mean?"

"They're wards. Talismans. Protections against evil. They keep me safe."

"Do you run into much evil?" I laugh.

He's silent for a while, and I'm terrified I've said the wrong thing.

"Every now and then. And if I'm right about you, Dylan, you'll run into it too one day. Most of us do. So…" He sighs. "You like comics?"

I'm so pleased he didn't say "graphic novels" that I start giving him the full geek chorus: how I first fell in love with The Fantastic Four when my dad bought me a colouring book at an airport; my Avengers-themed fifth birthday party, back when nobody knew who the Avengers were; my and Mike's invention of the candyfloss-themed supervillain Slaughter Master.

"Okay." El nods. "But why 'Slaughter Master'? Shouldn't he be, like, the Pink Peril?"

"Oh." I consider. "Yeah. Maybe."

"Or do you think that's a bit gay?"

"No! It's just, we were kids and probably didn't work it out properly and—"

"Frecks, I'm teasing."

"Oh." I press my hands between my knees. I want to hold his hand, but I've retreated again. "So, do you like comics?"

"Are you kidding? Steve Ditko's my hero! Those original Spider-Man designs? Wow. You know I draw a bit, right?"

"Yeah! I mean, I'd heard you do art A level."

Plus I've been sneaking into the school studios and looking at your portraits and sculptures every lunch break.

"I'm going to draw you when I get home," he says.

"Right. Are you?"

He shrugs. "I've got an idea. A hide-and-seek idea. We'll see... But first, Mr Frecks, will you leave your super-restricted lair and walk me to my car?"

I nod. It's all I'm capable of.

Mrs J is grinning like a loon when we pass the issues desk. I think she's dying to give me a thumbs up as well but she manages to resist, so I throw her a quick smile.

We walk side by side, out across the street and right through town. It's busy, shoulders barge me, but I hardly notice. I'm now fixated on how close our hands can swing without actually touching. I think he knows this game and he's teasing me, letting his little finger arch outwards then pulling it back, but I've discovered something about myself today. I like being teased. At least, I like being teased by Ellis Bell.

El knows. He must. Anyway, I've decided that I'm going to tell him. And maybe I'm completely misreading things, because I really can't see how he could ever be interested in *me*, but if he is then—

"What the hell?!"

We've turned down a side alley and El has broken into a run. I join him on the kerb in front of a rather beaten-up Nissan Micra. The driver's window has been busted in and a whole heap of rubbish thrown onto the front seat. A couple of bluebottles drone around the gloopy contents of old takeaway boxes while a random shoe pokes out from between a mountain of crisp wrappers. El looks up and down the street but no one's in sight.

"We should call the police. Hey." I click my fingers.

"Do you think this could've been Alistair Pardue? Revenge for how you kicked his sorry arse at the bonfire?"

He shakes his head. "No. No, I don't think this was Alistair. He wouldn't have the balls. I think…" He pauses for a second, his gaze roaming back down the street. "Probably just some silly kid." Ellis bends down and picks up something from under the front tyre. A shattered snow globe, a few specks of white still floating in the broken bowl. "Ah shit. My aunt gave me this as a moving-in present."

"I'm sorry."

He sighs. "I don't know how I'm gonna get the window replaced. If I make a claim my insurance will skyrocket."

"I can pay," I tell him.

"Frecks." He looks at me like I've just suggested handing over a spare kidney. "I couldn't. This'll cost eighty quid, easy."

"It's no big deal," I say. "You can pay me back later."

He looks all around, as if some other solution will appear out of thin air, before finally coming back to me.

"I *will* pay you back."

I shrug and we head off to a cashpoint. When I hand over the money, he takes this big journal from his bag and tears out a yellow page. Then he unclips a fine-point pen, jots something in this beautiful swirly script, and hands the paper to me.

I, Ellis Maximillian Bell, swear by all the most secret and solemn traditions of the ultra-secret restricted place (AKA The Library) that I will pay back Frecks, AKA Dylan Lemuel Jasper McKee, all his hard-earned moolah.
Signed EMB xxxxxxxxxxxx

"You should feel honoured," he tells me. "I never tear out a page from my Moodles and Doodles."

"Moodles and Doodles?" I grin.

"Don't you dare laugh! It's what I called my first ever sketchbook. I guess I'm superstitious and the name's sort of stuck."

I smile and fold up the paper and put it in my wallet.

"How do you know my middle names?" I ask.

"Dylan." He grins. "I'm your new gay BFF. I know *everything* about you."

Later, hours after I've helped him scoop the rubbish out of his car, I lie on my bed and read and reread the IOU. I know it's crazy, but I even put it to my lips and kiss the kisses back, then roll sideways and say his name, just a few dozen times. It takes me a long time to fall asleep that night, and when I do the yellow page is still in my hand.

NOW: Tuesday 28th April

12

I'm not embarrassed. Taking out my wallet, I retrieve the IOU you gave me the day your car was vandalized and show it to Mike. It matches perfectly with the torn page I received in the mail this morning. While Mike turns it over in his hands, I squat down and graze my fingers through Beckham's black and white underbelly. A deep, satisfied grumble rises up from the loveable old mutt.

We're sitting on the double swings that Mike's dad hung from the old beech tree in their garden a million summers ago. Mike's an only child but his dad didn't think twice about the second swing. I lean back and follow the creaking rope up to the sunlight, beams cutting through a cage of branches.

"Thanks for showing me this." He holds up the side with my picture and your words. "It's very special."

I'm not sure what to say, so I mumble, "He loved you too, Mike."

Mike nods, smiling. "Then we were both really lucky."

We were, El. Even with you gone, I know it.

He turns my picture over and studies the Gemma-witch on the back. She's levitating over your car, fingers twitching and twirling as her dark magic spews filth and rubbish through the broken driver window. In the foreground, and almost twice the size of the Nissan, lie the shattered remnants of the dashboard snow globe, Aunt Julia's moving-in gift.

"He knew she'd done it," I say. "She trashed the car as a way of getting back at him."

"For what?"

I sometimes forget there are big parts of our story Mike doesn't know. I wonder if this feels weird for him; we used to tell each other everything.

"For dumping her and chasing after me."

I tell him the story of that day at Hug-A-Book and the library. Usually with something like this I'd leave out the parts that seemed intimate and special for us, because they were our treasures and I lived for the hours when we'd relive them, sitting in your car or cross-legged in your bedroom, sorting through our favourite memories, laughing and arguing and getting hot over the details. But I only have Mike now to share these things with, so I walk him through every moment, even us on the library floor.

"I never thought to link her with it at the time," I say.

"It just seemed like this random act. But something about what El said that day, about how he looked... Right from the start, I think he knew it was her. You should've seen the look she threw him at Hug-A-Book when he came over and started chatting to me."

"Gemma doesn't deal with rejection well, that's for sure. Just ask Ollie."

"What happened with her and Reynolds?" I ask.

Mike shrugs. "Turns out he couldn't live up to her idea of the model boyfriend."

"Same with El," I say. "He was supposed to be her ideal gay BFF, but that didn't work out, and then he dumps her before she can dump him. She seemed okay with him afterwards, but they were never close again."

"Because she'd already got her revenge," says Mike. "What a psycho." He hands the paper back to me. "So who do you think sent this? One of our mystery guys? The porno perv? Whoever scared El at the dance?" He clicks his fingers. "Maybe none of the above! Maybe it was the stalker in the garden."

I frown. "Who?"

"Remember yesterday I thought I saw someone watching us in the crematorium garden?" Mike says. "Maybe that person overheard us talking about our suspicions. He wants to help but doesn't want to do it face to face for some reason."

"Okay…" I hesitate. "But how did he get hold of El's journal?"

"Loads of crap flew out of the car when you crashed, right? What if El's journal did too? Maybe it was thrown really far from the accident site. Our guy is out wandering by the lake, finds it, decides to keep it, then he overhears what we said at the funeral."

"I don't know." I press my hands between my knees. "Doesn't that all seem a bit coincidental? And why would he keep the journal in the first place? And why does he even *want* to help us?"

"Search me," Mike says. "But whoever he is, he's given you a start, hasn't he?"

I nod. "So you think Gemma could be the person who rescued me?"

"Or the person who scared El. I can't see her as the porno perv. But now we know that at least one person had a grudge against Ellis. The question is, what do we do about it?"

"We ask her," I say. "Confront her."

"All right, but…"

"But what?"

Mike looks again at the drawing. "You're sure you really want to do this, Dylan? I know you want justice for El, but I'm worried. I'm not sure when you get your answers it's going to make you feel any better." He catches my glance and looks away. "Okay, then I think there's something you should see."

He gets up and starts towards the house. Becks grumbles onto his paws and follows.

We enter through the patio door at the back and take off our shoes: Mumzilla Nest Rule #14. In the kitchen, Mike hunts through a pile of post on the breakfast table while I battle memories that try to swamp me: you at this very table, El, leaping to your feet as Carol and Big Mike bustle into the room with armfuls of shopping. We'd been secretly dating for three and a bit months, and I was so desperate for my surrogate family to fall for you. I needn't have worried, of course.

Mike shoots me a troubled look and hands over this stiff piece of card. It's designed to look like an order of service for a funeral.

TUES 28th APRIL @ GEMMA'S

THE WAKE
Put on your pearls and come party,
in memory of our boy Ellis

"I'm guessing you didn't get one? Dude, I'm so sorry, it's really sick."

I shake my head. "It's exactly what we need. We're going."

*   *   *

Mike potters around the kitchen, frying up one of my favourite junk-food breakfasts: a double-bacon cheeseburger. I know, El, my arteries, but I need this, and anyway my heart's already ruined. So my tally of high school parties is fairly pitiful, not only because of my crowds thing but, let's face it, before you arrived in Ferrivale, I wasn't exactly popular. Those shindigs (*shindigs?* I can hear you laughing) I did get invited to usually came my way because Mike had had a word with the host. But I'm genuinely puzzled by this Wake thing. Though Gemma and I have never been friends, I would've thought she'd want me there – the grieving boyfriend – as her centrepiece.

My burger lands, greasy and gorgeous. I take a bite.

"Mate, is it okay if I hang around here until the party?" I ask between mouthfuls.

Mike drops into the seat beside me. "What's happened?"

"McKee stuff."

He nods, because he's known my family almost as long as I have.

And so we have an old-fashioned Mike and Dylan day together. We battle the undead and get under Mumzilla's feet and eat family-size bags of crisps and start lots of conversations with "Remember when…?", and I suddenly realize how much I've missed this. Just the two of us, wasting hours.

145

Our Mike and Dylan day soothes me, although it isn't quite like old times. Around four o'clock he gets tired and has to go for a nap. I watch him lope upstairs, his chin sagging to his chest, knuckles white as he grips the bannister. He stumbles a bit and I jerk forward, but he waves me away. When he's out of sight, I feel an arm settle around my waist and I turn my head into the crook of Carol's shoulder. We stay like that for a long time.

"Sure you're up to this?"

"Dylan?"

"Yeah?"

"I am so going to out-party your ass."

Mike zips up his jacket and we head for the door. We're almost at the road when Big Mike calls us back and tosses his son a baseball cap.

"But, Dad, it's my plan to come out as a big bad baldy tonight. Girls are going wild for chemo-head this season."

Big Mike forces a wonky smile. "Wear it there and back. You can rock the cue ball as much as you like once you're inside. Oh! And, Dylan, if he gets tired and you need a lift?"

I wave my mobile. "I'll call you right away, Big M."

Big Mike shoots me a salute.

"My dad is such a tool," Mike sighs.

"Your dad rules and you know it."

"God, you're right," he groans. "It kind of kills me."

It isn't far from Mike's to Gemma's. Kids ride bikes in lazy circles, the setting sun thrumming off silver spokes. People in designer jumpers mow their lawns and leave the cuttings for the gardener to deal with.

As we walk, I'm reminded again how this side of town is a world away from your old estate, El. You said once that the "over here", as you called it, felt like a Hollywood film set, all cardboard houses and actor's smiles and scripted opinions.

"By the way," Mike says, "I've been doing some detective work."

"Okay, Sherlock, share."

"Alistair Pardue? Remember him?"

I do, El. I remember him flat on his homophobic arse after you belted him one.

"Well, he wasn't exactly Team Ellis, was he? Prime suspect for at least one of our mystery men. Unfortunately he was in Scotland camping with his family the night of the accident."

"Jesus, his poor family."

"And I've been thinking," Mike continues, "if we're saying Gemma could be the person who rescued you, well, I don't want to sound sexist, but could she really have dragged you out of a sinking car?"

"That *is* kind of sexist," I say, "and don't forget Gemma

is netball captain, swim team captain, and head ballbreaker of the new cheerleading squad."

"Don't remind me." Mike throws out his arms, waggling imaginary pom-poms.

"And maybe she wasn't alone," I say. "She's seeing Paul Donovan now, isn't she? A strapping rugger-bugger like him could do some serious heavy lifting. And Donovan has a car. If for some reason Gemma wanted to confront El that night, they could easily have followed us from the dance."

"Dude." Mike frowns. "Are you even allowed to say 'rugger-bugger'?"

I'm saved from answering this by my phone bleeping. A new message from Mum. Eighth since this morning. I delete it, along with the rest.

Looking up, I see we've reached a confluence of streets that all seem to feed into Gemma's. The invitation didn't mention a dress code but virtually everyone pouring down the road is in black. The mood doesn't entirely reflect the clothes, though. Kids are arriving in loose groups, fingers hooked through six-packs, passing around half-drunk bottles, everyone grinning and gossiping. Mike catches my eye.

"Sure you're sure about this?"

I nod and we join the swarm.

13

I don't know what Gemma's parents do for a living, but my guess is they either own an airline or run a drugs cartel. We reach the end of the drive just as the sun finally dips and the sleek modern house in front of us, all steel and glass, glows like an ember. Trance beats pulse through the open door and sheer white light flashes in time at the windows.

I don't want to go inside. This feels like what it is – an exploitative ego trip, an excuse for Gemma to insert herself into the narrative of your death – and it makes me feel nauseated. Plus, there are a lot of people already here: our year, lower-sixth kids, even a few of the cooler Year Elevens. I can see the masses heaving in the entrance hall and the thought of having to squeeze through them…

Can I turn back, El? Will you let me?

"Dylan?" Mike murmurs.

"I'm okay."

The entrance hall is all marble, what I can see of it. Heads bob around me to the music that seems to be coming from one of the rooms off the hall. It all looks pretty minimalist, with hardly any ornaments or pictures, unless that stuff's been packed away for the party. I'm guessing Gemma's parents have been packed away too.

Some kids come over and say hello. A few even give me a hug and say how sorry they are, and what an amazing couple we made, even though their knowledge of us together is based on that single dance the night you died. Prisha Banerjee even bursts into tears and I end up having to console her. All this is okay, nice even, but there's this other weird vibe going on – a kind of low-level hostility biding its time.

Mike steers us out of the entrance hall and into the kitchen. The Argyles have this Aga the size of a small family car and a huge wooden breakfast bar with a sink so big you could re-enact the Battle of Trafalgar in miniature, all seventy-four ships engaged. The music follows us into the room and I realize the beats are being pumped throughout the house.

It's here, in this oversized kitchen, that I find you staring back at me, El.

Mike grabs my arm. "Mate."

"I'm good," I say, walking slowly over to you. "I'm okay."

A massive free-standing poster of you dominates the

room. It's black-and-white and clearly a blown-up version of the headshot from our yearbook. Before I can reach you, this couple I don't recognize come blundering over and stand either side of the poster, grinning like they're in a fairground hall of mirrors. They cross their eyes and their buddy takes a picture. I just stand there. Then another group comes forward for a memento of the evening, and suddenly Ollie Reynolds is there, shouting and shoving them aside. Ollie's pretty built, so no one argues.

"Dylan, I'm sorry you had to see that." He comes over and places a hand on my shoulder. "This sucks on so many levels. I don't know what that crazy cow is thinking. Hey, Mike." He nods to his teammate. "Maybe we should all just get out of here? My cousin owns this bar in town and he can get us discounted beer, if you fancy it?"

I wonder vaguely why he's turned up at all, if he disapproves so much, and especially with the whole him-being-Gemma's-ex thing. I've always been on friendly terms with Ollie, mainly because he's Mike's footie pal. We don't have much else in common though, and I can't remember ever having a meaningful conversation with him.

"Maybe later," Mike says. "Me and Dylan have to do something first."

"Oh. Okay. But look…"

Ollie guides me like a geriatric over to the breakfast bar, where drinks have been set up. I'm still a bit stunned, and

151

I can sense you behind me, El, smiling in that yearbook way – not too formal, not too cheeky. Ollie busies himself pouring us all a glass of this gloopy yellow stuff called advocaat. He orders us to down it and I gag. It tastes like custard.

"So." He refills and chinks my glass. "I just wanted to tell you how cool Ellis was. He was, like, the coolest, wasn't he, Mike?" He slaps a frowning, nodding Mike on the back. "Never seen a left foot like it. And in bloody pearls! Guy was a beast. And you were so lucky, Dylan, you know? I don't give a crap who's gay or straight or bi or whatever, I know love when I see it. Not bullshit love." He bends down and breathes fumes into my ear. This clearly isn't his first drink of the night. "I mean proper twist-your-heart-in-two kind of love. You had that, man. 'Mazing. 'Mazing."

While he's talking my gaze has wandered to the open kitchen door. Gemma is in the hallway. She's wearing this beautiful black dress, slightly torn at the hip, as if she's been mourning in a post-apocalyptic wasteland. She's flapping at her face but I can't see any tears. The committee girls are gathered around her, offering Kleenex and comforting without touching. She's teetering slightly on her heels, so either she's really wasted or she's playing the role of grieving drunk. I think she's seen me already but suddenly her head twitches my way and she makes quite a display of looking me up and down.

"Didn't I say it was invitation only?" She sniffs and struts away, acolytes in tow.

I start for the kitchen door and Mike follows. Ollie's still mid-flow, praising El's keepy-uppy skills. He stumbles, literally and verbally, as he trails us through the hall and into this immense living room.

It's like a mausoleum decorated by Versace. Every surface is laced and ribboned and crêped in black and white and there are duplicates of that blown-up yearbook picture everywhere. She's trying to claim you, El. Remake you as she wanted you to be all along. You hated this kind of repetitive, lyric-less, meaningless music. You hated the idea that a single image could ever sum you up or define you. You even hated black and white, explaining once that your pencil sketches were all about gradations. How you pressed and held and feathered the pencil gave you an almost infinite variation of grey, each suggesting other colours.

"This is wrong," I tell Mike. "All wrong."

Maybe I said it louder than I intended. Maybe they'd been told to creep up and listen.

"You don't get to have a say," Katie Linton practically purrs in my ear. She circles us and comes to stand in front of me, committee sister Suzie Ford joining her. "You weren't even invited."

"He came with me," Mike says.

The girls give him this long sympathetic look. "Oh, you can stay, Mike. This isn't about you."

"What the hell is it about then?" Ollie fumes.

"Mike, will you please call these two a taxi?" Suzie pleads. "They're not wanted. Gemma's put a lot of effort into tonight's celebration of Ellis's life. She loved El."

"No," I say quietly, "I loved El. None of you even knew him."

Katie laughs. I don't think I've ever heard a sound like it before. It's all claws and blades and vinegar.

"*You* loved him? Then why did you leave him in that car? You might as well have murdered him. Hey" – she throws out her arms and twirls on the spot – "maybe you did! Who knows? No one was there. Maybe he passed out and you held him under the water."

"And why the hell would Dylan do that?" Ollie spits. "He was El's boyfriend."

"No one knows what goes on behind closed doors," Suzie says, suddenly soothing. She places a hand on Ollie's chest and he draws back. "Anything might have happened after the dance. Don't forget, the video came out that morning. What if Ellis posted it himself? What if he confessed to Dylan in the car and Dylan freaked?"

We have an audience now. Each stab from the girls gets a reaction. Some grumble discontent, others whistle like they're at a cage fight. I'd say the numbers in each group are pretty even. A smaller set smell blood and start hurling the accusation back at me:

"Yeah, McKee, what really happened?"

"Did you do it?"

Did you did you did you did you did you did you did you?

And through it all I can see Gemma in the doorway, smiling.

Suddenly she breaks in. "Stop it! All of you, just stop! Dylan?" She holds out a hand to me. "Can we talk?"

I don't need to be asked twice.

Mike and Ollie act as my bodyguards, clearing a route so I can follow Gemma out of the lounge and into a room across the hall. I give the boys a nod and they stay guarding the doorway like a pair of mafia goons.

Gemma closes the door behind us and the music fades to a dull throb. Unlike the rest of the house, this room is rammed with paintings, ornaments, antiques of every kind. A couple of what I assume are Argyle ancestors dressed in country tweeds sneer down at us from the walls. Decent paintings, but nothing compared to yours, El. The party girl goes and sits behind a long mahogany desk, kicking up her Valentino heels. She doesn't appear drunk or upset any more.

"Gemma, what is all this?" I ask.

She shrugs and examines her nails. "Aren't I allowed to give my friend a proper goodbye?"

I perch on the arm of a soft leather settee. "He wasn't your friend. He hadn't been for months. He knew what you did."

She blinks, and for the first time ever I see a quiver of self-doubt. "Me? I didn't do anything. You heard them all out there, Dylan. If anyone's got questions to answer, it's you, not me."

"You scripted that whole scene," I tell her. "Fed Suze and Katie their lines. Honestly, those two are just not that quick on their feet."

She shrugs in a *prove it* sort of way. Then pouts a little and changes the subject. "I've got a question for you, Dylan, if you're man enough to answer it. Who were you before Ellis came along? Really? A nothing, a nobody. Just some little freak who sometimes hung around with Mike Berrington and the footie boys. I was barely even aware of you."

I nod. "That's right. I agree. That's who I was."

"A nobody who no one even noticed. A whispery little gay boy too scared to say who he really was. I don't think I even knew your name before El picked you out and made you his pet project. Because that's what you were to him, Dylan. That's all you *ever* were."

It's weird, I should be angry. Screw that, I should be bloody furious. But I'm not, because I know none of this is true and that she's grasping for something she needs but can never own. She's grasping for you.

"And now you're a nobody again," she goes on. "Oh, I suppose you can carry on hanging around Mike and Ollie if you like, but Ellis is gone and he was the only one who gave you any meaning."

I nod again. "Gemma, you're absolutely right. He did give me meaning… And I gave him meaning too."

She looks at me and laughs. "*You?*"

I get up and cross to the desk. She draws back as if I might hit her. I wonder if she's been hit before. Not by Ollie, I'm pretty sure, but Paul Donovan? I wouldn't put it past him. I take out my wallet, unfold the paper with her picture and lay it in front of her. She starts to laugh, then stops. When she looks up at me, some of the bite has gone out of her.

"What is this?"

"He knew, Gemma. That day after he left you at Hug-A-Book, after he abandoned you for me, he knew what you did. He rejected you because you wanted him to be something he couldn't be. You wanted this make-believe gay best friend. He was to be your latest accessory, like your handbag or your dog, but El was larger and more complicated and too fantastic to be anyone's stereotype. And you hated him for it."

I round the desk and drop to my haunches in front of her. She has turned in her swivel chair and sits with hunched shoulders.

"Were you there at the lake, Gemma? Did you see him die?"

She looks up at me and a smile flickers at the corners of her mouth.

"You're right, I hated him that day. I gave him this amazing opportunity and he threw it back in my face, just to go mincing after you. Do you know how many kids would *kill* to be my friend? But he treated my offer like it was cheap. Nothing." The leader of the LGBTQ safe-space group grins at me. "He humiliated me, that pretty boy faggot. So yeah, I trashed his shitty little car. But if you're asking, did I follow you to the lake that night? Did I just stand there and watch Ellis drown?"

She draws back into her chair and shakes her head. Although she hasn't cried, her mascara is swimming down her face.

"No, Dylan, I didn't. Whatever you think, I'm not that twisted." She runs her fingers through her hair, scraping her scalp. "You know what I really think? I think that people like Ellis will always be vulnerable, just because they won't play the silly games that everyone else plays – to fit in, to be popular, to feel wanted. They're too brave for that. Too fucking brave to be anything less than what they are. I'm not sure that helps you, but it's all I know."

She reaches out for the drawing, turns it over and sees my picture on the reverse, and for a horrible minute I think she's going to tear it to pieces. But she folds it carefully and hands it back to me.

"He was too much Ellis Bell. Now get the fuck out of my house."

We say goodbye to Ollie and head back to Mike's.

"What was his deal tonight?" I wonder.

Mike shrugs. "I don't know. Nice of him to stand up for you like that though."

"I guess."

"So do you think she was telling the truth? That she had nothing to do with it?"

I let the question hang for a moment, replaying the scene over in my head. "I do," I say at last. "Look, I wouldn't trust her to take care of the family gerbil, but I also believe that she genuinely organized the Easter dance in your honour because she thought it was a nice thing to do. Don't get me wrong, she did it for the social kudos too. But I don't think she's evil enough to let someone die. So you know what this means?"

Mike slips on his baseball cap and grimaces. "That whoever's got the journal doesn't actually know who rescued you."

"Right. But they know *something*."

We part ways at Mike's house. I've done my duty – sworn

in secret to Mumzilla – and walked him home. When he mounts the front step and gives me a wave, I feel this lump lurch into my throat and stick there.

Death has taken you, El, and all the way along Mike's driveway it's as if I can see you walking with him, your hand swinging close to his.

THEN: Sunday 8th December

The Flat

A fresh breeze smarts my face as I come out of the forest and skirt around Hunter's Lake. I've always loved this place. Mike and I used to camp out in the woods with Mumzilla and Big Mike when we were kids. Snug in our two-man teepee, we'd wait until we heard his parents' snores from the neighbouring tent, then we'd sit up in our sleeping bags, turn on our torches, and scare ourselves stupid with the story of the lake ghost. They say a girl drowned here once, but on a day like this, with the midwinter sun icing the waters, it's hard to believe that anything terrible could ever happen here.

Okay, I admit my good mood isn't just because of the lake and the sharp piney smell of Christmas on the air. I've decided that today's the day. I'm going to tell him. El doesn't know that today's special for more than one reason – why should he? – but when his text came through this morning, it was the best birthday present I'd ever received.

Frecks, this is I, Ellis Maximillian Bell, and I am ready
to repay my debt. Any chance you could come over
to mine? Flat 123 (I know, ridiculous) Mount Pleasant,
the Estate, yadda yadda. I am putting the kettle on...
NOW! xxx
PS: bring Starbursts.

So it isn't exactly Shakespeare's 18th sonnet, but it'll do.

My parents are taking Chris to London for the weekend: a Spurs game and he needs some new clothes, Mum says. They tried to include me, it being my birthday and everything. (Mum: "Maybe we could pop into the Imperial War Museum." Chris: "*Again?!*") But I'd already made up my mind that five weeks since the bonfire, and two since the library, is long enough. I can't keep retreating from him.

Because that's what I've been doing. I know, it's mad. What clearer signals do I need than that moment on the floor of the library, his finger tracing my bottom lip? And I've seen loads of El over the past few weeks. In history, where I used to drink in the lives of the long-dead, now I can barely memorize a date. Instead I spend the lessons staring at those long black lashes, watching the flex and tone of those forearms with their paint splatters and their magical tattoos. Actually, me watching him is getting embarrassing, but El's like the aurora borealis or the Grand

Canyon, you can't *not* look. It isn't just history either. Cute Mr Denman, who I definitely would be lusting over if El didn't completely eclipse him, has caught me more than once wandering around the art block at break time, studying a certain student's sculptures and canvases.

It doesn't stop there. Mike has never known me to be so supportive of the footie team. Now, come rain or shine, I can be found sitting on the touchline, cheering the Ferrivale Falcons. If Mike isn't suspicious by now then I fear his chosen career as a CID detective is not looking promising. Anyway, every time El scores I seem to get my own personal goal celebration. He waddles over, sort of like a duck, and pats my head. The boys find it hysterical, but they don't see the wink he gives me when he has his back to them.

Most afternoons find us in the comics section of the Ferrivale library. We've become a bit of a fixture; Mrs Jackson even brings us hot chocolate. Mostly we sit and read, or El reads and I steal glimpses at him from behind my comic. We talk about lots of stupid, unimportant junk: favourite movies, TV shows, his art, my love of history and comics, my (according to him) appalling diet. Whenever his endless teasing (*"Why are your freckles so freckly, Frecks? Have you had them tested for their pure orgasmic properties?"*) threatens to plunge us into sex territory (*sex territory?* Jesus, Dylan!), I make my usual bumbling retreat.

But no more.

No. More.

Maybe no more?

Arrrrgggghhhhhhhhh!!!! Because what if his teasing *is just teasing*? I could be about to make a serious tit of myself…

Stop it. *Carpe diem,* Dylan. Seize the day by the balls.

I crunch to a halt in front of El's building and grip the gift in my parka pocket. Okay. Breathe. I plunge down the slabbed pathway to the main door of Mount Pleasant. Someone has attempted to cheer the place up, planting clumps of little yellow, white and purple flowers in beds on either side of the entrance. Because of those colours, his favourites, I think this is Ellis's doing, and I smile.

As I buzz flat 123, I try to lose the grin. It's difficult to talk when you're smiling. You tend to look like a psychopath. Anyway, my jaw is starting to ache. I rock from foot to foot and wonder if El will ask for his IOU back when he gives me the money. Honestly, I'd rather him keep the cash. I love my IOU.

The seconds stretch out and the old stupid doubts begin to creep in again. I get out my phone and reread the message. Is this jokey tone for real? Maybe he and Gemma wrote it together and they're watching from an upstairs window right now, giggling at me on the doorstep. My traitor brain invents dialogue for them:

Oh, poor wovesick wittle Dywan. I bet he's bought you a pwesent and evewyfing.

Not Dywan. Mister Fwecks. Oh my God, he might actually think I like him! Pass me a bucket!

But this is rubbish. Although he and Gemma haven't had any major fallout, there's definitely been this cooling off between them since that day at Hug-A-Book. I guess she didn't appreciate getting dumped for…

For *me*. For ME.

The intercom buzzes and the main door clicks. I take a breath and push through. A floor plan in the vestibule shows Ellis's flat on the first level. I'm too impatient to wait for the lift and so take the stairs, leaping three at a time. El's corridor suddenly stretches ahead of me and I force myself to slow down because if he glances out of his door and sees me running, a) he will think I'm completely desperate (which I am), and b) he will *actually* see me running, which Mike reliably informs me is pure comedy gold.

Flat 123. I count my heartbeats and they steady. I knock on the door. It swings open at my touch and a short corridor with pretty pink wallpaper banishes the gloom of the outer hall.

"Hello? It's, um, Dylan… Ellis? Is anyone…?"

"In here!"

I step inside and shrug off my coat. I'm looking for a hook, and breathing in this sleepy smell of jasmine, when El calls out again.

"We're in the bathroom. Please, Dylan, hurry!"

I drop my coat and start opening doors. Living room, broom cupboard, kitchen, a woman's bedroom, with colourful clothes and smart business jackets hanging on a rail and a straw hat perched on a dressmaker's doll. Bathroom.

"Oh God."

Ellis is sitting on the floor, his back propped against the toilet. He's cradling this middle-aged woman in a pink towelling dressing gown that matches the wallpaper in the hall. She seems to be semi-conscious, her eyelids fluttering, her mouth breathing unheard words. El's left hand is clasping her right, squeezing, comforting. His own right hand is pressed to her head and there are bright streamers of blood dripping through his fingers. He looks up at me and all I want to do is make this better for him.

At that moment the buzzer in the hall goes.

"Ambulance." He nods. "Can you let them in?"

I run back to the corridor; I no longer care who sees me running. The intercom's by the door and I buzz them in, then I return to the bathroom, where El's face is a picture of pain and worry.

"My hand," he groans. "Cramp."

I scoot down next to him. Up close I can see how badly he's trembling. I can also see the small white trails dribbling out of his aunt's nose.

"Take your hand away," I tell him. He looks uncertain.

"After three," I say, bringing up my palm to hover over his. "One. Two. Three…"

Our hands switch places, and in the millisecond before I press mine to the wound, I catch a glimpse of torn skin, thick and lolling like a curled tongue. My palm immediately feels hot and sticky. El makes a tiny shift in position and his aunt moans. They're both smeared with blood and the lino under my knees is slippery with it.

"It's going to be okay," he whispers to her, his voice hoarse and tender at the same time. "I'll look after you, sweetheart." He buries his face in her hair, then looks up at me, his eyes wet. "Bless you, Dylan."

"She'll be fine." I nod. It's the sort of thing you have to say, and I want it to be true.

Blood is beginning to pulse slowly through my fingers when a couple of paramedics shoulder their way into the bathroom. They're all fake humour – "Hello there, young lady, so what trouble have you been getting yourself into?" – while busily unpacking their kit. One of them edges around us and shines a penlight into Ellis's aunt's eyes, then gives her partner this psychic look and he starts tearing open plastic packages.

"You've done an amazing job, boys." She smiles. "But let us take it from here, okay?"

She cradles her patient's head, which allows El to slide out from under his aunt. When he's free, I notice his jeans are completely spotless but his George Ezra *It Don't Matter Now* T-shirt is flecked red. The paramedic gives me the nod and I remove my hand. Hardly any blood flows now and she takes her time assessing the wound. Meanwhile her partner sidles past us and grins through his beard.

"Give us a little space, hey, guys? She's in safe hands." As El starts for the door, the paramedic asks, "Do you know what she's taken?"

"Coke. Silly cow. I don't know how much."

"Anything else?"

El shakes his head.

We wait outside the bathroom, standing opposite each other, backs pressed to the wall. The corridor's so narrow I could reach out and stroke his hand, but would that be appropriate? I've no idea. So I just stand there looking at my shoes, and he stands there looking at his socks. Red socks with yellow lightning strikes. It's the insignia of The Flash. Is he wearing them for me? *Shut up, stupid brain! Not the time.*

"Bradley Hinchcliffe," he mutters.

I look up. Everyone in Ferrivale knows that name. My mum and dad had their twentieth wedding anniversary at Hinchcliffes last year. Mike and I had to act as if we'd never been before, and Mike almost overplayed it, walking around and pretending to be wowed by the glitzy nightclub decor, then pleading with my dad to buy us a couple of beers when we'd actually snuck in half a dozen times already. I'm not much of a drinker but on our last visit a supernaturally flexible Mike got so toasted he actually managed to throw up in the pocket of his pulling trousers. Yes, Mike has pulling trousers.

I'm about to ask El what he means when the paramedics trundle his aunt out on this mini-wheelchair thing. Her head's patched and her eyes are a little more focused. She calls out weakly and El grabs her hand.

"Can I come with?"

The beardy paramedic nods. "But only one of you."

"Dylan." His eyes cut to me. "Could you do me a massive favour?"

"Course."

He fishes in his pocket and throws me a set of keys. I catch them one-handed, which is a kind of miracle.

"Bring me some clothes to the hospital? I'm sorry, could you get a taxi or something? I'll pay you back."

The paramedics push on and the passage is so tight that El's forced to let go of his aunt. Before following, he closes the gap between us and cups my hand around the keys. A little of the terror has gone out of him and I tremble slightly when he brings my hand up to his lips.

"Thank you, I won't forget this."

And then he's gone and I'm alone in the flat.

A clock ticks, a radio plays. Someone downstairs starts

a washing machine. I exhale. There's one door here I haven't tried. With the keys still tight in my fist, I wander down the hall. I almost feel like I should knock, show some kind of respect, I don't know, because I'm about to experience a part of El that maybe he wouldn't have chosen to share just yet. I turn the handle and step inside.

His smell hits me first. Almost every library afternoon, I've found an excuse to lean over, showing him some passage or drawing in a book, just so I can drink in this smell. It's hard to describe: the citrus of his deodorant blended with his own natural El-ness. I paw at the wall and find the switch. A single bulb plinks on.

Drawings and paintings everywhere. Not a bit of wall left. El has made himself a cocoon, and it's papery and perfect. Aside from his smell, my senses catch the dustiness of his pencils and a sharp sting from the turpentine he uses to clean his brushes. The tiny room is overwhelming. So many spiralling colours and images: a teenager in a red coat swinging on a branch, her mirror-self caught in a puddle; our school at twilight, something creeping and monstrous at the windows; a prison cell holding a little girl, her pudgy hand reaching between the bars, something white and broken in her palm.

My eyes drift to his bed, neatly made. I want to fall into it, roll myself in the sky-blue sheets, but I have to get to the hospital. There's this neat built-in wardrobe in the corner where I find fresh T-shirts and a hoodie. I'm about to grab one of each when I realize my own black T-shirt is also smeared with blood. Will he mind? Trembling slightly, I take a canary yellow T – because El doesn't do black – and quickly change.

I press my hand to my chest. The shirt almost swamps me and it's garish and I love it. I can't help lifting the collar and breathing him in. I can't help kissing the fabric. Yes, I'm that pathetic. I carefully fold the spare clothes into El's gym bag, and I'm heading out of the room, when I see another drawing at the head of his bed.

I drop the bag. Zombie-walk across the room. Place my fingers against the yellow sheet tacked to the wall. It's me. Gangly, gawky, klutzy, freckly, bedheady me, and somehow he's caught me exactly as I am and *has made me beautiful*. I put my fist to my mouth and breathe slowly through clenched fingers. This is how he sees me. Beautiful. And then I realize how I'm positioned, smiling downwards, my eyes cast at whoever is sleeping in the bed below.

And I don't think any more.

I know.

I know I love him.

NOW: Wednesday 29th April

14

No one's up by the time I get home from Gemma's party, so I manage to creep into bed unnoticed. In seconds, I'm asleep, and for the first time since I lost you, El, I dream no dreams of you.

Opening my eyes the next morning, I raise a hand to the sunlight pouring through the window. I yawn, stagger upright, and stumble across the hall into the shower. Bullets of warm water drum my back. It feels good. But it was my need to feel good that got you killed, and so I turn the dial until the water scalds me raw.

Stepping out of the tub, I rub an oval in the bathroom mirror. I wonder what you'd say if you could see me now, El? My skin has this blotchy texture and the circles under my eyes are as bad as Mike's post-chemo. I cinch a towel around my waist and head back to my bedroom.

It stinks. Half-eaten sandwiches and mouldering bits

of fruit circle my bed like offerings made to a mummified pharaoh. I dry myself and search my drawers for a fresh T-shirt. I'm about to pluck out the inevitable black when a swatch of yellow catches my eye. It's the shirt I borrowed the day of Julia's accident. My fingers shake as I tease it gently from the drawer.

The yellow T hasn't been washed since that day. I can still see the sweat stains under the armpits. As I pull it up to my face, I pray to the god I don't believe in, and maybe He answers, because your smell *is* here. Oh, El, you've no idea how many hours I've spent ransacking this room for something that still held a trace of you. How did I miss this?

It's only when I catch the time on my Superman alarm clock that I break free of memories. 12.47 p.m. Crap. I place the yellow T-shirt back in the bottom drawer, promising myself that I'll vacuum-seal it, so your smell will be preserved forever, then pull on the usual black T-shirt and jeans and race downstairs.

No one's about. I grab the post from the kitchen table and flip through bills and postcards and junk mail, throwing everything down again when I'm done. Nothing from the mysterious journal-sender. Perhaps the Gemma drawing from yesterday will be the only time I'll ever hear from him. The idea scares me – because without him how will I ever find out what happened? – and so I push it away.

173

I make myself some toast and a cup of tea. I'm guessing Mum and Chris are on one of their mummy–son outings, probably slagging you off and swiping through Tinder in search of a safe replacement. It's nice outside and I decide I could do with some air. I grab my jacket just as Dad comes puffing through the front door. I try to shoulder past him but he grabs my wrist like he's about to judo flip my ass.

"Hold on, Dylan." He's blocking the door, and unless I want to drop-kick my old man I have to hear him out. "You should know you really upset your mum yesterday."

"Oh really?"

"You were rude."

"I slammed a door."

He breathes through his nose and his gaze flits to the ceiling. "I understand you may have overheard a private conversation between your mum and your brother. That was…unfortunate."

"No fucking kidding."

"Dylan," he barks at me. "I'm sure they meant well."

"Oh, did they? Because it sounded to me like they were doubting my relationship with the person I loved most in this whole shitty world. That Ellis was somehow not good enough for me." I laugh like it's the best joke I've ever heard. "I was in awe of him, Dad. Do you even understand that? I was in *awe* of him, because he was so far beyond good

174

enough it isn't even funny. The fact that he would even settle for someone like me—"

My dad's face turns this awful shade of red. "Don't sell yourself short. That boy—"

"What? You shook hands with him the night I came out. You congratulated us. Was that all a lie?"

"I don't care that you're gay," he mutters, "and you can choose to believe that or not. But gay or straight, your mum and I – and yes, even your brother – we only want what's best for you. And this, what you're doing now, giving up school, throwing away your future, do you think it's what Ellis would have wanted? Because I didn't know this amazing kid you're talking about – I never got much of a chance to know him – but I'm pretty sure he'd be appalled to see you like this."

Future? *My* future? Strangely, that isn't something I've even thought about. All I can concentrate on right now is finding out who left you to die, El. Anything beyond that is just a blank.

I thrust my face into my dad's. "You don't get to tell me what El would want. Not ever. Now will you please get out of my way?"

He looks like he's about to start in on me again, but then just sighs and stands aside.

"Dylan," he says as I pass, "there is something you should know. I'd rather you heard it from me."

But right now, I don't want to hear anything my dad has to say. I put my head down and storm out of the house.

I'm halfway along the drive when I consider calling Mike. But no, that's monumentally selfish. He's probably wiped out after the party. And so I make a decision: I'm going to the lake. Heading back there is asking for trouble, I know, but I slept soundly last night, and that feels like a betrayal. With images of the lake fresh in my mind, I won't sleep so easy tonight.

As I walk I think over what Gemma said: *People like Ellis will always be vulnerable, just because they won't play the silly games that everyone else plays – to fit in, to be popular, to feel wanted. They're too brave for that. Too fucking brave to be anything less than what they are.*

There's an ugly truth to this I don't want to acknowledge. You were always facing down what people thought of you, El, and though they were forced to turn away when you called them on their bullshit, they still thought it. Is that why you died? Because when you were most vulnerable someone who couldn't accept you held your life in their hands? For some reason I think of that couple in the hospital the day of your aunt's accident, the ones with the sullen eyes, and I wonder what they would have done if they saw you drowning.

I reach the lake and wander slowly down to the shore. Resting on the shingle there's a small collection of flowers.

I hunker over and examine a few of the tributes. One arrangement of purple, yellow and white has a card from Julia that simply reads, *Rest well, Angel boy xxx*. I know the name of these flowers now. Violas. It *was* you who planted them outside the flats, bringing beauty like you always did.

A huge bouquet to one side demands attention. I squat down because the writing's so small: *In memory of a truly amazing teammate. With love, Ollie x*. It's heartfelt and touching and weird. I think back to last night and Ollie's behaviour at the party. What is going on with him?

I spend the whole day at the lake. Memories don't invade; I don't really think about much at all, and feel as guilty as hell about it. The sun's setting when I drag myself to my feet and start towards home.

Lights are on in the sitting room. I slip through the front door and I'm heading upstairs when Chris comes out of the kitchen.

"Hey, bro," he says, a carrot clamped between his teeth. "Mail for you."

I tear back downstairs and grab the envelope from him. No postage this time, hand-delivered. But the same packaging and the same unidentifiable handwriting.

"When did this arrive?"

"S'morning. I meant to tell you, but you were still asleep."

"You fucking idiot!"

He looks at me like a stunned rabbit, the carrot making

circles in his mouth. My mum comes out of the kitchen, wondering what's wrong. I don't give her a second glance.

Outside again, I open the envelope as carefully as I can and slip out a single yellow page. The next second, I'm calling Mike.

HINCHCLIFFES. The neon buzzes above my head and the lack of an apostrophe, as usual, bugs me. Everyone knows that our local self-styled businessman-guru is an only child and unmarried, so I don't care how many charities he funds, how many floats he sponsors in the Ferrivale parade, or how many drug runners he has operating across town, his punctuation is atrocious.

As we shuffle forward in the queue, I shoot Mike a concerned glance. He came running over as soon as he got my call but last night is clearly telling on him. Under our phone lights, he examined the new picture I'd been sent from El's Moodles and Doodles book – this time a drawing of Bradley Hinchcliffe, the sharp nose, small eyes and ferrety mouth so familiar from local newspaper coverage of a million ribbon-cuttings. Only El had drawn Bradley's mouth to resemble a leech-like hole, a disgusting dripping cavity ringed with needle-sharp teeth. From out of this alien mouth, gluts of white powder fall like snow over Ferrivale.

In a few short sentences, I told Mike about that day at

your aunt's and my theory as to why Bradley might have wanted you out of the picture.

"I think it must be someone who was at Gemma's 'wake' party," I said. "The journal-sender, I mean. They assumed from what happened last night that we've ruled Gemma out, which pretty much confirms our theory about them not knowing who rescued me. They're using the journal pictures to help us identify suspects, but it's just guesswork on their part. They don't know for sure, so they send us the next most likely suspect from El's drawings."

An idea then popped into my head. Could it be Ollie? It would fit in with his ultra-protective behaviour at the party... But something about that didn't ring true.

"So from what you say, this picture might indicate that Bradley Hinchcliffe had a grudge against El and that he's our lake suspect," Mike said. "We can pretty much rule him out for the porno perv or whoever frightened El at the dance. Someone would've noticed if he'd been hanging around the school. Okay, so what's the plan?"

It's a pretty terrible plan, but it's the only one I could come up with, and so here we are, at the front of the queue – and for the first time in our Hinchcliffes history, a bouncer is barring our way.

"IDs."

Crap. Neither Mike nor I look eighteen and we've both left our IDs at home.

"Um, we don't really want to come in, necessarily."

The man-mountain gestures with two fingers and the people behind us start funnelling past. "Oh yeah? So you're just turned on by the queueing part then?"

"No." I shake my head. "But me and my mate… Well, we want to buy some… You know…"

He looks down at me and breaks into this huge grin. "Now you *are* yanking my chain. Look, little boys, run on home, will you?"

I'm at a complete loss when Mike pipes up. "Hey, that notice above your door? Your premises' licence to sell alcohol?"

"What about it?"

"It's a legal requirement that the person nominated to sell alcohol must be clearly identified on the sign," Mike says, parroting something he's probably picked up from Carol's work as an events organizer. "As you will see, Mr Hinchcliffe's name is currently hidden by a huge dollop of bird shit. That means you are in breach of the law, and if I call the cops, they *will* shut you down. So unless you want to get a ladder and some marigolds and start scrubbing?"

"You cheeky little—"

A hand reaches up from behind the goliath. "It's okay, Tommo. Let them in."

Tommo moves aside and Bradley Hinchcliffe himself beckons us inside. Reaching the cloakroom, the small, sleek, well-dressed figure stops and indicates a girl behind the counter.

"Talk to Yaz here," he says. "She'll sort you out."

He's about to move on when I catch the sleeve of his immaculate pinstripe.

"We're not here for that," I tell him. "Mr Hinchcliffe, I want to talk to you about a boy who died."

Bradley hesitates, then shrugs and leads us through the painfully purple heart of his club, past the glittering bar and private booths, across the slightly sticky dance floor and beyond the DJ box. People barge and jostle us but it's only 9.45 and the banter's friendly. One girl tries to grab Mike and twirl him but he offers his apologies and keeps pace with us. My heart is hammering. Scenes from a dozen Hollywood gangster movies flicker through my head: scarfaced henchmen hauling traitors into the presence of cat-cuddling mafia bosses, bodies stuffed into trunks and dropped off piers. What have I dragged you into, Mike?

Hinchcliffe opens a leather-padded door and ushers us into his office. Then, while we stand in audience, he rounds a big glass desk and sinks into his chair.

"So what's this all about?" he asks casually.

And suddenly I'm not one bit scared. Fuck this guy. Fuck him for what he did to you and Julia that day, El. "I want to know if you had anything to do with the death of Ellis Bell."

He steeples his fingers and looks up at us. "Who?"

I take out your drawing and smooth it down on the desk. He grins. "Nice likeness. What is this?"

"You must have known Ellis," I say. "Your runners sold your shit to his aunt. Exploited her for years before El showed up and put a stop to it. Not good business for you, him sticking his nose in."

Bradley twirls his finger. "Right. I know the name now. The lad who drowned in the lake a couple of weeks back? Yes, my girlfriend read about it in the *Chronicle*." He cocks his head to one side. "Wait a minute, were you the boyfriend? Oh, kid. Well, you have my condolences, of course. But let's see, you think because this Ellis got his aunt sober, I what? Tampered with the brakes of his car or something?"

I shake my head. "The brakes were fine. But I think it's possible that you held a grudge against El for losing you a customer. Maybe a good enough grudge that, if you happened to be near the lake that night, you'd happily watch him drown."

Bradley rocks back in his chair, laughing his arse off. "Oh, but you are pure entertainment, kid. Better even than Netflix…" He clicks his fingers at me. "What's the name?"

"Dylan. McKee."

"Oh yeah. Your dad's that probate solicitor in town. I've chatted to him once or twice, felt like I was drifting in and out of a coma. Okay, Dylan, so I'm going to tell you two things, but first I am going to make a prediction. Are you ready for this?"

I nod, though my insides are churning, like one of those razor-teethed leeches is going to work in my stomach.

"Prediction: when you hear my two little facts I will offer you a free night in my club, all the booze you can drink, and you will take my offer and say, 'Thank you, Mr Hinchcliffe, you're a gentleman. I'd like that drink now.'"

Mike laughs and I almost join in.

Bradley allows us our moment, then begins: "Little fact number 1: *if* I was this big bad drug lord you seem to imagine, then I probably couldn't care less whether Ellis's aunt continued to buy my shit or not. She would be an infinitesimally tiny speck in a very large operation. Certainly not significant enough for me to hold a grudge. Moving on, little fact number 2... Now are you watching very carefully, Dylan?"

He retrieves a remote control from the desk drawer and, rising from his chair, moves towards us. Honestly, Mike and I could take him easily, and I'm hardly the Immortal Iron Fist, but there's something about this guy. He reminds me of one of those wicked imps in old fairy tales, the ones you can sell your soul to without even realizing it.

Bradley thumbs the remote and the TV on the wall blinks into life.

"I remembered this while you were talking. Had to

check the CCTV after we had a fight in here on New Year's Eve." He glances at us over his shoulder. "I *do* recall your boyfriend. Yes indeed, he made quite the impression. Just after midnight, main bar. And here – we – go!"

He clicks and a black-and-white image stutters into life. It's you, El, bright and alive, on one of those nights over the Christmas holidays when you mysteriously disappeared on me. I stand and watch and the bottom drops out of my world.

"Woo-eeee!" Bradley chuckles. "I gotta admit, this is some steamy action. So, Dylan, I'm not sure you can hear me right now, but I want you to know that I'm doing this as a favour. You see, you can stop grieving now, because that boyfriend of yours? Well, he obviously didn't give a crap about you, did he? So why not just let it all go and take me up on my generous offer?"

I stand and gaze through tears at the TV, watching you in the arms of a stranger, kissing, grinding, lost in him. What had I been doing on New Year's Eve? Staring at my phone, praying that you would answer one of my texts, wondering what I'd done wrong.

I turn to Bradley. "Thank you, Mr Hinchcliffe," I say, "you're a gentleman. I'd like that drink now."

THEN: Sunday 8th December

The Bedroom

I find El sitting on a plastic chair in A&E, twisting his pearls between his fingers.

"How is she?" I ask, dropping into the seat beside him.

He looks up at me, and at first I'm not sure he knows where he is.

"Oh, I don't know. No one's come out to tell me anything yet."

I nod and slide my hands between my knees, clamping them there, because that's my go-to when I don't know what to do. After a minute or two, El rocks against me and I feel his head droop against my shoulder. His hair tickles my cheek, and I'm about to rest my head against his when I see this couple sitting opposite us.

They're dressed in those gigantic coats that old people seem to wear in all weathers, and they're giving us this sullen-eyed stare. It's difficult to describe exactly, but it's a bit like they've seen a gang of kids scraping dog shit off the pavement and are suspicious that said shit might be posted through their letter box. The old man curls his lip and his wife mouths something. I think it might be the F word.

"Tea," I say, getting to my feet. "There's a machine in the corridor."

"Wow." El nods. "These places are really cutting edge."

He follows me to the vending machine and watches me feed coins into the slot.

"I was supposed to be making *you* tea, remember?"

"I do. White? Sugar?"

I punch in our order and the cabinet grumbles, then chucks out two plastic cups before vomiting liquid and powder into them. I pinch the scalding rims and hand El his cup. He sips and grimaces.

"This is awful."

"I think it's supposed to be. I mean, it has to be intentional, doesn't it? You couldn't *accidentally* come up with something this disgusting. I'm picturing a secret laboratory where retired PE teachers dream up the drinks that go into hospital vending machines. Sure it's a far cry from the old days, but sadism's sadism, right?"

He bursts out laughing. I love how El laughs, full and musical and like nobody's in the room. I wish I could laugh like that. We wander back to our seats, where we grimace at our undrinkable tea. We're quiet for a while, then El says –

"She saved me, you know." He holds the steaming cup to his chest. "When my parents threw me out, she was the only one who showed me any kind of support or sympathy. Do you know what that's like? To have just this one person who's prepared to offer you some security? It's like you're attached to the world by a single thread, and if that thread snaps?" He looks at me with these huge eyes. "What's going to happen to me then?"

He tells me his coming-out story, and it shatters my heart. I travel with him from closed door to closed door, the money in his pocket transforming from paper to coins, from silver to bronze, until he ends up cold and starving in Ferrivale, where his mum's second cousin takes him in. She gives him food and a bed and, most important of all, wraps warm arms around him and tells him he's wonderful just the way he is.

It was a week later that he first discovered her passed out in the kitchen.

El's face turns dark. "Bradley Hinchcliffe. His boys have been dealing to her for years."

"But everyone knows the guy," I say. "He was in school last year talking about ethical investments and community spirit."

"Oh, on the surface he's Jesus reborn." El smiles. "But if you look a little deeper..."

He crushes his cup and some of the tea spills onto his

shirt. It's only then that I remember he's sitting in blood-stained clothes. I rummage in the bag I brought from the flat and take out a fresh T-shirt. He thanks me and we head to the bathroom. It's a single toilet so I pass El the shirt through a crack in the door. Long seconds drag as I stand outside.

"Are you okay?" I ask at last.

"I can't," he murmurs. "My hands are shaking too much. Dylan, I'm sorry, can you help me?"

"Oh. Yeah. Course. No problem."

I check the corridor for sullen eyes, then slip into the room. It's a small space and the smell of industrial cleaner makes my eyes itch. El stands in front me, the T-shirt in his hands. It's then that his gaze flicks to my own shirt.

"Oh, I'm sorry." I blush. "There was some blood on me and I—"

"It's okay. More than okay. Yellow suits you. It brings out the gold in your hair and the little amber flecks in your eyes. I never noticed before…"

He touches a strand on my head and I feel that touch in every cell of my body. My heart drums, and when I look down a canary-yellow patch over my chest is fluttering in time.

El pulls off his stained George Ezra T in one smooth motion. I'm sorry, I can't help but look. His body is a toned, honeyed brown, broad at the shoulders, tapering down to a narrow waist with those plunging hip lines you only really

188

see in magazines. I watch as he turns, and my heart roars. I want to kiss that firm chest and flat stomach, explore each tight curve and sweeping plane, watch how the subtle shifts in pigmentation define his body. And at the same time I need to run and hide from this intimidating perfection.

I do neither. I hand him the shirt.

"Thank you." He grins as he pulls it on. Is it a knowing grin? My blush reaches supernova.

"Bell?" A voice echoes through the door. "Ellis Bell?"

We exchange a look and duck out of the one-man bathroom. A doctor with a clipboard gives us a wry smile as we tumble into the corridor.

"Mr Bell?"

"Is she okay?" El cuts in.

The young doctor guides us into a side office and we take a seat.

"Your aunt is doing well. The cut from her fall was pretty serious, but I'm sure the wound will heal quite nicely. We've sedated her and we're going to keep her in—"

"Why?"

The doctor makes a soothing gesture. "An overnight stay is pretty standard in these cases. We want to make sure she isn't suffering any concussion. She should be released first thing tomorrow. However, there is the other matter. Do you know how long she's been using?"

El shakes his head. "I only moved in a few months ago, and before that…I didn't really know my aunt very well. I think she's been on the stuff a while."

"I see. Well, look, it's important we get her some help. I'm going to talk to her tomorrow and see what kind of treatment will work best, but I won't lie to you, she's going to need a lot of support going forward."

"She'll get it," El says firmly. "No question."

The doctor makes a quick note and gets up to leave.

"Can I see her?" El asks.

We're shown through to a curtained-off cubicle just past the nurses' station. All at once El comes undone. He drops into a seat next to his sleeping aunt and covers his face with his hands. A fresh bandage has been taped around her head, her face has been washed, and for the first time I can see the resemblance between aunt and nephew. She looks kind, even in sleep. I give El a moment, then fumble in my pocket and place a hand on his shoulder. He looks up, sees what I'm holding, and laughs through his tears.

"Starburst! You're a mind-reader, Frecks."

We spend the next few hours keeping watch. I pop out every so often for drinks and snacks. When a porter arrives to take Julia to a proper ward, El insists on going with her. That's when the young doctor pokes his head into the cubicle.

"You boys still here? Look, nothing is going to happen to your aunt tonight, and if it does, we have your number.

Go home. Get some rest. You'll need it if you're going to support her in the coming weeks."

"Why don't you stay at mine?" I say. "My family's away for the night, and I heat up a mean frozen pizza." He starts to shake his head but I put my foot down. "You owe me, remember? So I'm going to trade the cash for your company." He immediately objects, digging in his pocket for the car-repair money. I take his wrist and draw him into a handshake. "You, Ellis Maximillian Bell, do hereby swear you will endure the close proximity of Dylan 'Frecks' McKee for one evening, in full and final payment for any and all outstanding debts. Plus, you will not request anything green to go with your pizza because, just no."

El shakes. "If you're sure? Okay then, deal."

We're heading back through A&E when he loops an arm around me. And it seems impossible, but sitting in the exact same spot are the old couple in their big coats. I don't know, maybe they make an all-day outing of their hospital visits. Anyway, they see us and start radiating the stink-eye, and before I know it, I'm stink-eyeing them right back. Then I wrap my arm tight around him and, with my free hand, I flip them a glorious middle finger.

"Sorry," I say, as we stand shivering in the hall, "heating's gone off for some reason. Just be a minute."

I leg it upstairs to the boiler cupboard and click a switch. Something roars somewhere, and I guess that means heat sometime soon. Skipping back into the hall, I find El looking for a place to hang his jacket. I take it from him and drape it over this weird alien sculpture my mum made in one of her night classes.

"You know, my mum's an artist too." I grin.

"I see that."

"Yep... So, she sucks, doesn't she?"

"There is potential," he says, drawing his bottom lip between his teeth. "But, yeah, sorry, mostly it's suckage."

The temperature is almost bearable by the time I take my *pièce de résistance* out of the oven. El looks from me to the pizza and back again.

"And we're supposed to do what with this, exactly?"

"Dude. Do not dis the kebab-meat deep pan."

"Is that what this curly grey stuff is on the top? I thought a dog might have sneaked in and rubbed his flaky balls all over the base."

I shrug. "More for me." I grab a greasy slice from the plate and stuff the whole thing in my mouth. "Ah, man, heavenly."

"McKee D, you are all kinds of revolting." El shakes his head, picks up a slice, and takes a nibble. He tries a few experimental chews, then begins to wolf it down like it's the last morsel of food he'll ever consume. Mid-gorging, he lifts an oily finger. "No one must ever hear of this. Promise me."

I give him a scout's salute, then rub my hands on my jeans.

"Crap, I forgot. Hold on a minute."

I run out to Mum's alien creation and grab El's present from my coat pocket. I'm officially the world's most inept wrapper of gifts, and I really tried with this one, but it still looks like random bits of silver paper sellotaped together in a darkened room by a poorly coordinated chimp. El gets a napkin from the sideboard and cleans his fingers.

"Wow. It's a gift, right? I mean, you don't hate me or anything?"

"Just open it, smart-arse."

It takes him a minute to wrestle with the tape but eventually he's holding a brand-new snow globe in his hand. He stares through the falling flakes at this grim little elf who appears to be guarding a sack of presents.

"Dylan, I think this guy is trying to steal Christmas. No, don't laugh, just look at him. He's clearly broken into Santa's workshop and pinched St Nicholas's magic sack." I clap a hand over my mouth to stifle giggles. "Frecks, please don't be a child. Yes, I said 'pinched his magic sack'. He's an elf on the run."

"Okay." I stroke my chin. "I can see that. He is kind of gangsta."

El throws his arms around my neck. "I love it. Thank you. Gangsta-elf-on-the-run will take pride of place on my dashboard."

"So," I say, coughing as he releases me, "did the police figure out who trashed your car?"

"Nah. I didn't report it."

"What? Why?"

"I don't know. I sort of feel sorry for them, I suppose. You've got to be really unhappy to do something like that."

He looks away, and I wonder then, just wonder, if he knows who it was.

"Hey, you want to see my room?"

I lead the way upstairs. The heating's definitely kicking in now. I feel sort of flushed and sweaty anyway.

I open the door, and although my room is more than twice the size of his, I'm suddenly aware of all its lameness and inadequacy. Everything here – the superhero posters on the wall, the historical quotes and mottos painted over my bed, the old toys and action figures on my bookcase – it's all the work of someone else. I have contributed absolutely nothing to this space. I think back to the individuality and sheer effort that made El's room so special, and it's like I've been stripped bare and found wanting.

He wanders around, picking stuff up, smiling. I want to tell him how I feel but I can't put it into words. Then he notices the cards on my desk and stops short.

"Frecks, it's your birthday? Today?"

I nod.

"And you got *me* a present?"

I shrug. "I've had my present." I dig out the IOU from my wallet. "It's the best thing anyone's ever given me."

He doesn't tell me I'm crazy, just nods. And then he's tearing out of the room, calling over his shoulder, "Hold on, I need something from my bag."

I drop into my desk chair, swing around, count and recount my cards, get up, throw my dirty underwear into the laundry basket. Then El's back and flourishing his journal.

"Moodles and Doodles." I smile.

He takes my chair and pulls a black felt-tip pen from the journal's elastic band.

"Can I see?" I ask, holding out my hand.

He shakes his head. "Everyone needs a secret corner all to themselves, Frecks."

I go and sit on the bed. "Even from me?"

His eyes are serious but there's a kind of laughter there too. "Even from you, sweetheart. You'll have that corner too. It might not be a book, but there's some place you keep all to yourself and I won't be there. Now lean back against the wall and stay still."

What follows is just about the best fifteen minutes of my life. I cross my legs and put on this stupidly serious expression, until El scolds me and asks for a natural smile. Every so often I steal a glance at him while he works. He's even more beautiful in these moments. There's this single deep furrow in his brow and a little twitch that leaps at the side of his mouth and his long dark lashes quiver while his eyes dart over the page. And his fingers *sing*. That's the only way I know how to describe it. They sing like the fingers of a conductor stirring and then lulling an orchestra. At last he stands up and brings me my present.

"Sorry. I can never really capture what I want to." He flops down beside me and scoots in close. "Do you hate it?"

I can't speak. This isn't me. It can't be.

"Why…?" I swallow hard. "Why are you so obsessed with my freckles?"

He leans in close and kisses the speckles that run across my nose. "Because they're yours."

This is it. No more retreating. I take my chance before my courage fails.

"Ellis?"

"Yes, Dylan?"

"I'm gay."

It's the most obvious statement in the world, but he doesn't tease. Because I think he knows I had to say it out loud. He kneels beside me and cups my chin, inviting me to look at him.

"Dylan?"

"Yeah?"

"I think I like you."

"Yeah?"

"I like you very, very much."

He kisses me again. On the lips this time, the lightest, most feathery kiss, and I kiss him back. He runs those brilliant dancing fingers through my hair, trails them down the back of my neck, lightly scratching my skin. He presses harder and I open my mouth and very softly feel the tip of his tongue against mine. And then he's kissing my jaw and my chin and the nape of my neck, and his hand is inside my shirt, *his* shirt, grazing fingernails across my chest.

And then, because I'm Dylan, I say something stupid.

"So, you've ruined history for me."

He pulls back, lips smudged, grinning. "What?"

"I know absolutely nothing about the French Revolution, and we've been studying it for a month. Basically because I can't stop looking at you, and I just—"

El's phone starts to buzz. We exchange a glance and I can see the panic in his eyes. Julia. Something's wrong. He fumbles in his pocket, pulling out his second-hand Samsung with almost Dylan-levels of clumsiness, thumbing the screen and then dropping the phone on the floor. Leaning over the bed, we both stare down at Mr Denman, El's hipster art teacher.

"Oh." Denman blinks at us from the screen. "Hello,

Ellis. And is that…Dylan McKee? Sorry, am I interrupting something?"

El shoots me a wicked side-eye. "Not at all, sir. Everything okay?"

"Yes, Ellis, no, everything's fine. I just thought I'd call to say how impressed I am with the latest improvements to your sculpture. With this as your main project, I can't imagine you're going to have any trouble getting into the uni of your choice." He moves to one side and I see that he's standing in one of the school's art studios. Behind him is this incredible model of a winged monster, its body a see-through string of wires, its insides veined with red ribbons. I've seen this sculpture slowly taking shape during my secret visits to the art block. It's startling and it's perfect. Of course it is. "However, I do think it needs just a few more touches," Denman goes on. "Could we maybe get together after school one day to discuss?"

El nods. "Sure. Thanks so much, Mr D."

Denman gives us both a knowing grin. "Okay, boys. As you were."

El lets out a long breath and ends the call.

"Wow." I elbow him in the ribs. "Your art teacher has your number. And I thought I was the world's biggest dweeb."

"Oh, Dylan." He smiles. "You are *so* the world's biggest dweeb."

"What?"

I throw myself at him and we roll across the bed. I'm kissing him and I know I'm doing it right because I can feel him, hard and aching against my thigh. After a delicious forever of this, we turn onto our backs, faces to the ceiling, where a million years ago I stuck a galaxy of fluorescent stars.

"Are you my boyfriend, Ellis?" I ask, my voice tremulous.

"Dylan…" He rolls to face me. "Know this one thing if nothing else…" He kisses me again, soft and deep. "I am *very definitely* your boyfriend."

NOW: Wednesday 29th April

15

I hate you, El.

I *hate* you.

I stumble out of Bradley Hinchcliffe's office and push my way across the dance floor. Someone shouts "Hey!" and starts to follow. There's a huge mirror lined with shelves and bottles behind the bar and I can see this twenty-something reflected there, twice my size with murder in his eyes. I don't give a shit. Let him beat the crap out of me, who cares? But then Bradley grabs his shoulder and spits a word in his ear and the guy holds up his hands. By the time I reach the bar he's back on the dance floor, grinding against his girlfriend.

Bradley's reflection makes some signal to the barman, who scurries over.

"Yes, sir?" I plunge a hand into my jeans pocket. "No, no, sir. On the house. You're Mr Hinchcliffe's guest, aren't you?"

"Sure." I give him this death's-head grin. "Can I get three flaming sambucas to start with?"

I have no idea what a flaming sambuca tastes like, but Chris has told me they're the bomb. Anyway, my own personal cocktail waiter doesn't blink.

"Coming right up."

I wait, drumming my fingers on the sticky counter. In the mirror I see Mike walking over with these huge worried eyes. The fuck has he got to be worried about…? Oh God, what am I thinking? I feel thoroughly ashamed of myself, which makes me more bitter and more angry. In fact, I'm kind of surprised I'm not crying…but no, all I can do is replay the CCTV footage in my head.

I thought I was empty before today. I was wrong. Turns out there was a tiny part of me you hadn't taken with you into the darkness, El. Well, you've taken it now. Scraped it out of me and left me hollow. You weren't who I thought you were, Ellis Bell.

Mike pitches up just as the drinks arrive. I turn to him and slap his shoulder, as if we're regular drinking buddies.

"Michael, my man. Flaming sambuca? It'll put hairs on your head."

Okay, I hate myself, but I said it. I can't unsay it now.

"Dylan, don't."

As pleas go, it's pithy and to the point. I hand him a shot glass and blow out my own blue flame.

"Don't let me drink alone, Mikester." I swallow and my whole head feels like it's been pumped full of aniseed. It's disgustingly glorious. "Dude! You have to try this." When he doesn't, I take back the glass and down it, then turn to the one on the bar. "I'm not kidding, Mike, you really need this awful stuff in your life."

I gesture to the barman who nods, pours and ignites.

So which was your secret identity, El? Your Bruce Wayne? Your Peter Parker? Because if I had to make a guess based on what I've just seen, I got your mild-mannered schoolboy while the guy in the vid got your Dark Knight. It seems impossible that there was a side to you more intense, more passionate than the one you showed me. That first night, my birthday, when my parents were away, I thought that was as perfect for you as it was for me. But it fits, I guess. Your jackknife moods maybe echoed your jackknife affections, constantly and secretly switching. And now, downing my fourth sambuca, I remember what I once thought about you: *El's passions are intense but fleeting.* I tried to fool myself then that I was the exception.

I stare at my reflection. I'm coming apart. I know it and I don't care. But no, let's be fair – I lift my glass and raise a toast to your ghost – I always knew this was going to happen. How many times did I tell myself you were too good for me? That it made no Earth logic, as Mike might say, that someone as talented and clever as you would ever look at someone like me. The shy, awkward, geeky kid who can't even take a packet of sweets out of his pocket without turning it into a comedy routine.

In my mind I see Bradley Hinchcliffe's video playing on an endless loop. You pressed against the boy in the denim shirt, mouths locked tight, your hand fisting his hair, his hands slipping under the band of your jeans.

I turn to Mike.

"He never kissed me like that. Not once."

"I'm glad."

"What the hell does that mean?" I throw out my arms, spilling a fifth sambuca.

"I mean—"

"New Year's Eve," I cut in. "We had two good weeks before all the weirdness started. You know when we got together properly?"

"Your birthday," Mike says. He tries to put an arm around my shoulder but I shrug him off.

"Right. That whole time before school broke up was amazing. I still didn't want to tell anyone, and El respected that, but every chance we could get… It wasn't just sex. It was holding hands, talking. And then the holidays came and he just disappeared on me. It scared me, you know? I kept going over and over things, wondering if I'd done something or said something."

"It wasn't you," Mike soothes.

"I thought so too, after all my usual self-accusing. You guys screwed up your last few games before term ended, and I know El thought he'd let you down. Then he was worried about his art project, with Mr Denman nitpicking all the time. So when he stopped answering my calls and texts, I thought I'd give him some space. Except it killed me, thinking he didn't want me any more. That he'd got tired of me that quickly. I went round to his place a couple of times, but Julia always said he was out or asleep and that he'd call me later. I could tell she was covering for him because she'd give me this really guilty look.

"And then we got together again a few days after New Year and everything was fine. He was the same old El. But I could never get him to tell me what had happened over Christmas. Well, I guess now we know."

I snag my fifth sambuca, or is it the sixth? Another thing I'm shit at: drinking.

"Nothing had scared or upset him, he told me," I say. "He just wanted a bit of time to himself. Turns out he obviously got sick of all my amateur sex and wanted to fill his boots somewhere else. You know, he told me once that we all need this secret corner for ourselves that not even the people closest to us can invade. I guess this place was his corner."

"Dylan, you need to stop this right now."

I stare blearily at my best friend. "Stop what?"

"The self-pity," he says. "You have absolutely no idea what was going on with El. You've seen a twenty-second clip of him making one massive mistake—"

"And that makes him cheating on me okay?"

"No, of course not. And if I'd been there, I would've kicked his arse for you. But you knew El better than anyone. He was a decent guy."

I snort.

"And he was lucky to have you."

My gaze flicks along the bar and I spot this adorable kid propped sideways, a beer at his elbow, listening.

"What's your problem?" I grunt at him.

He shakes his head and turns away.

"Mate, I want you to come home with me right now," Mike says. "I have something important to show you. Something you missed on the video."

"Is it some big reveal that explains why my boyfriend was snogging some other dude's face off?"

"No, but, Dylan, we need to talk."

"We're talking now. And I'm getting free drinks. Are you going to pour me flaming sambucas at Casa Berrington? Because I'm not sure Mumzilla and Big M would be cool with that. Look, Mike, it's okay." I waft my hand towards the door. "You go if you want."

He can tell it's pointless, and I almost give in when I see his faith in me drain away.

"All right then," he mutters. "If you insist. I'll talk to you when you're Dylan again."

I almost call him back. Almost.

A smoke machine rolls mist around my feet. Red and orange lights dance on the fog and make me queasy. I think of Gemma's party, of kids gurning in front of your picture. I think of mist on a lake and the headlights of a car flickering in the depths.

A cool hand runs down my arm and slips over my drink. The kid takes it from me and downs it in one.

"Hey," he says.

"Hey."

At first I think he might be the boy from along the bar, but this kid has bright red hair and sea-green eyes. He asks me if he could have another drink and I call the barman over. My new friend grins. He's all teeth, but sort of cute.

"I'm George."

"Dylan."

"This place is so lame."

"Why are you here then?"

"All right, Oscar the Grouch." He bats my chest. "It's okay, I guess. Especially if handsome young men are buying me drinks. I'm not going to ask you if you come here often, because that's so—"

"Lame?"

"Wow. You *are* moody. Okay, so here's a plan: buy me five more of these and I promise to put a smile back on your face."

Time seems to shift, running through my fingers like sand. One minute we're at the bar, George telling me about his bitch mum and his bitch sister and their bitch cat and the bitch manager at his bitch work, and then we're in this toilet cubicle and I'm standing with my back to the wall. I guess it's okay as nightclub cubicles go, my experience is limited. Anyway, George reliably informs me there's no wee on the floor, so that's fine. My brain is whirling now, turning everything over and over like one of those rolling barrels they have in funhouses. I'm not sure I want to go through with this, but George assures me I do, and I don't have the words to argue.

It's like an out-of-body experience. I'm watching him but all I can think of is you. How you showed me this stuff and did it patiently and gently, talking me through what you liked, asking me what I liked. You were kind, El. You made all this scary sex stuff safe and wonderful. And I don't believe you were that person in the video. Not really.

I love you.

I'm sorry.

"No," I mutter. "Please. Don't."

I try to swat George's hands away but he pins my wrist to the wall.

"What's your problem?" he snarls. "It's only a bloody blow—"

And then someone wrenches the door and, thank God, the lock is damaged and flies off. It strikes George in the mouth. A spray of blood hits the partition wall. Then a pair of hands reaches into the cubicle and drags my drinking partner out into the bathroom. I blunder after him in time to see the adorable kid from the bar pull George to his feet and throw him against the wall.

"Get your dirty little hands off him."

"Or what, Raj?" George sleeves the blood from his mouth. "Or what?"

Raj crosses the distance between them. "Or I'll tell Bradley you're hustling in the toilets and not cutting him in."

Raj releases him and George grumbles his way to the door. When we're alone, Raj gives me a pained grimace.

"I think you need some water."

I shake my head. Something familiar about this kid. Can't quite…

"You're him," I murmur. "You're the one who was with Ellis at New Year."

Raj nods. "Okay, Dylan, I think we need to talk."

NOW: Thursday 30th April

16

The digital clock above the counter flashes 00.14, and for the first time in my life I push away a slice of perfectly edible pizza. My stomach feels like a sack of rubbish churning in the machinery of a refuse truck. Whenever I look at the neon in the window of the takeaway, stars explode behind my eyes. The table's greasy but I don't care. I have to rest my face against something cool.

When Raj returns with a bottle of water, I lift my head a couple of centimetres only to find a cold chip stuck to my cheek.

"Wow." He nods, handing me my drink. "I can totally see why Ellis fell for you."

I unpeel the chip. "Yeah, he thought I was a real catch, clearly."

This is the ultimate in weirdness – my dead boyfriend's fling being kind and buying me food. I'm not really sure how we got here, either. One minute I'm zipping up my fly in the bathroom, next I'm waiting for a slice I never asked for, sweaty palms pressed between my knees.

Raj takes the seat opposite and swigs his own water. And honestly, El, I can see what attracted you to him. This boy has serious eyes. I mean, onyx-dark and so freaking fathomless I can't look away.

"So, I heard you and your incredibly gorgeous friend talking at the bar."

"Yeah. Mike. He's straight."

"The world is full of such tragic stories."

His finger makes patterns in the spilled salt on the table, jags and little darts that make me think of a pale blur on a dark road.

"Okay," he sighs, "I'm guessing from what you said that Bradley showed you a video of me and Ellis at New Year? So there are a few things you need to know about what you *think* you saw. First, and most important, there was nothing going on between me and Ellis."

"Really?" I arch back in my chair, suddenly wanting to put some distance between us. "Gotta say, you had me completely fooled."

He leans forward. He won't let me get away. "Yeah, you know something, Dylan? A twenty-second snapshot of a person's life can be pretty deceptive. Your regrettably straight friend was right about that. So let's get this clear:

I kissed Ellis once. *Once*. And what you saw on that video was the first Act, the interval, and the final curtain of our entire whirlwind romance. So I thought he was cute when I saw him come into the club that night. Are you going to blame me for that?"

No, El, I can't blame him for that.

Raj scrunches up his face, trying to remember, or perhaps searching for the right words. "He looked so sad and, I don't know, desperate."

"Desperate?" I nod. "Cheers."

"Dylan, please stop being so touchy. From what I know about you, this moody teenager act isn't a good fit."

"And what exactly *do* you know about me?"

"Quite a bit. Literally, after the twentieth second of that one and only kiss, Ellis broke down. Whatever you saw tonight in that video wasn't love or affection or even lust. I've been around a bit, believe me, and I know what those kinds of kisses are like. All Ellis needed at that moment was someone to hold."

"Then why didn't he hold *me*? I would've been there for him. He only had to pick up the phone or answer one of the million messages I'd been sending all week."

"Maybe he cared about you too much to bring all that darkness down on you. Because it was darkness, Dylan." For the first time, Raj cuts his gaze away from me. "I saw it. He'd experienced something very bad."

My thoughts fly back to the night you died. Instinct still tells me that the darkness Raj is talking about is somehow linked to whatever frightened you at the Easter dance. But how can those two events be connected?

"Anyway," Raj continues, "I helped him to a booth and we pretty much talked all night. Not about whatever was upsetting him, he wouldn't discuss that. But you know what we did talk about? What obsessed him and took up virtually every thought in his stupidly handsome head?"

Raj grins and, reaching across the table, flicks my nose with his finger.

"You, you moron. God, I know every little thing about you! How you can't go five minutes without making some comic-book reference; how crappy your taste in music is; how when you were eight years old you stood up at a wedding and told the vicar the happy couple couldn't get married because your mum thought your cousin's partner smelled a bit like cat food and that he had these weird tiny feet."

"Weird tiny hands," I correct, and suddenly I'm smiling.

"Whatever. I knew enough to order you that revolting pizza, didn't I? Look, I don't know what happened leading up to New Year's Eve but I do know one thing. Ellis *loved* you. He was in pain that night and he made a stupid mistake. And God, if he *had* been single, I would have snapped him up then and there. But he wasn't. And he felt so bloody guilty after he kissed me."

Raj's grin is infectious, and I can't help it, I like the guy. If you had to cry on someone's shoulder that night, I'm glad it was his.

"You are one lucky nerd, Dylan McKee. To be loved like that, even once in a lifetime…" A shimmer glazes those deep onyx pools. "It's something, anyway."

I get up slowly from my chair and Raj mirrors me. Jeeze, this kid is psychic, I swear, he just seems to *know*. Anyway, before I can hold out my arms he catches me in this hug that seems to go on forever. I hug him right back. It's nice to be held like this, and for once I don't feel any guilt. I even hope that one day we might be friends.

I find you again in the night. In the winding country roads we used to walk, holding hands and feeling safe holding hands, beyond the gaze of Ferrivale. I find you in these moonlit fields you loved to sketch. I find you in Raj's words and in my renewed certainty of who you were.

The night's warm but still my skin goosebumps whenever I hit a familiar spot. Behind me, the town lights glower like the eyes of the old couple at the hospital. But here's the stile I stumbled over before you caught me, swinging me in a huge circle until my feet touched back down on the ground. And here, far across the yellow field, the footpath with its wonky signpost pointing to *Ferrivale, Givesby,*

Goodstone, Dorral; a signpost you climbed, laughing and splaying your hands over letters until all I could read was "Gives Good orral".

I walk the night thin and, reaching my destination, sit on a tombstone and wait for morning. I leave it until 10.30 before taking out my phone and calling Mike. I tell him I need to see him, but only if he's up to it.

"Give me an hour," he groans, and hangs up.

I know, El, you don't have to tell me. He's a better friend than I deserve.

I try not to look at our place. Not until Mike's here with me and I can take some of his strength. I try not to think or remember anything at all. I just sit and wait…

Something pale circles and snuffles through the mid-morning mist, threading between the trees, picking its way over the tumbledown wall until it finds me. I reach down and cup my hand around Becks's snout. Dogs never judge, do they? Not even when you've been the most unholy of dicks to their master.

"Hey," I say, as Mike steps into the graveyard.

He moves slowly between the stones, his gaze drifting from inscription to inscription. I know he can't read them. You and I examined every crumbling slab during our hours here and, even crouching up close, could only ever make out a few random words and dates. I wonder how many love stories have been worn away in the years since this place was abandoned. Their grief must have seemed as powerful and unique to them as mine is to me, and yet now their romances are forgotten. Ours will be too, one day. This should give me some perspective, I guess. It doesn't. It's still wrong that the world hasn't stopped and broken into pieces because you're no longer a part of it.

Mike takes the tombstone next to mine and hands me a thermos and something warm and delicious-smelling wrapped up in tinfoil. My stomach grumbles. While I unwrap my bacon sandwich, Mike fills two plastic cups with hot sweet tea.

"Have you been home?"

"Uh-uh." The bacon's salty and crispy and the nearest thing to heaven I've ever tasted. Mike lets me finish.

"You're an unbelievable tool, Dylan. You know that, right?" I wipe my mouth and nod. "Okay, just as long as that's clear."

I feed Becks a bit of bacon rind. The sun is throwing long graveyard shadows and the mist is starting to clear.

"Mate, I'm sorry."

He sighs. "All right. But you do realize what this calls for?"

"Dude, no."

He licks his forefinger. "Take your punishment like a man, Dylan." I sit perfectly still while he waggles a wet digit in my ear. Becks yips at us and chases his tail, wanting to show that he can pull off slapstick humour too.

"Am I still one of the Incredible Twat Brothers?" I ask.

"The twattiest." He nods.

So I dive straight in. I tell him about my encounter with Raj, leaving out the part with George and the aborted BJ in the cubicle, because there's only so much shame a boy can bear. Mike listens, fussing with Becks, throwing him bits of stick. Then I tell him about my renewed certainty that whatever scared you over the Christmas break must be connected to the thing that freaked you out at the Easter dance. He nods, thoughtful, so I know these aren't just drunken ramblings.

"I should get home," I say. "Another page from the journal might have turned up. You know, it's crazy, but it doesn't feel as if this thing only started two days ago. It feels like I've been receiving these pages forever."

Mike shoots me an uncertain glance. "Dylan, you know that none of this is going to bring El back."

"Jesus, Mike." I stare at him. "I get that I'm an idiot, but I'm not that stupid."

He runs a hand under his baseball cap and fixes his eyes on the old church, the western elevation black as night in the morning glare.

"I don't know, mate. All this stuff, it's like it's freezing you in the moment. You're not grieving, not properly. You're—"

"Not moving on?" I don't want to argue, not when we've only just made up; and anyway, I don't have the energy for this. "Listen, I'm not letting this go," I tell him. "I won't ever stop, Mike, not until I find out what happened to him. If I don't understand what scared him, I think I'll go mad. But you don't have to help me." I reach out and rub his shoulder, and feel sharp bone where healthy muscle once sat. "I can do this on my own."

He breathes deeply, and despite what I've just said, I feel kind of terrified, because I honestly don't think I *can* do this on my own.

"Then we go on," he says at last.

He puts down his tea and rummages in his coat pocket, bringing out his phone. "Now you've stopped being a colossal dick, there's something you need to see." He thumbs his gallery and brings up a blurry image. "You were so focused on El and that Raj kid that you didn't see what was going on in the background of the shot. I tried to tell you in the bar, but you weren't having it. Now look, I don't know what this means, but it's weird, right?"

He hands me the phone and points to a figure in the background of the video snapshot. At first I don't understand what he's trying to show me. And then I recognize the wavy hair that almost curtains his eyes, and that weirdly defensive way he always stands, one arm draped across his stomach. He's half-turned away from El and Raj, as if he

217

isn't really interested in what's going on. Except that would be odd in itself, because practically everyone else in the place is gawping at the show. And anyway, the act isn't convincing, because Ollie Reynolds is filming the whole thing on his phone.

I turn to Mike and see my disbelief reflected back at me.

"What the hell does this mean?"

THEN: Thursday 2nd January

The Church

I sit on a tombstone, hands between my knees, breath billowing. There's hardly any wind and the countryside all around is crisp and white and still. Even the abandoned church, which is always creaking and groaning, keeps its silence. I check the road for the fiftieth time. No car belching its way down the lane, bringing El back to me. I kick my toe against all the junk at my feet and pray he'll show up soon and tell me what I did wrong.

For twelve days we were happy. Julia had started her treatment and was doing well, Ellis was working hard on his sculpture, and we were grabbing every second we could to be together. Twelve days of free periods when we'd race back to mine before my parents got home and tear off each other's clothes. Twelve days in which we talked politics and movies and music and history and all the weird stuff I thought I'd never share with anyone. Twelve days in which we didn't talk at all, but just lay there, lost in each other.

Okay, so we had the odd disagreement. El couldn't understand why I didn't want to tell my parents. He hadn't met them properly yet, but from everything I told him I guess they sounded fairly cool. I just couldn't make him understand what telling them might mean for us. Anyway, he accepted my decision and assured me that, whenever it felt right, he'd be there for me.

Then term ended and everything changed. We were supposed to meet the following day. The new Star Wars movie was out and I'd convinced El that adventures a long time ago in a galaxy far, far away were not just for little kids. In fact, they weren't for little kids at all, and if some snot-nosed brat started talking during a lightsaber battle? Well, I would not be held responsible for my actions. El laughed and promised he'd be there.

He never showed. I called and texted. Nothing. It was weird. I thought about calling Mike and offering him El's ticket, but two things stopped me: first, Mike hadn't been feeling all that great and was off school the whole last week of term; and second, suddenly I was stupidly worried about my boyfriend. In the end, I abandoned the movie I'd been waiting two whole years to see and headed over to Mount Pleasant.

I wasn't bothered about Julia being there because El had already told her about us, and of course she was cool. In fact she gave me this very random double Snickers bar as a coming-out present, even though I'm not out, and kissed my cheeks until it looked like I'd been mauled by a grizzly wearing Ruby Woo red (I now know heaps about lipstick, thanks to El). Anyway, I realized on the way over that Julia was on a late shift at the bakery.

The "123" on the door of 123 shuddered a little when I knocked. Just like with the phone, no answer. I was about to knock again when I glimpsed a shadow wavering under the door.

"El? El, it's me." The shadow froze. "Is everything okay? We were supposed to meet for the film, but if you're not well…? Come on, El, this isn't funny. Is it…" I tried to swallow but couldn't. "Have I done something? Are you upset with me?"

Silent darkness under the door.

"C'mon, are you messing with me?" I tried on a grin but it slipped like water from my face. "Ellis, what have I done? Why won't you talk to me?"

I'm Dylan McKee, I don't make scenes, but right at that moment I started hammering on the door.

"El, please, just say something!"

But he didn't, and in the end I had to stop because neighbours were poking their heads out of doorways and throwing glares at me.

Another twelve days passed, this time spent in hell.

I texted and texted and texted, but the only messages I received were from Mike and a couple of kids at school asking about essay deadlines. So the days crawled by and I did what I could to reach out. I sent emails, even wrote a letter, and all the while the ingenious little torture device between my ears went into hyperdrive: *Dylan, it was the sex. Hey, he tried his best, but there's only so much he could do with a pure clueless virgin… Dylan, it was the comic-book stuff. You bored him rigid, and not in a good way… Dylan, it was you. Weird, klutzy, awkward little you. He came to his senses at last, that's all.*

I listened to these scenarios daily as I trudged over to my spot outside Mount Pleasant. Even on Christmas Day, I haunted the pavement while little kids wobbled their new bikes around me. And though I bumped into Julia a few times, who always said you were ill, always avoided my gaze, I never once saw you. I didn't think then that I could ever be more miserable.

I was wrong.

The day after New Year I was sitting on Mike's bed, beheading vampires, when I tossed the controller onto a pile of pillows and turned to him.

"Mike?"

"Yup?"

His tongue was clenched between his teeth as he executed a sweet headshot. I took the controller from him and he started to complain, then clocked my expression and frowned.

"Are you okay? Mate, what is it?" He turned his body towards me. It was now or never. If Mike ended up hating me, I wasn't sure what I would do, but I couldn't get out of it now. There was no revelation about myself that I could substitute and that he'd believe…because, you see, I was crying.

"I'm not straight," I said.

He laughed, because how I'd said it was perfectly Dylan-ridiculous. Then he stopped abruptly and nodded.

"So you're gay?"

"I am."

"Are you sure?" He lifted a quizzical eyebrow.

"Why wouldn't I be sure?"

He puffed out his cheeks. "I don't know, bro, you are like the least stylish person I have ever met. Plus your dancing is atrocious."

"Hey." I elbowed him, grinning. "You know it's kind of homophobic, presuming that all gay guys are amazing dancers?"

His smile faltered and he gave me a long look. "I'm sorry, Dylan."

My heart went right through the floor. He was sorry. Sorry he couldn't be my best friend any more? Sorry I was a freak? Sorry, but he'd pray for me?

"All those stupid jokes," he sighed. "All that crappy gay banter stuff. Christ, it's making me cringe, thinking back. You know if I'd had any idea, I would never…" And suddenly he was crying too and throwing his arms around me and crushing me in a typical Mike bear-hug. "I'm just so sorry, dude. Me being a complete moron must have made this even more difficult for you."

"It's okay," I said, patting the blond head that was now tucked into my neck. "I accepted you as a complete moron when we were three."

He laughed and drew back. "You know, whenever you want to come out, I'll have your back. Any idiot messes with you at school?" He made a slicing motion across his throat. "And…" He made the same motion across his groin.

"You'll cut their dicks off?"

"Damn straight. Or damn queer. Or whatever you prefer." Then he dabbed a finger in his mouth and waggled it in my ear. "I love you, bro."

"Thanks, mate."

"So." He let go of a huge breath. "Gay. Cool. Have you told anyone else?"

That was when it all came rushing out about me and El. As I recounted the early days of teasing and flirting and me retreating – or the Dance of the Dylan, as El liked to call it – Mike sat there with this cringing grin on his face. Then I reached our first twelve days of being boyfriends and, in my torrent, I let one or two pornographic details slip. Mike buried his face in a pillow and mumbled, "TMI, dude. T-M-fucking-I!" and I could feel the mother of all blushes sheet my face.

Then we came to the past week. Mike listened and slipped a hand around my shoulder.

"Bud, I don't know what to tell you. El is a good guy. Honestly, I've got to know him a bit on and off the field, and I couldn't have picked a better boyfriend for you. I just don't understand."

"That makes two of us."

We sat there for a while, listening to Mumzilla downstairs practising for choir. Carol has this amazing melodic voice that I've always found really soothing. But not today.

"Dylan," Mike murmured.

"Yeah?"

"As it's a coming-out kind of day—"

I spun towards him. "You're not!"

"Nah." He gave me this sad smile. "But I do have something to tell you…"

I check the road for the fifty-first time and bolt to my feet. A beat-up old Nissan is trundling towards the church. My heart jerks against my ribs. I think back to the phone call this morning; the call where I could barely get the words out for crying.

"Ellis, please pick up… It's not about us. It's Mike… I don't care if you don't want me any more, but I have to talk to you. Mike. He's…he's not well. In fact, he's really, *really* sick. Please, El… *Please.*"

"Dylan?" Your voice when you finally, *finally* called me back, enough to collapse me. "Are you okay? What's up with Mike?"

I didn't want to say that scary word, but somehow I managed it, and El went so quiet I thought he'd hung up. Then:

"I want to see you, Dylan."

"Where?"

"You choose."

So I stand at my tombstone, not daring to move. The car brakes. El gets out. He comes around to the front and – I can't help it – I run to him.

He catches me and holds me tight, hands gripping all across my shoulders and back and neck as if he's terrified I might slip away. And I know right then that all the poison my brain's been spewing this past week or so is bullshit. He loves me. He does. I pull back and take his face in my hands. He tries to look away but I won't let him.

"What happened?"

"I'm sorry." His face screws up and I thumb hot tears

from his cheeks. "It was the first Christmas away from my family, from my sister, and…I don't know, I kind of lost it for a few days. Can you forgive me?" He cups my hand and kisses my palm, then looks sort of disgusted with himself, as if this was a cheap ploy. "Shit, what am I saying? *I* wouldn't forgive me, so why should you?"

I want to believe him, I really do, but the way he vanished on me was just too extreme.

"I could have helped," I say, turning and taking a couple of steps away. "Like I said in the billion messages I left, if you had something going on, I'd have been there for you."

He catches up with me, grabs my hand. "I know. I know. I've been an idiot."

"You have."

We stand in silence for a time, just the skitter of leaves between our feet.

"Have I lost you?"

I shake my head and stretch onto tiptoes. A tear – his tear – slides between us when we kiss.

"Are you sure you don't want to tell me anything else?"

"No. No thank you." He nods. "And I won't ever shut you out like that again. I promise."

And although I know he's holding something back, I also know that's all I'm going to get. Because, just like his journal, El has this secret space inside him that I don't think he will ever let me into. It hurts my heart, but I guess

227

I can live with the majority of him in my life. And the honest truth is, I'm a coward – I'm frightened that if I push too hard I might lose him forever.

"So," he breathes, "Mike."

We sit among the tombstones and talk. I give him Mike's diagnosis and he holds my hand as I rehearse all my hopes and fears for my best friend. El can't make this better, he can't guarantee that Mike will be okay, but he listens and comforts and in doing so he *does* make it better. A little.

"We'll see him through it," he says. "He's a strong mofo is Michael."

After a while we get up and I collect the provisions I've brought along, just on the off chance that today would work out. El grins as I drop half the bags and trip over the rest, then glances up at the boarded doorway of the church.

"So what is this place?"

I stumble after him, throwing a bag his way. He collects it with ease.

"You have your Moodles and Doodles…well, this is my secret place. I've been coming here ever since I spotted it on a family bike ride. Don't ask. We abandoned them after Chris blindsided my dad and broke his ankle. Anyway, I kind of thought it looked romantic so I started imagining all these histories for it in my head."

"I bet you researched the hell out of it. Typical Frecks."

"Actually, I didn't. I wanted it to be this blank canvas

228

where I could imagine my own stories."

I move the rotten board aside and we squeeze through into the porch and the echoey vastness of the nave. A burst of feathers erupts somewhere in the rafters; a flurry of winter birds tumbling through holes in the roof. Half the pews have fallen like dominos and most of the stained glass has been smashed, the eyes of the church blinded by metal sheets. But the light that plays through the roof gives it all a fairy-tale sadness that's always haunted me.

I take El's free hand and guide him down the central aisle.

"It's got a kind of hideous beauty, don't you think? I used to imagine it was once part of this huge abbey with choirs of monks chanting this amazing music." I blush and I don't care at all that El notices. "So there were once these two novices, Lukas and Matthew, who spent their days inside these cold stone walls. And while they prayed and fasted and praised God, they were always careful never to let their thoughts wander. But then one harvest time, Lukas was injured in the fields and was taken to Matthew's infirmary. The wound was deep; fever set in. None of the remedies Matthew tried could stop the infection. It was while holding his brother's hand on Lukas's final night that Matthew admitted there had been moments between praying when his eyes had strayed to Lukas and, seeing his gaze returned, he knew Lukas had felt the same. But now it was too late. And so he crawled onto the bed beside his brother and took the dying Lukas in his arms, so that at least they might have this one honest moment together."

El smiles. "And Lukas wakes up and kisses Matthew and they run away on a medieval cruise."

I smile too. "It's about missed chances, El. I could feel myself missing them back then. Back before we met. I don't want to miss any more."

I guide him to the north transept and the winding stairway hidden there.

"Is this safe?" El asks, climbing up behind me.

"I doubt it."

High in the bell-less tower, a gentle wind stirs our hair. Laid out before us are acres of snowy countryside with Ferrivale and the blue glint of Hunter's Lake beyond. I move across the creaking floorboards and introduce El to my non-human best friend. El pretends to shake him by the claw.

"What's his name?"

"Um…"

"The great storyteller hasn't given this poor guy a name?" El strokes the horned head of the crouching gargoyle. "Monster, I dub thee Stanley. May you always watch over my Frecks and keep him safe."

"Stanley?" I laugh.

El shrugs. "Dude looks like a Stanley."

We put down our provisions and, while I unroll a two-man sleeping bag, El takes out his Moodles and Doodles and starts sketching Stanley.

"Gargoyles are supposed to ward off evil," I say. "A bit like your tattoos."

He looks at me over his drawing. "So we're doubly safe."

He's right. That's exactly how I feel. After all the fear and heartache of Christmas, I feel safe again. At least, I think I do.

When he's done sketching, I snuggle myself into the sleeping bag and call him over. He snakes his way inside and we lie facing each other, breathing slowly.

"Thank you for showing me this," El murmurs. "I get why you love it. The stories and the history."

"It reminds me of how small I am," I say. "You know, in the grand scheme of things. That whatever I think and feel right now doesn't matter. Not really. Because we're all just history in the end."

He doesn't say anything for a while, then hugs me to him. "That sounded profound, Frecks. And it's also the stupidest thing I've ever heard you say. You *matter*." We part, and for that split second the secret thing that's haunted him this past week returns. "You matter so much to me. Don't you understand that at all?"

NOW: Thursday 30th April

17

I stare at the image of Ollie filming you and Raj. Mike's sent it to my phone, and even as I trespass into my old school, I can't stop looking at it. How does this sly, sneaking Ollie fit with the kid who leaped to my defence at Gemma's party? Honestly, I don't have any theories. After last night at the club I'm tired and jittery, and the note I found on the fridge when I got home a few minutes after one this afternoon hasn't helped.

The house was empty when I crept in through the side door. As it's a Thursday, I was fairly confident Dad would be at work and that Chris would have hauled his lazy arse out of bed to take Mum to Zumba (he has to justify his existence in these ways from time to time). Although Mike's bacon sarnie had helped with my hangover, I was still aching for a shower and a couple of hours' rest. Of course, when I first saw the image of Ollie, all I wanted to do was head straight over to his house – but one look at Mike told me that was a no go. In the beams of light among the gravestones he looked almost spectral. Anyway, Mike had a better plan...

Back to the note: I was grabbing a carton of milk when it caught my eye.

Dylan, Michael has kindly informed us that you are safe and alive. Now – there is something important we need to discuss. Please be home this evening – your mother is worried and we can't continue living like this.
Love, Dad.

I tore down the note and crumpled it in my pocket. *We can't continue living like this.* Were they planning to throw me out? I supposed from their point of view, they'd feel justified, what with all my hostility and sullen silences. Well, if that was their plan, maybe it was just what I needed. I was too cowardly to leave home myself – being chucked out might be the best thing that could happen.

No one returned home unexpectedly during the afternoon. Mum's Zumba routine usually involves a pretty phenomenal lunch afterwards, then she and Chris will catch a movie in the afternoon. And so by three o'clock I'd caught up on some sleep, taken a long scalding shower, changed into my old uniform and was heading back to Ferrivale High.

My biggest fear as I enter the school is bumping into a random teacher. Other kids I can fool – *Oh yeah, just back for the day, checking out how it feels* – but teachers know the score. Even if I wanted to come back, there would need to be a discussion about that assembly in which I called a police officer "Shit-for-Brains" in front of a bunch of Year Sevens. I suppose Chief Dementor Harper would be the nightmare scenario, but I sort of dread encountering Mr Morris even more. That look he gave me when I told him I was quitting, a bit like a sad-eyed beagle that's just been informed his favourite pup has pissed all over the kitchen floor. I can't pretend it didn't tug a heartstring.

But it isn't Harper or Morris I collide with. It's your old art teacher, El, the adorable Denman. We run into each other outside the boys' changing rooms. Mr Denman apologizes, though it was me who crashed into him, and starts picking up the brushes and sticks of charcoal he was carrying. I don't think he's actually realized who I am, and I could step over him and be on my way. But then I see how he's holding his right arm, all stiff and claw-like. That car accident really did a number on him.

Suddenly a thought occurs: what if it wasn't some huge thing that derailed you at Christmas, what if it was a gradual accumulation of stuff? Maybe you were telling the truth about missing your sister. Then there was all the stress of those last few games where the team kind of sucked, and then this guy, your mentor, smashes himself up a month before your major project was due to be assessed. That kind of drip-drip-drip of stress could have been too much.

Except, if that was the case, why wouldn't you just have told me?

I scoot down beside Denman and help him collect up the charcoal into its packet.

"Dylan?" He's crouched awkwardly in front of me, his hand held out for the charcoal. "I'm sorry, I didn't… Look, are you supposed to be here?"

He glances over his shoulder, back down the corridor towards the staff room. I remember teasing you about how you crushed on this guy, and he is still pretty cute, especially for a teacher. Blond flyaway hair and these clear blue eyes. Okay, so he's a little bit "catalogue model", with the distant stares and those so-ancient-they're-cool cardigans, but I get the attraction.

"Jesus." He staggers to his feet. "I'm sorry. Did that feel like an interrogation? Who gives a toss why you're here, right? You do whatever you need to do." He shoves the packet of charcoal under his arm and pats my shoulder. "This is so bloody awful for you, Dylan. I just want you to know that you shouldn't listen to any of the crap my colleagues might be giving you. It's important that you take whatever time you need. And look, if you ever want to talk to anybody, my door's always open, yeah? We could even grab a coffee. I'm always here after school, pottering around in the studios. Just know, you don't have to be alone in all this."

So yeah, he's sort of cool, and at least he isn't threatening to bar me forever from these hallowed halls of learning. I nod my thanks.

Suddenly Mike appears from behind Denman, takes me by the elbow and drags me away. Denman does this double-take, which I've only ever really seen in cartoons, and the next second Mike and I are through the changing-room doors.

"Dude," I breathe, "what the hell?"

Mike shrugs. "We don't have much time. Ollie's out on the field but practice finishes in about ten minutes. I'm heading over there now. When Mr Highfield calls it a day, I'll keep him talking, but you need to be out of here before the lads come back."

He guides me round to Ollie's locker and starts spinning the wheels on the padlock.

"How do you know his combination?" I ask.

"Because Ollie has no imagination. It's bound to be his date of birth."

The padlock clicks, proving Mike's a genius and Ollie is not. Mike slams open the locker and gives me the nod. "Ten minutes."

I watch him head out. There's something going on with my best friend. Even when he told me his diagnosis, even when I've sat with him in the hospital chemo suite, desperately inventing funny stories to keep his mind off the inevitable upcoming vom sessions, he's always chilled. Hell, he was chilled last night when I was provoking the crap out of him. But right now his jaw is twitching and I don't like the look in his eyes. Is he really that angry with Ollie? It's possible. Ollie was *his* friend and, if I'm honest, I only put up with him for Mike's sake. With all his football stats and rambling jokes that go nowhere, Reynolds can be about as entertaining as watching the Berringtons' dog lick its balls. Scratch that. In comparison, Becks licking his balls is like an Avengers movie marathon. So yeah, Mike might well be taking some of the guilt of Ollie's betrayal on his own shoulders. Which is ridiculous.

Anyway, much as I'm concerned about Mike, I don't have time to think about it right now. I plunge my hands into Ollie's locker, grimacing as I throw aside crusty socks and sweat-stained boxers. It takes me a minute to find what I'm looking for, and at first I miss it completely because security-conscious Ollie has stuffed it into the toe-end of an old Nike. Finally, I pull out the phone and swipe the screen.

It's password-protected. Three failed attempts and I'll be locked out.

I try to remember everything I know about Ollie

Reynolds, and even though I hate him right now, I'm ashamed to say there isn't much. It's a bit shocking when I think about it. I've hung with Mike's footie crowd ever since Year Seven, and yet I know practically nothing about them. Maybe they don't know anything about me either, but that's not really the point.

Why is it that, when we get to secondary school, we stop being interested in each other? I mean, *really* interested. I remember back in little school when we all delighted in everyone's tiny triumphs and tragedies, as well as all the boring stuff too, and it suddenly occurs to me that if I'd known I was gay at nine or ten I wouldn't have worried one bit about coming out, probably because my classmates would already have known. It's only when we hit puberty that we close down like this and become mysteries, even to ourselves.

Okay, El, I can almost hear you whispering in my ear: *Very impressive philosophizing, Frecks, but the phone's still locked, so get your arse in gear.*

I hop awkwardly across the changing benches and climb up to the slit windows high in the wall. Far across the pitch, Mr Highfield is checking his watch, a whistle poking out of his beard. Faces keep twitching from him to the ball and back again. Crap. I jump down, plonk onto a bench, and put Ollie's phone on the slats next to me. I guess I could just take it with me and try to crack the password at my leisure, but even if I'm right about what I'm going to find on it, that's still theft. Theft, the ransacking of a locker, trespass on school property and illegal use of a uniform. More ammunition for my parents, if they really are planning to evict me.

Drips from the leaky shower in the stalls drum like a countdown – ten, nine, eight, seven – and…

An idea.

Ollie's a simple soul, Mike said, and if he was obsessed for some reason, then… I type E L L I S, and the phone screen flips to the menu page.

Somewhere far off I hear a whistle blow. Minutes now. Maybe seconds. I head straight to his gallery and the videos section. My hands are trembling; the end-of-school bell almost shocks the phone out of my grasp. Feet thunder in the halls, teachers bellow, echoing the thunder and bellowing inside my chest. I scroll through half a dozen clips of Ollie practising keepy-uppies, a snippet of his mum's birthday, a fragment from some concert…

I find it.

The thirty-second slice of film that changed my life forever.

I don't want to watch it again, but I can't help it. I thumb the screen and the blurry, disjointed game-changer leaps into life. The cleft of a buttock, a grasping hand, lips meeting flesh, a sweeping glimpse of pubic hair, our faces pressed together, and my voice, tinny and mortifying.

It wasn't our first time, El, not even close, but it was the time you told me that we would always be together.

I stop the clip and shove the phone into my pocket just as the changing-room door bursts open. Footie lads swarm in, tearing off shirts, laughing and ribbing each other. I push through the crowd, my face burning, fists clenched. Someone tries to catch my arm.

"Hey! Dylan! Man, are you back? It's good to see you, bro."

I shrug him off and shoulder my way to the door.

18

So now we know the identity of our pervy porno guy. Only the bastard who frightened you at the dance and whoever abandoned you at the lake left to unmask. And whoever's posting the journal pages to me, of course. Could that be Ollie too? I've considered this before, back when I found Ollie's flowers down by the lake, and just like then, the idea doesn't seem to fit. But why, out of all our suspects, do I keep forgetting the journal-sender? Maybe because the others feel like enemies while he/she/they seems to want to help us. Some shy individual who can't come forward and just hand me the diary, perhaps because they're embarrassed they took it in the first place. Except why don't they just post the whole bloody thing? It all seems so random and clumsy somehow.

Anyway, time to confront Ollie Reynolds. Right now, I honestly have no idea why he's done this thing – my brain's too scrambled to even begin to guess – but one way or another, I'm going to find out.

I bang out of a side door and start across the field. Up ahead, only Ollie and Mike remain on the touchline, Mike running his hand repeatedly under his baseball cap while Ollie scoops footballs into a net bag. The wind's picked up since this morning and I can't hear what they're talking about, but Mike is a picture of pure agitation.

An unwanted memory hits me as I stalk towards them. The "Guy for the Guys" Bullshit Bonfire; me, Mike, Ollie, Gemma and the rest of the committee witches all huddled around that huge unlit stack. Those were the last moments of the BE era. That's how I divide up my life now: Before Ellis and Anno Ellis. It's monumentally unfair, how these portions of my existence are divided: seventeen years of BE, six months of AE. But who knows? Maybe there is a gay-friendly afterlife where we can add immortal years to AE's tally; a kind of endless LGBTQ safe space designed just for us.

Ollie is just straightening up when I reach them.

"Oh. Hi, Dylan," he says, his grin shaky. "You hanging with Mike today? That was some effed-up shit at Gemma's party, I'm sorry you had to go through that. She can be insanely vicious sometimes. Probably why I had to call it a day with her."

"Probably?" I smile back at him. "You mean you're not sure?"

He grabs the net of balls and shrugs. He's about to head back towards the school when Mike, stony-faced, blocks his way. Ollie laughs, then stops. His gaze flicks between us.

"Guys? What is this?"

I don't say anything, just take his little movie camera from my pocket and wave it in front of him. He drops the net and footballs scatter as he makes a grab for the phone.

"How'd you get that? Give it back."

Mike blocks him again. I don't know whether Ollie can't bring himself to wrestle a cancer patient or if Mike's whole attitude is intimidating him; it's definitely starting to scare me.

"Hey, come on, this isn't funny. What the hell are you trying to prove anyway? Mike? C'mon, man, we're buds. Whatever you think you know, I just—"

I've heard enough. It makes me sick to do it, but I thumb the screen and my voice cuts across the field. Mike doesn't turn to look. His gaze is laser-focused on Ollie, who stands as if he's just been condemned to the gallows. He wets his lips, tries to speak. Can't. Tears brim but he has the sense not to let them fall in front of us. And I think I could forgive him, he looks so miserable, but then he ruins it with a coward's smile.

"I just copied it off the internet. Honestly, I don't know why I did it, but everyone was just going on and on about

243

the vid and…I'm sorry, Dylan. I guess I forgot to delete it."

"You're a shitty liar," I tell him. "I checked the properties on the file. This was created the day before the video of me and El hit Instagram. It's the original."

My hands tighten into fists. I've never hit anyone in my life, never even been in a playground fight, but right now I want to hurt Ollie Reynolds. I lunge forward, and suddenly a blur erupts in front of me and Mike is going to work.

Ollie staggers backwards at the first blow, tripping over the loose footballs. He almost regains his balance but then Mike punches him again and this time Ollie hits the deck. At first I can't seem to move. I just stand and stare as Mike presses his advantage. I don't care what happens now. In fact, I'm enjoying the show.

And then I hear you, stern in my head: *Stop it, Frecks. Stop it before it goes too far.* You're right, El. This isn't like how you schooled Alistair Pardue at the bonfire – that single, smart, prove-a-point punch. This is manic and I love Mike too much to let him do this, both to Ollie and to himself. It takes all my strength but I manage to scoop Mike under the arms and drag him away.

We all take a minute. Mike and I standing together, breathing hard, Ollie on the ground, bleeding, shaking. After a while I go over to him and help him to his feet. He wipes his nose on his bare arm and stares at the blood.

"Is it broken?"

He shakes his head. He's hurt but he seems to accept the hurt.

"Ollie…" I close my eyes then open them and stare at him. "What the hell?"

He looks at us with such a face. I don't know. Even Mike has to turn away.

"I liked him," he sobs. "I liked him, that's all."

Mike looks skyward. "You idiot."

"I know," Ollie says, touching his cheek and hissing. "I know… It's why I broke up with Gemma. El, he made me realize. I don't mean we had some big talk and I had a eureka moment about myself. Not that. It's just, when I looked at him, I felt these things that had only been, I don't know, like background shadows before. Maybe I kept them that way on purpose. My parents…" A single tear tracks down the side of his face. "They drag us to church every Sunday, and then it's prayers every mealtime, and I just always knew what they'd say if I ever turned out to be… And so I made-believe I wasn't. You know, you can convince yourself of anything if you try hard enough. But then El. He just…"

"Bursts in."

Ollie looks up and gives me a smile that makes me want to hug him. I don't, but still.

"Yeah. I think 'bursts' is the word. There was no hiding any more. Not from myself anyway. So I called it off with Gemma. I thought I was being noble, not using her as my alibi. I wasn't ready to come out so I told her I wasn't good enough for her, some crap like that, but I think she knew what was really going on. You can't hide the stares when you're obsessed with someone, can you? On the field, in class…"

This echoes so much of those klutzy days before El and I got together it almost feels like an invasion. I thought I was the only one stealing glances.

"She knew why," Ollie continues, "so all I got from her afterwards were these little innuendos. '*Oh, Ollie, yeah, I guess I was too much of a* woman *for him.*' Crap like that. She had some grief with El before we broke up, so this just added to her hating him – though how any of it was his fault, I don't know. Gemma logic," he grunts, then suddenly tries to reach for me. My hand flies out, pushing him away, and he nods. "Dylan, can you understand? He was everything I wanted to be. Out and proud and brave. But I'm not brave. I know my parents would just sit me down and say they still love me, and then we'd get together with our pastor and I'd get the talk: *You're confused, Oliver. God never made you this way. Now let's pray for His guidance.*"

"Okay," I say, "but they wouldn't break your teeth and throw you out, would they? El had it harder than any of us, and he was still El."

"I didn't know that. About his family…" He balls up his hands like a frustrated child trying to understand. "I was obsessed, okay? And I know it's mad, but yes, I started following him around. Taking pictures and… God, I'm sorry. It sounds so weird."

"It *is* weird!" Mike snaps.

"What do you know about anything?" Ollie shoots back, but there's no anger in his words, just a sadness that I recognize all too well. "When you can't be all of who you are, I think it does things to you. Twists you somehow. Drives you crazy. I know what I did was wrong, but even to have his picture… And following him was my way of building up some courage."

"To do what?"

"To ask him out? To tell him how I felt?" He shrugs. "I don't know. Eventually I did get my shit together, the day before the Easter dance. It was after practice and we were joshing about, just us two, putting some gear away. I leaned in and he… Dylan, he told me no. I knew about you two by then, of course."

"How?"

"Like I said, I followed him about. You were careful, but there's only so much hiding you can get away with. I saw you together one night out by the old Megadeal supermarket."

My breath catches. I remember:

It's March, long after the weirdness of Christmas and just before the Berringtons' barbecue, and you're taking your life in

247

your hands. You're teaching me to drive. Not a single obstacle in the abandoned car park, yet I'm certain I'll hit something. On the Nissan dashboard, the gangsta-elf-on-the-run seems to be winking at me.

"Ignore him." You reach across from the passenger side and plant a hand over the wicked imp. "Hands at nine and three on the steering wheel. Then mirror, signal…"

My foot jolts against the accelerator and we bunny-hop to a standstill.

"Manoeuvre."

I shrug. "At least I didn't hit anything."

"I'm afraid you did." You look down into your lap, gaze full of sorrow. "Frecks, I'm sorry to tell you this, and it will affect your no claims bonus, but your reckless driving has bruised my dick."

I arch an eyebrow. "Is this some kind of fake claim?"

You make this little outraged "O" with your mouth. "I am shocked and offended. I swear, your honour, on the holiest of holies that the seatbelt cut right into my package and I am now in mortal fear that my dong will drop off. Unless…" You smile mischievously. "…it gets some emergency attention."

"Well," I say, shrugging off my seatbelt, "you are the instructor…"

I stare at Ollie. "You were there that night?"

He closes his eyes. "I'm sorry. I don't know what else to—"

"So El rejected you," Mike cuts in. "Just finish it."

"I misinterpreted stuff, all right? It was just El's normal kindness, I know that now. But I thought he was flirting with me and I…I put my heart on the line. That sounds lame, but it's true. I tried something and he put a stop to it."

"Why didn't he tell me?"

"He knew me and Mike were friends," Ollie says. "He probably didn't want to make things awkward for everybody."

"But you didn't take El snubbing you well, did you?" Mike says.

"You want the truth? I hated him for it." Ollie wraps his arm around his stomach, a defensive gesture that reminds me of Mr Denman. "I'd already dumped Gemma and she was spreading shit about me. I was jealous of what you guys had, Dylan. And I just felt so…lonely, I suppose. All I could ever think about was El – so when he shot me down, yeah, I wanted to vent. I followed you that night onto the school roof and… Well, you know the rest."

"But Ellis must have known it was you," Mike says, "or suspected anyway, when the video was put on Instagram."

"Maybe he did. I thought he would and so I stayed away from the dance."

"You wanted to punish us," I say quietly. "Because we were happy."

"No, Dylan. Because I was *unhappy*."

I nod. It kills me to admit it, but I understand. If I'd

been in Ollie's place – and I could quite easily have been – then… I don't know.

"And this was why you were so defensive of Dylan at Gemma's party?" Mike says. "You felt guilty."

"I'd like to think I'd have stood up for him anyway." Ollie nods. "But yes, I suppose."

"And the flowers and the card at the lake?" I ask.

He's sobbing again, quietly now. "If I hadn't posted the video you wouldn't have felt forced to come out, Dylan. And then El wouldn't have taken you to the dance to make that big show of being together. You'd never have been on the road later and the accident…" He draws back and covers his face with his hands. "It's my fault. I killed him."

"You didn't kill him," I murmur. "You hurt us very badly, Ollie, but you didn't kill him. Don't carry that weight around, it isn't yours."

His fingers part and I almost break. I don't hate this kid…but no, I can't forgive him. I just need to close the book on Ollie Reynolds.

"Is there anything else you want to say?"

"No," Ollie says quietly. "Except…Dylan, I know I was obsessed with him. I think in a way he inspired obsession. Not deliberately, not consciously; he was just Ellis. But maybe being Ellis could be a dangerous thing. Obsession can turn to hate. It did with me."

Mike and I leave Ollie alone on the field and traipse

homeward. Mike's knuckles are raw and bruised, but he doesn't complain. While we walk, Ollie's words float around in my head. You inspired obsession, El. Is there some clue in that? Some larger message that I just don't understand yet?

We're at my door and Mike looks like he's about to drop.

"Mate," I say, "are you okay?"

"Yeah." He shakes his head wearily. "I've texted Mumzilla to pick me up. She'll be here in a sec." He claps my shoulder and sets off down the drive.

I feel like collapsing too. I watch until Carol draws up and give them both as cheery a wave as I can muster, then I take a deep breath and head inside. It's time for the McKee showdown, invitation by fridge door. I don't really know what my parents want to say to me, but I feel certain it must end with my bags packed and at least a night or two on Mike's camp bed.

The hall's empty. I dump my coat on Mum's alien sculpture and wander into the kitchen. I'm drifting over to the kettle with vague thoughts of tea when I see the post lying on the countertop. A familiar brown envelope pokes through the heap. The third envelope in three days. Will this one finally give me the answers I need?

My hands don't shake this time. I'm too tired to be nervous. I rip open the envelope and a single yellow sheet flutters out. I unfold the carefully torn-out journal page and your artwork stuns me, as always. This time it's a series of Disneyesque cartoons. In the first panel an exaggerated, red-faced version of my father is outside your door at Mount Pleasant. He's jabbering away while you stand before him, shaking your head as gluts of money pour from his lips. In the next panel, you're weeping, thrusting the money back at him, and then Julia is there beside you, indignant, furious, screaming at my father to leave...

Our front door opens. I hear Mum and Chris bustling through with shopping, then Dad's voice following them, asking if they've bankrupted him again. They all chuckle. Ha-de-fucking-ha. And then the chatter stops. They've seen me, but I can't turn and look at them because my eyes are resting on the last panel of the cartoon. You, alone in your beautiful bedroom, holding your bleeding heart in your hands. A price tag is attached to it: £100.

"Honey?" Mum says. "Are you okay?"

"Dylan?"

"Bro?"

I turn around slowly.

"What did you do?" I say. And when they don't answer, I scream it: *"What did you do?!"*

THEN: Saturday 14th March

The Barbecue

"Frecks, you're being silly. I think we should just tell them."

We're catching a quiet five minutes in Mike's kitchen, sitting around the breakfast table that's been the scene of a kajillion Marvel vs DC action-figure wars. Because practically everyone he has ever met loves Mike, there are about two hundred people in the Berringtons' huge garden, all bearing gifts for the birthday boy. As it's weirdly warm for mid-March, no one's even close to the house, so I lean in and grab a kiss.

"Don't push your luck," I tell El. "I agreed to you meeting my incredibly lame kinfolk today on the basis we're friends."

"And I agreed to leave the pearls at home. Which feels all kinds of weird, by the way."

I hold his hand to my cheek. I hate this. Asking El to adapt because I'm too much of a coward to allow him to be himself in front of the people I love. It's wrong and selfish,

253

but I can't seem to get past this pathetic version of myself. Other than this, things couldn't be better. It's two-and-a-bit months since the Christmas weirdness, and although it still bugs me that El won't fully confide, I'm ridiculously happy. Just spending time with him is sort of magical (I know, barf bags ready) and the sex is pretty freaking awesome!

So okay, it was awkward and klutzy at first, but the second, third and every other time has been amazing, mainly because El is a very tender teacher, and I guess a slightly embarrassing and slightly painful first experience goes for straight sex as well as gay (not that I ever plan on finding out). Anyway, last night is still playing on a loop in my mind, not because it was ultra-romantic or anything – the gearstick stuck into my backside and left a bruise – but it was still pretty hot for a Friday night in an abandoned supermarket car park.

At that moment Mumzilla and Big Mike bustle in, bickering in that adorable Berrington way of theirs. Seeing them laden down with boxes of burgers from the freezer in the garage, El jumps up to help.

"Thanks," Carol smiles, then turns to her husband. "I swear to god, Michael, you did *not* tell me you'd invited your idiot running-club friends. Now it's going to take at least an hour to get all these extra people fed, and I just…"

Big Mike plants a kiss on Mumzilla's brow. "Light of my

life, can we agree to differ? We have company. So, Dylan, are you going to introduce us?"

I turn from unpacking a stack of burgers. "Oh. Course. This is El. Ellis."

Big Mike grins. "I'm kidding. I know this guy. Carol, I want you to meet one of the most spectacular strikers ever to grace Ferrivale High. Honestly, bit of a rough patch before Christmas, but you guys really pulled it out of the bag in the new year. It's just a shame Mike couldn't…"

His smile becomes tight and the crinkles around his eyes deepen. Carol steps forward and rubs his arm.

"Mike'll be out there with us soon enough," El says. "We actually really need him, so after his last chemo session, I'm not accepting any excuses. It's practice with me, one-on-one, every day after school."

Big Mike rubs his eyes, then slaps his hands together. "Right," he announces, "burgers."

El and I pitch in with Mumzilla cutting rolls, while Big Mike hooks his *Hot Stuff Comin' Thru* apron around his neck. There's a picture of these impossible abs on the front, and Big Mike knows his son finds this mortifying, so of course it has to make a birthday appearance every year. El chatters away to Carol as we slice, joking and lifting the mood. When he goes to the bathroom, Carol nudges my elbow.

"I love him."

255

I stare at my pile of rolls. "Oh, you mean El? Yeah, he's cool."

I can feel her watching me, and when I dare a sideways glance she wrinkles her nose and gives me this impish smile. So my surrogate mum knows, and I'm one hundred per cent certain Mike hasn't told her. Mumzillas have psychic powers, it seems. Anyway, she's sensitive too, so changes the subject.

"How's my little dude doing?"

Mike is now a head taller than Carol, but he'll always be her little dude.

"He's playing Subbuteo with some of the footie lads. He seems in good spirits, doesn't he?"

She stops handing me rolls and places both palms flat on the counter, then nods, head down. "Thank you, Dylan."

"Don't be silly." I nudge her. "I'm only cutting bread. Although it is cool you trust me with a knife again after the ninth birthday A&E incident."

"You daft apeth. I mean thanks for coming to his chemo sessions. They're hard days for him, for all of us, and you sitting with him all that time, making him laugh...really, I don't know what we'd do without you." El walks in at this point to find both me and Mumzilla blinking hard. Carol gives this shivery laugh and holds out her hand to him. "Thank you, both. Mike told me how you've been a good friend to him too, Ellis."

She draws us into a huge hug. And with my arms wrapped around my boyfriend and my second mum, I take a moment to imagine how easy everything would be if I really was a Berrington. I certainly wouldn't waste another minute of my life pretending. I'd tell Carol and Big Mike everything and I know there would be zero awkwardness, just laughter and love and support.

"Anyway," Carol giggles, "stop helping. Go play."

"You know we're not eight any more, Mumma Z?"

"You'll always be eight to me, Dylan."

We're about to head out the patio door when Big Mike sticks his head in for more rolls. I say I'll grab some and tell El to go see how Mike's doing. He gives me a scout's salute and I walk with Big Mike onto the terrace.

"How're your folks, Dylan?" BM asks. "Has Chris got a job yet? You know, I'd kill that boy if he was mine."

"The position of Chris-assassin is open and very well paid," I tell him.

I stand with Big Mike for a moment behind his pride and joy: a gleaming barbecue of almost impossible size. We chat about my school work, plans for uni, my love life. It quickly becomes apparent that Big Mike does not possess the mind-reading abilities of his better half. Anyway, I'm just telling him about El's amazing 3D collage project, a replacement for the harpy sculpture he junked just after Christmas, when I see my boyfriend in deep conversation with my parents. My blood freezes.

"Gotta go," I babble, and launch myself across the terrace.

I take the steps down to the garden three at a time, my gaze never leaving that terrifying huddle of four standing by Mike's old trampoline. I dodge between Berrington family friends I vaguely know, smiling as best I can, when Gemma Argyle steps into my path.

"Gemma," I breathe. "Hi."

"Dylan McKee." So it seems she's finally learned my name. She presses a gaudy yellow and pink flier into my hand. "Easter Dance. Couple of weeks' time. Be there. It's for a good cause."

"Oh," I say, "there's dancing? Um, yeah, I'm not sure that's really my scene."

I don't tell her that me and Mike have long ago dubbed it the Dipshits Ball. She shrugs in a who-cares-what-your-scene-is-McKee? kind of way and moves on.

I move on too, and a random realization hits me as I reach the huddle. This time last year I'd never have been able to dash through that crowd. I would have walked slowly, murmuring hellos, keeping my head down. I know what's changed in my life, though I'm not sure how he's done it. I guess El is just a bona fide miracle worker. But he can also be a monumental pain in the arse. For example:

"What charming pearls, Mrs McKee! I have a set at home just like them."

I close my eyes, plaster on a grin, and join the party.

"Hey, guys, what's going on?"

Dad is holding a paper plate bearing a wedge of cheese while Mum sips a small white wine. Lager in hand, Chris is watching El like he's on safari and has spotted a rare and baffling specimen. El sidles closer to me and I inch marginally away.

"So Ellis here…" My mum seems at a loss. "He's a friend of yours, Dylan?"

"He's all our friend," I say, which sounds horribly ungrammatical. Anyway, I reach onto my tiptoes and knuckle El's head. "This joker."

Mum sips, Dad nibbles, Chris slurps.

"Ellis tells us he lives with his aunt on the new estate. Are they nice apartments, Ellis? Gordon thought it was a real boost to the town when the flats were put up, didn't you, dear?"

"Mount Pleasant is good for the local economy, certainly." Dad nods. "Just as long as the newcomers try their best to fit in, I think it's great."

El smiles. "What exactly does that mean? Fit in?"

"Well, it's obvious, isn't it?" Dad says, munching his brie between sentences. "Like any community, we have our standards and traditions. It's up to some of the new tenants on the estate to respect our way of doing things, that's all. Especially those from other cultures and viewpoints."

"But what if people like me want to make changes?" El shrugs. "Maybe we'd like our little bit of Ferrivale to reflect our culture too. Instead of us just fitting in with you, perhaps you'd like to fit in with us too? That way, we could all learn something about each other."

"Yes, Ellis," my dad says, putting down his fork and casting a condescending eye. "That's all very idealistic, I'm sure. But, well, you must understand, we were…"

He seems unsure how to finish his sentence, and so El nods.

"You were here first?"

Dad turns scarlet. "No! I didn't mean that at all!"

"So," Mum cuts in, "you were saying you live with your aunt? How lovely. And what does she do?"

"El's aunt manages Bettison's bakery," I say. "Sixty hours a week, plus overtime. I don't know how she does it."

I dig my nails into my palms. El has shot me this tiny smile but I know how my praise of Julia has come across: as if I'm overcompensating for a failure that doesn't exist.

"I've got a question." Chris raises his beer like he's in one of the classes he flunked four years ago. "Have you ever been in a gang, Ellis?"

"I have not," El says, "but if I ever form one, you can be my first recruit." He gives my brother a brief up-and-down look. "But I don't know, Chris, maybe you're already a member of my gang and you don't even know it yet."

260

Chris follows my dad's lead, face turning beetroot.

"Are you in all of Dylan's classes?" Mum twitters.

"Only history. But Dylan's a passionate supporter of our football team."

Before Mum can wonder at my sudden interest in sweaty men running around chasing a bit of thermally-bonded polyurethane, Chris butts in with:

"*You* play footie?"

"Bet your ass, Christopher."

"Okay." Chris hands me his beer and goes off to steal a ball from Mike's little cousins. Cue tears, but Chris is oblivious. "Quick kickabout then, one on one."

El snatches the ball and sets it dribbling at his feet. "You're on."

Chris is wearing shorts and the brand-new pair of Adidas Ultraboost that Mum bought him during a post-Zumba shopping spree. Meanwhile El is in skinny jeans and biker boots. A little crowd, including Ollie Reynolds and the footie lads, form around this clash of the titan and the goon. El doesn't need the encouragement but a general chant of "El-lis! El-lis!" starts up. I know Mum and Dad keep stealing glances at me but, screw it, I'm grinning anyway.

El annihilates my brother. I mean, just *annihilates* him. Chris keeps trying to take the ball from him, even attempting sly shin-kicks and blatant shirt-holding, which provokes boos from the lads, but El coasts serenely above it all. I remember thinking once how his fingers dance, actually *dance*, when he's sketching. It's the same with his feet. He manoeuvres the ball like it's a part of him, waltzing it above and below and around his adversary's clumsy lunges. In the end, Chris doesn't get in a single touch and El exits the field of combat to rapturous applause. Most people would now bow out gracefully, but my brother is the King of Cockwombles.

"So you should know," he pants, as he and El rejoin us, "Mum and Dad are big supporters of your lot."

"Oh yes?" El takes a sniff under his collar, though I can't see a bead of sweat on his brow.

"Yep. Big gayers, my parents. Civil partnerships, queer marriage, the whole thing."

El sweeps my folks with a beautiful smile. "That's awesome of you, Mr and Mrs McKee."

"Well," my dad blusters, "it's only right that we should grant the privileges we enjoy to those who choose a different path."

"Choose?" El rolls the word around. "Okay."

"Anyway," I say, "we really ought to check in on Mike."

"Charmed," El calls over his shoulder as I march him off. I don't even care that I'm holding his elbow, it has to be done.

"Babe, I love you," I say, "and I know they're awful, but that was just…I don't even know what that was. I think you've

262

managed to piss off my entire family in five minutes flat."

"Do you think so? I thought they liked me."

"Yeah," I inform him, "but you live in Ellis World, where everyone wears novelty Ellis ears and thinks all your rides are cool."

We find Mike sitting on a deckchair, surrounded by unopened presents, shaking his head and smiling at us.

"Dudes, you know you're getting pretty obvious, right?"

I snatch my hand away from my boyfriend's elbow. El pouts. Whatever. It's time to focus on Mike. My best friend looks pretty well, considering. His cheeks are a bit pinched and his clothes are sort of baggy, but when you're puking up your guts every couple of weeks, that's bound to happen. We sit on the grass either side of him, like lackeys to an emperor.

"Presents?" I suggest.

"Presents!" He grins.

While I rummage in the pile around him, El tries to direct me, even though he has no idea where I dumped my gifts. I snap back at him and Mike laughs.

"You guys are becoming old-couple-cute."

"Bingo!" I say, lifting three parcels and plonking them in Mike's lap. "This one first."

Mike's fumbling is too slow for El, who decides to help, and after a manic flurry Mike holds up a rainbow-coloured mini umbrella attached to a headband.

"Okay, I know you hate hats," I tell him, "but you're getting a bit thin on top and it'll be summer soon. So…"

El curls his finger through Mike's corn-coloured locks. "You should just shave it off. You have cool hair, Mike, but I really think you'd rock the skinhead biker look."

We all laugh. I don't know how he does it, but El can make the most uncomfortable conversations fly. Maybe you have to have lived a harder kind of life to become an expert in that sort of thing. I realize I feel like this a lot when I think about him – my admiration for his grace and talents tinged with sad thoughts of how he came to be the Ellis I know and love. Thinking this, my mind returns again to Christmas. I still don't buy the explanations he gave me for his vanishing act, and every so often I'll catch a darkness in his mood that worries me.

When I look up again, Mike is holding the footie shirt I bought him and the set of colouring books.

"The shirt because you wanted it," I say. "And those are chemo colouring books: Batman villains and alien planets of the DC universe. I'm going to time us on my phone. Fastest colourer wins one those free NHS barf bowls. And I don't want any but-my-colouring-arm's-hooked-up-to-a-drip excuses."

"Me next," El says, jumping on the spot. "I haven't wrapped it, sorry."

He reaches into his shirt pocket and takes out this little

onyx pendant on a piece of multicoloured string. I know straight away that El has fashioned and polished the stone himself, because he'd never give a gift that didn't have a personal touch. He turns its face to the light and I see a staring symbol picked out in tiny silver pointillist dots.

"It's the Eye of Ra," he says, tying the string around Mike's neck. "An ancient symbol of protection. It'll watch over you, keep you safe."

Mike's voice is hoarse as he touches the stone. "Thanks, mate." Then he rallies himself. "Okay, so there's cake in fifteen minutes, but in the meantime, my bedroom's empty."

"Dude," I say, "no way! That's where we've had sleepovers since were six."

"Dylan, we're not six any more. Anyway, you have my permission for fifteen minutes of kissing and heavy petting." He raises two fingers, like a blessing. "It is *my* gift to you on this auspicious day."

Me and El exchange a quick glance, then head as nonchalantly as we can back into the house. Seconds later, I'm closing the bedroom door behind us. El pulls me to him and we lose most of our time just kissing. Precious minutes hurtle by until we suddenly hear Big Mike bellowing "*CAKE!*" and we part, groaning in unison.

"I hope it's a Starburst cake," El says. "That would be some compensation."

"I don't think such a cake exists."

He rolls his eyes. "I hate this universe."

"All of it?"

He grabs my waist and pulls me back from the door. "No, not all of it."

"C'mon." I drag him with me into the corridor. "Mike's day, remember."

"Oh!" He slaps his forehead. "I forgot your present! So, I thought you'd get jealous of my amazingly thoughtful Mike-gift, and I didn't want a pouty boyfriend pouting at me all day with his beautiful pouty lips, so here you go."

He takes a single yellow sheet from the same pocket as Mike's amulet and hands it to me. I unfold the sketch and blood courses into my face.

"You are so adorable when you blush." El grins.

"This is…" I stare at the image. "This is pure filth, Ellis Bell!"

El's smile drops. He takes the drawing and holds it between us.

"No, Dylan, it's me and it's *you*. You are the most beautiful thing I have ever seen in my life, and I want you to see yourself as I see you. Stop hiding away, stop doubting yourself. I love you because you're kind and clever and funny and you're freakin' hot! Do you understand?"

"Okay." I don't quite believe him, even though I know El wouldn't lie about something like this. But my boyfriend isn't infallible and… Well, I can't look like this in real life, can I? "But where will I keep it?"

He slings an arm around my shoulder. "Tape it under your desk drawer."

We separate on the bottom stair and head out through the empty kitchen. Down in the garden, Mike is being paraded around in his deckchair by the footie guys, all chanting his name, while Big Mike follows, holding the cake aloft. He really does look like a Roman emperor. Suddenly Carol's calling me down to help cut the cake.

In the minutes that follow, I lose track of El. Mike and I are laughing our arses off at Ollie Reynolds as he tries to beatbox along to "Happy Birthday To You" while Big Mike is showering everyone with party streamers. The crowd ebbs and flows around us. And then I catch sight of El talking again to my dad. Heart in my mouth, I'm about to head over when Ellis spots me and breaks off the conversation.

"All good?" I ask as he reaches me.

He looks lost for a moment, then scratches his elbow and gazes towards the road.

"Yeah. But wow, your dad really doesn't like to be contradicted in a debate, does he?"

"Oh God," I say. "What's he said?"

"Nothing, it's cool. But look, Julia has this therapy meeting and I promised I'd go." He glances at his watch.

"Will you tell Mike I'm sorry I had to bail?"

"Of course."

And with that he's gone.

I look over to where my parents stand with Chris. I just know Dad has said something to upset El, and I'd like nothing more right now than to have it out with him. But I remind myself again that this is Mike's day, and so I plaster on a smile and rejoin the birthday boy.

NOW: Thursday 30th April

19

My gaze returns to the cartoon. To my father throwing money at you while you weep and while Julia screams at him to leave. To the drawing of you holding your heart in your hands and to the price tag valuing your love for me at a hundred measly pounds.

"What did you do?" I ask them again.

Dad starts forward, then stops dead when I hold up your drawing. It takes a moment for the images to sink in.

"Dylan," he begins, his eyes wide. "Dylan, we were going to talk to you about this tonight. You have to understand—"

I hold up my forefinger. Suddenly I don't want to hear any more. "You shut the hell up."

"Don't talk to Dad like that!" shouts Chris from the kitchen doorway.

"All of you," I shout back, "shut the hell up until I'm done!"

I take out my phone and watch them wait in silence while the call connects. When Julia picks up, I find I can't look at them any more. I swing around, my free hand grasping my wrist because my phone hand's shaking so badly. Maybe it's a mistake on your part, El. Maybe I'm misinterpreting your cartoon. Because my family can't be this horrifically soulless, can they?

"Hello, sweet boy." Julia's voice breaks into my thoughts. She sounds tired and raspy, but there's not that telltale drowsiness and I don't think she's been using again. "How lovely to hear from you. I was worried, you know, after the funeral."

"I'm sorry. About what happened," I tell her. "I'm fine now."

"Are you, Dylan?"

I'm glad my back's turned to them. "No. No, not really."

"No," she echoes sadly.

"How are *you*, Julia?"

"Oh, you know. It's funny, really, because I didn't know our boy at all until he turned up at my door back in…when was it?"

"November. I mean, I met him in November. He came to you at the end of October, I think. Around Halloween."

"Poor kid. He looked a bit like a Halloween ghoul when I first saw him. 'I'm your nephew Ellis,' he said, 'and unless you're as shitty as the rest of our family, I'm hoping you'll

270

let me stay.' He was dirty and stinking and his poor tooth was missing, but I don't know, those words just made me chuckle. It always amazed me how he could do that; make you smile when you ought to be on the floor crying your bloody heart out. I miss that about him most."

"Me too." Just then Mum drifts into my field of vision and I thrust out my arm and she drifts away again. I won't let them invade this moment with the only other person who loved you as much as I did. "Julia, I need to ask—"

"He's here!" she says suddenly.

And I almost lose it. There's a brightness to her voice that I remember from all the other times I'd call and she'd open with "*He's here!*" – so excited to tell you that your boyfriend was on the line. I feel the tiles shift under my feet. I imagine that you're there, El, snuggled up in bed at 123 or sitting at your drawing board, your fingers dancing. That none of it was real. Not the Dipshits Ball nor the accident nor the lake nor the funeral – not a single awful second of it actually happened. It was just me retreating from you again. My coward brain conjuring this nightmare in which I was rescued and you were left to drown. A smile flutters at the corner of my lips. Of course it wasn't real. Nothing this terrible could happen to someone who loves another person the way I love you. The universe would have to be completely purposeless or else designed by some psychotic comic-book villain.

"They sent the urn round this morning," she goes on. "So he's here, Dylan, if you'd like to come and take him home with you."

I think for a minute my legs will give way but I manage to stay upright.

"Are you still there?"

"Yeah… Yeah, I… Julia, I couldn't take him away from you."

"Dylan," she says slowly, "he was *always* more yours than he was mine. You belonged with him and he belonged with you. But it's your decision."

I can't put it off any longer. I have to ask her the question. "Julia, did my dad ever visit Ellis?" I sense movement behind me, hear a dry cough as if someone might be about to interrupt. No one does. "Did he…" It takes all I have just to force the words out. "Did my dad offer Ellis money to stop seeing me?"

Silence down the line. Silence that confirms everything.

"Dylan," she says. "Oh, sweetheart. I'm not sure I—"

"Please just tell me," I say. "I have to know."

She takes a moment. "All right. It was a month or so back. I was sitting in the kitchen when I overheard your dad speaking to El out in the hall. I couldn't believe what he was saying, so I marched straight out there and told him to sling his hook. Afterwards, we talked. I thought you had a right to know, but El, he made me swear I'd never tell you.

272

He said it would hurt you too much."

I grip the phone hard and close my eyes. "Thank you, Julia."

"Dylan, wait. What your parents did, it was cruel and thoughtless." She sighs. "But they're still your parents."

I tell her I'll come round soon, that we'll go through your room together, El, and that I'll help as she packs your life away. And then I hang up and turn back to face them.

Another secret you kept locked away in your journal, El. Why didn't you tell me? Because it would smash my family to pieces? Didn't you understand that some things are already so broken a little more smashing won't do them any harm?

I can't rage at them any more. I just ask my questions.

"Why did you hate him?"

"Dylan…" Mum begins, her face ashen.

"Here we go," Chris cuts in, "melodrama hour."

"Shut up, Chris," Dad says, which seems to startle both Mum and my pea-brained sibling. Dad spreads his hands like he's making an appeal to the jury, except he isn't that kind of solicitor. "Look, son, we thought you might possibly find out about this. That Ellis's aunt might let something slip. That's why we've been trying to sit down with you these past couple of days, in case you heard it from someone else and got the wrong end of the stick."

"The wrong end of the stick?" I brandish the cartoon. "How am I possibly misinterpreting this?"

273

My mind flies back to the night of the Easter dance and my conversation with Mike. *"And they're cool with El?"* he'd asked, and I'd cut him off. Because even to Mike, who knows the McKees and their funny little ways, I couldn't straight out admit that they *weren't* cool with you. That look Mum and Dad shot each other when we told them, the look you didn't catch, it said it all really. By then they had already tried to bribe you so that you'd stop seeing me.

"When did all this start?" I say. "Did you suspect we were together at the barbecue? I guess you must have. Then, what? You popped round to Mount Pleasant for a little word with El? You're all such bloody hypocrites," I mutter. "You signed the petitions to give people like me the rights we should have had anyway. You pretend to hate the people who hate us. But you're as bad as they are. You only really want to accept the 'safe' gays, like me. The ones who find a nice quiet boyfriend and go away and do our gay stuff out of sight and don't insist upon ourselves."

Chris laughs. "Have you been taking your mental pills, bro? Because it sounds like you need them."

This time it's my mum who surprises herself by telling Chris to shut up.

"I want to ask you something," I say.

Dad nods. "I'll give you an honest answer, if I can."

"Always a qualification, isn't there, Dad? Always a get-out clause. All right, here it is: if any of you had been there

274

that night at the lake, would you have let him drown? Just because you thought El monopolized me and made me gay and that sort of disgusted you." I look directly at Chris and he looks away. "Or because you thought he was corrupting me somehow?" I turn to Mum, who has her hands covering her mouth. "Or because, on the basis of one meeting, you decided he wasn't good enough for your precious son?" My dad returns my glance but I see something change in his face. A certainty gone, a doubt creeping in. "You won't know this, but El's parents beat him senseless and disowned him when he told them who he was. They threw him onto the street and forgot about him. You're not as bad as them, not even close, but by rejecting him you've rejected me too."

"We thought we were doing the right thing," my dad says slowly. "We didn't think he was... Yes, all right, Dylan, yes, we didn't think he was good enough for you."

"And he wasn't!" Chris spits through drawn-back lips. "We all said it. Who knew where that dirty little estate rat had been putting his prick. Did you want to end up with AIDS or something, lying in a hospital bed next to Mike?"

"Get out!" my dad roars at him.

Chris looks dumbstruck. He turns to Mum, who has no words for him. After a few miserable seconds, he lopes out of the room.

"We just thought, if we could put a bit of distance between

the two of you, this whole obsession would blow over." Mum begins to move towards me, then sees something in me that clearly frightens her. I don't want my mum to be frightened of me, but I don't know how else to look. "I was just concerned about your safety, Dylan. To look at you, no one would know…but Ellis? I was frightened that by being with him you were putting yourself at risk. You know how people can be. But maybe we were wrong." She pauses and glances at my dad. "I think…I think we were wrong."

I shrug. "It's too late now, Mum. He's already dead. But there is one thing I want you to know – Ellis was determined that he'd never, *ever* tell me what Dad tried to do. Because he wanted to protect me from my own family, I guess. This kid you doubted and despised? He was better than all of us."

I start towards the hall and Mum reaches for my arm.

"Dylan, what are you going to do? Please, we just didn't realize how deeply you felt about Ellis. If we had—"

"If you had? You'd have done exactly what you did. Mum, do you know what I thought when I saw that note on the fridge this morning? I thought you might be getting ready to throw me out."

"No! We wouldn't. Not ever."

"Doesn't matter. I was too much of a coward to take this step before, but I'm not frightened any more. I guess if you had anything to hate Ellis for, it might be this."

I shake off her hold and head to the stairs. Chris is sitting there sullenly on the bottom step.

"I have to go," I tell them over my shoulder. "This isn't my home any more."

20

The next twenty minutes pass in a blur.

Dad remains stationed at the bottom of the stairs, still in his work clothes. Chris is playing thrash metal in his room, his way of screaming for attention because, just for once, no one is giving him any. Mum stands in the hall outside my room, watching me throw clothes into a backpack. I know she wants to help – it's what mums do when their kids are making a mess of packing – but I think she understands now that I won't be coming home from this particular sleepover. When I go to close the door on her she rocks back against the wall.

I move to the desk, pull out the drawer and untape the sketch you gave me the day of Mike's party. I can't look at it. Not this misguided perfection you saw in me. I fold it up and slip it into my top pocket.

Only Dad remains when I head back downstairs. We

stand in silence for a minute, listening to Metallica drown out Mum's crying.

"I can wait at the bottom of the drive," I say.

"This is still your home, Dylan," he answers. "You can wait here, if you like."

I want to say something to him, comfort him, I don't know. I can almost feel you willing me to, El. But your heart was an ocean and mine's the meanest little pavement puddle. So we stand and wait.

This doesn't feel like the huge moment it should. I was actually born in this house, my mum too far gone to get to the hospital, paramedics delivering me, furious and screaming and disgusting, on the kitchen floor. I chipped my front tooth on this stair post, playing Star Wars with Chris, him as Han and me as Chewy – which was ironic, as chewing was painful for a week afterwards. Dad's office across the hall was the scene of the infamous "sex talk", a cringe-fest that lasted three minutes and that has haunted us both ever since. My mum taught me how to tie my shoelaces on this bottom step, patient and consoling and ridiculously proud when I accomplished that first bow. And under the stairs was where Mike and I practised kissing. It wasn't a gay thing, Mike insisted, it's just we couldn't convince a single girl in our year to teach us how it was done.

I have never fancied my best friend, but I still remember

his mouth on mine, warm and trembling. I thought of it every night for months afterwards, touching the place where his lips had been, grateful in ways I couldn't understand for that moment between us.

All these memories, acres of them, each in their way defining who I am.

A knock. Big Mike stands on the doorstep, looking awkward as hell.

"Hey, Gordon," he says, waving and then closing his fist.

"Michael, thank you for doing this."

"No problem. We're always happy to have him, as long as he's still house-trained."

The two dads share a smile that you probably have to be a dad to understand.

"C'mon then, kiddo. Mike's got some popcorn on the go and some movie that would've scared the hell out of me when I was your age." He grabs my bag from my shoulder and stands back from the door. "Say hi to Barbara for me."

I glance over my shoulder, wondering if Mum might appear. She doesn't.

We walk in silence to Big Mike's four-by-four and I climb up into the passenger seat.

"Buckle up, Sonny Jim," he tells me, and starts the ignition.

I don't know what to say to Big Mike. Within minutes of sending the text to Mike, I got the green light to come and stay at the Berringtons'. I'm family, after all. But I know I'm imposing. Mike needs his rest, and all I've brought him these past few days is a barrelful of my unrelenting crap. I feel awful about it, but I just don't have anywhere else to go.

Big Mike reaches out and shakes my shoulder. "All good?"

Trees rustle by, budding now that the long winter's finally over. Life invading all this death. I shake my head and look down.

"Nah," Big Mike murmurs. "Silly question. But you know you can talk to me and Carol, right? About anything. Carol's great with advice and I can cook a mean double-bacon cheeseburger, which is even better than good advice. Am I right?"

"Right."

A few minutes later, we're home. That's how the Berringtons' feels. How it's always felt. A refuge when my real home became confusing and unbearable. Big Mike grabs my backpack and waves to Carol and Mike, who are waving back from the open doorway. Honestly, I want to just sit here and cry my eyes out.

In the end Mike comes to get me, pulling me out of the car with diverting talk about popcorn and horror movies. Mumzilla ruffles my hair and says it's dinner first, then popcorn, which makes Mike wonder aloud if she might have been a torturer for the Inquisition in a previous life.

"Yes, Michael, I'm a bloodthirsty tyrant, and waiting thirty minutes for popcorn is my modern version of the rack. Now go and wash your hands."

"Sadist."

I'm about to follow Mike when Carol calls me back.

"I just got off the phone with your mum."

"Is she okay?"

"No, sweetheart. I'm not sure how she could be. Look, I don't know what's happened tonight, and maybe it's not my place to know, but one thing I'm certain about: your family love you." Big Mike puts both hands on my shoulders and Carol lifts my chin, so I'm forced to look at her. "Even that idiot brother of yours likes you quite a lot. Now, I want you to give your mum a call tomorrow, just a few words to tell her you're okay. It's my only condition."

"And she will kick your arse if you don't," Big Mike adds.

So I say I will, and I don't think I'm lying.

We eat Mumzilla's trademark dish: incredible home-made pizzas with curly fries. No one talks about the elephant in the room, even though it's parading around the breakfast table, leaving huge steaming dumps in its wake. Big Mike regales us with his collection of lame dad jokes and we all laugh in the right places, mainly because we've heard the routine a million times before.

After dinner we head up to Mike's room and grab our

beanbags, bowls of warm popcorn nestled in our laps. After half an hour of serial-killer carnage, Mike pauses the movie.

"How's stuff?" he asks.

"Stuff sucks."

He nods and flips the remote like it's a six-shooter in an old Wild West movie. He's about to restart the film when I catch his eye.

"All this time, Mike, everything we've found out, every secret El kept from me, you know what I keep coming back to?"

"What?"

"It's us. Something rotten in us. You know how we like to present ourselves in Ferrivale? This brilliant, modern, tolerant community? Just so lovely and friendly and accepting of everyone. So we're super-nice to the gays but we're also accepting of that church group that pushes their *It's Adam and Eve, not Adam and Steve* fliers through every letter box. But we can't be okay with everything. In the end, we have to choose. And I'm not talking about freedom of speech – let the haters hate, let them post their fliers – but *we* need to have some idea of what we stand for and what we oppose. Because if we don't decide, then we leave these gaps where good people get swallowed up.

"We all wanted El to be something he could never be. And we thought us wanting that was somehow acceptable, but it's not. It's not about El fitting into some idea of what

283

he should be. Tolerance isn't conditional. It's absolute. It's not on your terms, it's on *his*. Even I wouldn't accept El for who he was. Not at first. And that's what makes kids like El feel rejected and puts them in danger, because we're not strong enough to say, 'This is where we as a community stand. Ellis Bell is one of us and we will look out for him. Even those among us who would never be his friend and don't like his choices, we stand with him because he has a right to be whatever he chooses to be and he lives here, in this town, where our tolerance isn't this shallow thing that makes us feel virtuous. It's real. It's powerful. It protects.'"

I don't know where these words are coming from, but they feel like they go to the bone of me.

"We're all responsible," I say. "But I have to know who it was, Mike. Who left him to die like that? Who hated him that much? It's killing me."

Mike nods. He's taken the amulet you gave him for his birthday from under his shirt and is stroking the protection symbol.

"Dylan, I just…" He looks away. "I wish I could help you."

"You are helping." I throw a cushion at his head; he doesn't smile. "You've always helped me."

Eventually, we continue with the movie. When it's done, I unpack my night stuff and we make up the camp bed. Mike strips to his pants and T-shirt and turns off the light.

"Need anything?"

"No," I lie. Because what I need, he can't give me.

I'm still wide awake when Becks snuffles into the room and curls up beside me. I run my fingers through the white fur of his belly and he stretches up and licks my face. It doesn't matter. It was already wet.

I wake to find Mike's bed empty and Becks gone. The alarm clock on the window sill blinks back at me: 10.56 a.m. It seems unreal that your funeral was only four days ago. In that short time, I've learned so much more about you, El. Now I wonder if a fourth picture will find me here and what new secrets it might reveal.

It always makes me feel weirdly guilty when I sleep in at Mike's, probably because the Berringtons have this "up and at 'em" attitude, though no one's ever said anything. Wandering downstairs, I give Mumzilla a smile and sink into "Dylan's seat" at the breakfast table. I'm instructed to sit and drink tea and eat toast. Sounds good.

"Don't forget our deal," she tells me, pouring tea from the arse-end of her comedy cow teapot. "Call your mum."

I nod. "Where's Mike?"

"Taken Becks for a walk. He's feeling a bit groggy so I've let him skip school." I start to say something when she holds up her hand. "Dylan, he's fine. He'll be back soon…"

So I've read about "pregnant pauses" in books, but I never experienced one until now. There's this almost unbearable pressure slowly building up between me and Carol, and I have no idea what it is, but I get the feeling that whatever's about to be delivered will be painful, for both of us.

"I'm so sorry, Dylan," she begins, "I really don't want to have to say this."

My gaze is fixed on my cup. "It's okay."

"No. No, it isn't okay. Not one tiny bit. Because we love you very much and we all hate what you've been going through. You know you're like a second son to us, don't you?"

"Yeah," I croak. "Yes. Thanks."

She grabs my hand across the table. "Don't thank me. Thank *you*, Dylan. Thank you for being the best friend Mike could ever have asked for. God." She wipes her eyes with the corner of a tea towel. "This house is as full of you as it is of any of us. You know I still check around my feet when I'm carrying food to the table, just in case little Mike and Dylan are playing tag under me. That's what makes this so hard."

"It's all right," I tell her, because I know what's coming. "Don't worry."

She takes a huge breath and exhales. "You can't stay here, sweetheart. I wish you could. But Mike, he's my little dude, you know?" I nod and she erupts into floods of tears. I get up from my chair and hug her as tight as I can. "He's still got such a long way to go," she sobs. "That last chemo was brutal on him, and he should be further ahead anyway, but he—"

"I'm not good for him," I say, straightening up. Outside I can see Mike's old trampoline, rusted and silvered with webs, its creaking laughter just a memory.

"You *are* good for him. Of course you are. But, Dylan, it's taken such a toll on you. Me and Big Mike, you know we love you and we'd do anything, *anything* to make this better for you, but I listen to my boy crying himself to sleep every night and I… Mike has to be our priority." She closes her eyes. "We can't have anything distracting from his treatment and I just—"

"Please, Carol, you don't need to say anything. I shouldn't have asked to stay. It was selfish."

"Don't be silly, of course it wasn't selfish. And you can stay, for a while. Until you fix things up with your parents or find somewhere… And me and Big Mike, we can help with that. We can talk to your folks, contribute something towards rent for a new place for you. I don't know. But we won't abandon you, Dylan, not ever. It's just right now—"

"Carol, it's okay. Really. I'll sort something out. Please don't worry."

I finish my tea and help her with the washing-up. We

don't say anything else but I can feel the guilt radiating off her. I hate it. Can't stand it. I'm like a poison here, and she's right, I have to go.

I'm just heading upstairs when Big Mike comes panting through the front door. He's about the only dad I know who can pull off Lycra. He shoots me this look and I know he's wondering if Carol and I have had "the conversation". I give him as carefree a grin as I can.

"Hey, been for a run?"

He looks down at himself.

"Gay bar." He winks. "Just don't tell Carol."

I laugh and start again for Mike's bedroom, but Big Mike calls me back.

"I was passing your house and your dad waved me over."

"What did he say?"

"Not much, kiddo. He just wanted me to give you this. Said it arrived this morning."

Big Mike hands me a familiar brown envelope. Whoever our mysterious journal-sender is, he clearly isn't keeping up with my accommodation arrangements.

"Everything all right?"

"Yeah," I say, "all good."

I take the envelope from him and race upstairs. In Mike's room I turn on his desk lamp and drop into his chair. How long is this going to go on? I wonder. How many more brown envelopes containing single yellow sheets containing terrible secrets? Each step I take with these pages feels like walking on a turntable, an endless, soul-destroying merry-go-round that only appears to move me forward but actually keeps me stuck in the same place.

And then I open the envelope and unfold the sheet and look at the drawing you made, and I know, straight away, that this isn't like the others.

Finally, El, we've reached the end.

In this single, crashing moment, I know what happened to you in December, and the horror of it is almost unimaginable. And yet it all makes sense now. Why you withdrew from me at Christmas. Why you acted so strangely at the dance. Why you wouldn't tell me what was going on with you. Because, more than anything else in the world, you'd want to protect me from this. Because if I knew, then your pain would be my pain too.

Because you were raped.

21

The drawing: you're on the floor of the school art studio, naked. It's night. Surrounding you is your sculpture; a beautiful winged harpy, her body a see-through wire mesh, her insides a helix of red ribbons. Your main A-level project, finally completed. Your fingers reach through the mesh, the ribbons wrapped around your wrists and taped across your mouth, binding you, silencing you. The details are so painstaking it hurts to look at them. Your sculpture, this beautiful monster, has become a prison.

It was such an awesome piece; I never did understand why you destroyed it after Christmas. Thought it was just you being tough on yourself. Now I get it. Because *his* fingerprints are all over her.

A frosty moon glares behind the windows of the studio. There's no one around to see, and so the featureless man looming above you, towering over the sculpture, has no fear.

He's smaller than you in real life, weaker, but none of that matters. Words circle the image, writhing around your tortured face. Words I know he must have implanted in your head: *IF YOU TELL, NO ONE WILL BELIEVE YOU.*

Your face is slack, your eyes huge. Haunted windows looking out at me, asking where I am. Playing video games with Mike? Watching TV? I don't know. I can't remember.

No one will believe you.

But *I* would have believed you, El. Of course I would. So why didn't you tell me? Because he got inside your head? Because he made you believe that you were somehow to blame for what happened to you? You were raped, El. None of this was your fault.

Why didn't I understand what you were going through? Why didn't I put the pieces together? It all seems so obvious now. But when you came back after disappearing on me for that week in December, I was just so relieved to have you back that I stopped looking for answers...

Okay, stay calm. Think it through. What are you going to do?

But I can't stay calm. My hands can barely hold the yellow sheet. Cold beads skate down my back. My mouth and throat and tongue are like bits of roadkill roasting in the sun. I can't breathe or swallow. All I can do is sit and stare at the trembling devastation in my hand.

Oh God, Ellis. I get it now. It's like Raj said, you cared about me too much to bring this darkness down on me.

And Jesus, this is the worst kind of darkness I could ever have imagined. I want to cry and scream and rage against it. Christmas makes sense. Easter makes sense. You pulling away from me, filled with all that misguided shame; I understand everything.

I don't know how long I sit there, frozen, screaming inside my head, but suddenly I'm moving, slowly, deliberately, pulling fresh clothes from my backpack and changing into them. The internal screams continue all the while. They follow me into the bathroom, where I mechanically brush my teeth. They echo round and round as I splash cold water on my face and watch the droplets cascade in the mirror. They almost drown out my voice as I speak to Carol and Big Mike in the living room:

"Hey, guys. I'm going over to see Julia. I can probably stay with her a few days. Will you tell Mike I'll see him later?"

"Honey, are you sure?" Carol asks.

"I can drive you if you like?" says Big Mike.

I shake my howling head. "No need. I could do with a bit of fresh air."

Outside, I huddle inside my jacket, every part of me shivering as I make my way down the road. A George Ezra tune you played on the Nissan's stereo randomly invades my thoughts. I don't know the title or the lyrics. Why didn't I pay more attention to the things you loved? Too late now.

Birds caw overhead. Blackbirds, eyeing me from twisted branches. It's strange. Despite the screaming in my skull and the sickness in my stomach, I feel floaty and elated, like in the very last seconds of the very last exam before school breaks up forever. We'll never know that day, Ellis. Never know that giddy wonder as we burst out through the fire doors, setting off alarms, consequence free, grabbing at each other's autographed school shirts, running and sliding across the football pitch only to catch each other, laughing and hiccupping, dreaming dreams of that little university flat that awaits us. This mad lightness I feel now is the closest we'll come.

My phone rumbles. It might be Mike or my mum or Carol. I don't want to talk to any of them. I whistle George Ezra and watch the blackbirds in the trees.

The only annoying thing is that I have to wait. Reaching the edge of the woods that border Ferrivale High, I hunker down, elbows planted on my knees. My watch tells me it's 12.36. Three hours, maybe four, and finally I'll have my answers.

I watch the rhythms of the school day from my vantage point. Lunch is over and kids swarm out onto the field for twenty minutes of texting, bullying, consoling and running around in pointless circles. Then they crowd back in, only for some to swarm back out again, a few scrambling about like puppies, others dawdling towards the unbelievable agony of PE. I catch a glimpse of Ollie as goalie, an unusual position for him. He barely moves during the game and concedes four goals, winning the middle finger from his teammates. Then Mr Highfield whistles them all back inside and I watch an hour of Year Nines trying to stay awake as Mrs Gupta reads aloud from *Of Mice and Men*. I know it's Steinbeck because Gupta always stands on her desk to read the Lennie parts.

The end-of-day bell makes my heart leap into my throat. Flexing the cramp from my fingers, I call Mike. Kids are flooding through the gates as the call connects. I think I see Gemma and the committee girls, but maybe I'm imagining things. It would only be right to glimpse them before the end.

"Dylan," Mike blurts. "Where the hell have you been? Is everything okay?"

"Yes, mate. I hope it will be."

"What..." I hear him swallow. "What does that mean?"

"I know who it was," I tell him. "The person who scared El at the dance. The one who..." I can't say it. I don't want to put the image from the yellow paper in Mike's head, so I simply say, "I know what happened to him at Christmas. It was someone from school. They did something very bad to him and I need to ask them why."

"Okay," he breathes, "but, Dylan, you shouldn't be doing this on your own... Dylan?"

"I love you, Bitch."

"Dylan? Dylan! Talk to me. Whatever you're thinking of doing, just—"

"You can't help me, Mike. Carol and Big Mike would never forgive me if I got you mixed up in this. But things might get a bit crazy after today, so I just wanted to say thanks. For everything you've done this past week. And I wanted to tell you…" I rub my eyes with the back of my hand. "Mike, you were *always* my best friend. Even when El came along, you and me…" I grip the phone, force myself to keep going. "You were never second-best to him, you know? You were always my brother."

"Dylan, you need to listen—"

"I have to go."

"No! Dylan!"

I end the call. Then I thumb quickly through my apps, select the one I need, and rise. Pushing my way through the undergrowth, I emerge onto the field. The sun throws my shadow like a cloak, draping it across Ferrivale High.

Some dawdling Year Seven kid with half his shirt tail hanging out emerges from the science block just as I reach the main building. I ask him to hold the door. Year Sevens usually obey sixth-former commands, even if the older kid does have a strange look in his eye.

I pass quickly through the corridors. I don't think there's anything quite like that echoing, eerie emptiness of a school

295

at five-to-four on a Friday afternoon. I jog past abandoned classrooms, my ears keen for a teacher's step or a cleaner's trolley. I have to be fast now. You told me how he hovers late on a Friday, unloading the kiln, placing pottery projects in the drying room.

And this is where I find him.

"Hello, Mr Denman."

Your old art teacher jumps, his claw-like hand sweeping across a drying shelf, knocking red clay bowls to the floor, where they shatter like fragments of frozen blood. He turns to me, breathing hard.

"Dylan, what the hell? You don't just come into a room like this without warning. Look at the mess. Who's going to—"

"Clean it up?" I shrug. "I don't know."

His gaze cuts from the shattered fragments to my eyes. Maybe he sees something there. Anyway, he gives this tremulous little smile and I wonder how I ever thought he was attractive. Slowly, I move across to him and place my hand on his arm. Touching this man, being anywhere near him, makes my skin crawl, but I force myself to lean into him, my lips close to his ear.

"I've been thinking about your offer, Mr Denman."

"Wh-what offer?" he says.

I pull back and smile. "Coffee. And a chat. About how I'm feeling? About Ellis." A tiny bubble of saliva foams at

296

the corner of his mouth. I should be afraid. I'm not. "Maybe we could take our drinks up onto the roof?"

He swallows hard. Hesitates. "Yes, of course. Coffee. I keep my own private stash in my office. Special blend. Teachers are notorious when it comes to stealing each other's coffee. It'll only take a second to brew."

He squeezes past me and I let my hand trail across his lopsided shoulders. That accident at Christmas? It *really* did a number on him. At the door, Denman looks back.

"But why the roof? You know it isn't allowed."

"It's private," I say, leaning as casually as I can against one of the drying shelves. "El and I used to sneak up there all the time. And I'd like to talk to you where no one can overhear us. You see, Mr Denman, there's something that's been worrying me. About El. About what happened to him last December. I really think you'd be interested in hearing what I have to say."

"Of course." He gives a sharp nod. "Of course. I understand perfectly. Be right back."

I follow him, quietly, discreetly, none of my usual Dylan-clumsiness. Through a crack in the office door, I see what he puts into my coffee, then head back to the drying room where I wait. And although I don't know what exactly will come next, I feel strangely serene.

When Denman returns, I reach for the mug in his outstretched hand, making sure my gaze doesn't linger on that dark, swirling surface. The drying room is at the back of the largest art studio, miles from the rest of the school. No one sees us as we head to the stairs, steaming cups cradled in our hands.

I lead the way. As we go, I try to shut out the memories of the last time I mounted these steps. You were with me then, and everything in my life had seemed sweet and perfect. Now when I push through the door marked *ROOF ACCESS*, all I sense is the steady tread of darkness behind me.

The metal door opens and a wash of daylight floods my face. I pull down a huge breath. The door slams shut behind us. Crossing the flat roof, I give in to this single, shining memory of you:

A tartan blanket thrown over the gravel at the very edge of the roof. Our view is the football pitch, scene of a hundred Ellis Bell victories, the trees swaying gently beyond. You unpacking the hamper, me complaining about the food. What even is quinoa? *The setting sun in your hair, gold rippling in a black and shining sea. A hand, a touch, our mouths pressed together, eyes closed, hearts in sync, the cherry of your lip balm on my tongue.*

"Forever's a long time, Frecks."

It's a memory, an echo, a romcom acted out in my brain. It has no weight or reality or value to anyone else, but in this moment I will treasure it. Stay with me, El. I need you now.

Moving to the edge of the roof, I place my cup on the shallow parapet. There's a snap of gravel behind me; Denman approaching.

"We were happy here," I tell him, my eyes skirting the distant trees. "The night before he died, we were so happy."

And then I reach into my jacket and take out the drawing from my inner pocket. I know what's sketched on this sheet, I don't have to look at it again. It's an image that won't leave me while my heart still beats. Turning, I hold it up to Denman.

22

"The last time we met I felt really sorry for you," I tell him. "There you were, scrabbling around on the floor for your precious bits of charcoal. *Poor Mr Denman*, I thought. *What shitty luck he had with that hit-and-run over Christmas.* Your recovery must have been very slow and painful, sir; over three months before you could come back to school. But what I didn't realize until today was that El never uttered a word of sympathy for you, even though before the holidays he was your favourite pupil and you were his favourite teacher. I must admit, I used to get a bit jealous sometimes."

The art teacher has stopped dead, his coffee mug dangling from his finger. His eyes are rooted on your drawing, El. A nerve jumps in his neck and he passes his tongue over his teeth.

"Yeah, El was a great tease," I continue. *"Don't you think Mr D has the cutest bangs? Have you seen Mr D's eyes?*

You could just drown *in them. But that's all it was. Teasing.
Problem is, I don't think you understood that. Well…"
I shrug. "Even if you did, you didn't care."

"What is this?" Denman laughs.

"It's the truth. Or as much of it as El could ever face.
You raped him."

He jabs a finger at the unidentifiable figure lurking
behind the sculpture. "You think that proves something?
I mean, I don't even know what that's supposed to be. Look,"
he draws his hand across his mouth, "you have to understand,
Dylan, Ellis always had a very vivid imagination. It was a
wonderful thing. But…but obviously it could get the better
of him."

I start to refold the drawing, replacing it in my pocket.
"So you're saying he made this up?"

"Well…" Denman juts his chin at me. "It isn't true,
that's all I know. I mean, whatever it's supposed to represent,
it isn't real. Now listen, if you leave here right now we can
forget this ever happened. I won't tell anyone what you've
said today, I swear."

I stare at him. "But why wouldn't you, if the drawing's a
lie? I've just accused you of a serious crime, Mr Denman.
That must mean I'm dangerously deluded. *If* the drawing's
a lie."

"I feel sorry for you." He tries on a shivery smile that
doesn't reach his eyes. "It's awful, what you've been through.

Watching the boy you love drown. Blaming yourself for not being strong enough to save him. That's what you've been thinking, isn't it? All that guilt, Dylan, it's bound to have an effect."

I won't listen to this. I change tack.

"You know something, sir?" I give him a long up-and-down look. "You really are an *awful* mess. Remind me, how did you get so spectacularly fucked-up in the first place? Crossing the road, wasn't it? Hit-and-run? Did they ever find the driver?"

"Dylan, listen…"

"Listen? Did *you* listen when El begged you to stop?" I've had enough. It's time to end this bullshit. "I agree, the drawing proves nothing. It's too abstract, too vague to ever stand up in court. But the coffee you just gave me? What exactly is in your special blend, Mr Denman?"

His gaze darts to the mug resting on the low parapet.

"I think the police will be interested in the contents of that cup, don't you?"

He threads his fingers together until his knuckles stand out, sharp and white. "There's nothing distinctive about that mug," he says. "Nothing to connect it directly to me."

"Isn't there?"

Reaching into my trouser pocket, I take out my phone and show him the screen. A red circle flashes and a counter marks the thirteenth minute of the recording. "I started

302

this just before I entered the school," I tell him. "It's being automatically uploaded to a file-hosting service. The recording will cover our entire conversation up to this second, including your offer of coffee. And when the police analyse whatever's in that cup? Well, I think that'll be enough to put you under suspicion for at least the attempted rape of a student. Then the police will probably get a warrant to search your house. I wonder what they'll find there?"

You used to love my klutziness, El, but I think you might have been even prouder of my lack of it now.

"Tell me about your accident," I say. He stares back at me, his clear blue eyes as black as ink in the failing light. "It wasn't a hit-and-run, was it? Ellis came for you. He spent a week trying to recover from what you'd done to him, shutting out the world and everyone who loved him, but then, slowly, gradually, he began to re-emerge. El was never really the same again. I can see that now. Something was taken away from him that night, but you couldn't eclipse him. Not totally. He was just too strong for you. Too bold and proud and brilliant. He came back to the world. Back to me. But before he could, he had to reclaim some of that power you'd stolen from him."

For a second it looks like he's going to start protesting again. But then his gaze shifts back to the coffee cup and something new enters his tone.

"Outside my house," he says slowly. "He waited outside my house. New Year's Day. It was still dark. I had to let my cat out and when I opened the door, he…"

"I know what he did to you," I say. "I can see it."

"He said he wouldn't go to the police," Denman says. "That they'd never believe someone like him. But he told me never to come back to Ferrivale High. That if I did…" He runs his good hand over that crooked claw. "So I stayed away as long as I could. I tried to respect his wishes."

"You fucking liar," I spit back at him. "You stayed away because you're a coward."

"But I had to come back," he insists. "In the end, I had to. Because of my contract. Even if I wanted to go to another school, I needed to work out my notice. I had to live, Dylan. I had to work."

"And your first day back was the day of the Easter dance. El didn't see you until then because we'd taken the day off after Ollie's video hit the internet. He had no idea you were back until he spotted you with the other teachers in the gym."

I flash to you in the car, perfect pink lips trembling, your gaze flicking to the gym doors again and again. In those brief moments you couldn't bear for me to touch you because my touch, any touch, would remind you of his.

I get it now. My own flashbacks have haunted me since the lake; I know how these trauma triggers work. Seeing

Denman set you off, and although you had reclaimed so much of yourself since Christmas, just that glimpse of your abuser regressed you into a living nightmare. Your self-control, your amazing jackknife ability to shift your mood, pulled you back to me, but I wonder how long that would have lasted, if you'd lived.

"I thought he might have recovered," Denman says. "Forgiven me, I don't know. But that look he gave me? So frightened and hateful."

"But it didn't stop there, did it?" I say. "You knew from that look that Ellis would never forget or forgive. And so when we left the dance you followed us in your own car. Maybe you thought you could talk to him, get him to see things your way? But then fate gave you the sweetest chance. You saw us go off the road. You saw the car go into the lake. Your first instinct was to save us. You ran down to the shore, waded in, dragged me out. There was still time to save El, and you were halfway back to the car when you realized what an opportunity this was. El drowns, your problem disappears. You can go on teaching at the school, the hero who rescued at least one dying kid. Except you'd then have to explain why you were following us in the first place. Might lead to awkward questions. And so you just stood there and watched the car sink, taking your secret with it."

"No." He shakes his head. "I didn't follow you. I didn't

305

let him die. I'm not a monster. And I have witnesses. Everyone will tell you I stayed at the dance."

"It was you," I say. "It had to be. You had the most to lose if El lived."

"I swear to you, it wasn't."

"You're full of shit."

But now he's making excuses. He starts to blather, telling me he'd been suffering from depression for months leading up to that day; his partner of five years had left him the week before; he'd been put on these mind-altering meds by his doctor and wasn't thinking straight. In fact, when he looks back to that night and imagines the person who did those awful things, it doesn't seem like him at all.

He takes a step towards me, hand outstretched, almost pleading.

"You know what Ellis was like, Dylan. He was always so provocative, wasn't he?"

I step back.

"Always teasing, always flirting."

I don't want this man anywhere near me.

"And you know something else?"

Denman's lip curls. The coffee cup falls from his hand.

"Deep down, he *wanted* it."

Suddenly he's lunging at me, an awkward, loping thrust. That same unreadable face from your drawing has fallen like a mask over his features. He darts past me, kicks at the coffee cup on the parapet, sends it flying. I turn too late and watch the dark liquid arc into the air. Seconds later, there's the crack of cheap china on the concrete below.

In the next moment, Denman's good hand, surprisingly powerful, is shunting me backwards. My heels hit the parapet. I grasp at his face, try to tear the skin, but his attack has unbalanced me and I'm finding it difficult to breathe. Meanwhile he grabs my phone with his bad hand and sends it skipping across the rooftop.

He shoves again and the soles of my trainers teeter on the precipice. Grabbing my shirt with that strong right hand – a sculptor's hand, used to moulding tough clay – he wraps his fist around the material and pivots me over the drop. My arms windmill. I hear trees rustle and the breeze snatches at my hair. I know if I fight him now, if I startle or hurt him in any way, he'll let me fall.

His face swims before me, blank and hideous. I don't want this to be the last thing I see. And so I close my eyes and let memories play in the dark. Not the horror show of the lake, but all the small and beautiful moments that were ours: a bonfire, a bookshop, a library, a bedroom:

Fingers trace the bridge of freckles across my nose.

"Who's going to be first to sign my petition?"

Like electricity moving across my face.

"Friends until our dying day."

The sweetness of your fingers.

"Be seeing you, adorable Frecks."

Starburst-sweetness.

"Are you my boyfriend, Ellis?"

I stare out across the spaces between us.

"He wanted it," Denman insists, invading my thoughts. "They pretend they don't, but they always want it, in the end. I don't even have to drug their drinks. Knew I didn't have to with him anyway. As soon as I started, he wouldn't struggle. And he didn't, because he *wanted it.*"

"He didn't want it," I gasp. "He was scared. Traumatized by what you were doing to him. But he came for you later, didn't he? When he was Ellis again, he came for you."

Denman extends his arm and I pivot further over the edge. I don't want to, but I have to open my eyes. I need to see that he understands this.

"Whatever happened that night at the lake, I want you to know that you killed Ellis."

Movement behind Denman. The gentle opening of a door. I drag my eyes back to his; I keep him focused.

"You took a part of him. And although he was brave and clever and wonderful, he could never drag that part back into the light. I want you to remember that."

Denman's expression is impassive. No anger, no outrage, no lust. Just the deadness that I'm sure lies at the heart of him.

"I'm not a killer." Tears swim in his eyes – pity, but only for himself. "I never wanted to hurt anyone. But I have my life, my job. Even my partner's come back to me. Felt sorry for me after my accident. I can't lose these things, Dylan. I won't." His grip on me begins to loosen. "I don't believe you're uploading that file, and even if you are, I'll delete it before anyone finds it. So here we are. Do you know what everyone's going to think happened here today?" A bead of sweat trickles down his brow as he strains to hold me. "They'll say you jumped. Why wouldn't they? Such a sad and damaged little boy. What else was there left for him but this?"

"There's justice," I say. "Justice for El."

A thick arm loops around his neck and Denman screams. In the next moment, he's released me and I'm falling backwards. I grab at the air, frantic, because I want to live, El. I do. Even if it's without you.

And then a hand snatches mine and I'm reeled away

from the brink and onto the hard shingle of the rooftop. I fall with my rescuer, sprawling into him, knocking heads with him, then resting, face to face, breathing hard.

"Dylan!" Hands in my hair, hands cupping the back of my head, pulling me close. "Jesus, Dylan!"

Sprawled together, I lock eyes with Mike. He's laughing hysterically and I can feel his heart slamming against my chest.

"You stupid, *stupid* prick," he says. "Why didn't you tell me?"

We rise together and watch as police swarm the rooftop. One officer shouts at Mike, reminding him that he was told to stay downstairs. Meanwhile Denman is face down in the gravel, a burly constable wrenching his arms behind his back and fitting the cuffs. His pale, sweat-soaked face turns sideways and the art teacher looks across at me, that emotionless mask firmly in place.

Suddenly I recognize the officer snapping the handcuffs. It's PC Shit-for-Brains from the hospital and the cycle-safety assembly. He gives me a knowing grimace and a very official shake of the head. Another officer collects my phone from where it landed and I find myself babbling some explanation about the recorded confession.

Then a team of paramedics come over and Mike and I are separated. They guide me gently downstairs to an ambulance and I sit in the back, answering questions in a dull monotone. Through the open doors I see your rapist escorted to a waiting car. I won't look at him. He's nothing now. Meaningless.

And anyway, there's another question that I'm only just starting to turn over in my mind.

It's the last question of all, and for once, I'm not sure I want to know the answer.

23

We sit side by side on our old swings in the Berringtons' garden. Above us, through shreds of cloud, the moon rides high.

It's been an hour since we got back from the police station. Our parents met us there after Denman's arrest and stayed with us while we gave our statements. The inspector who interviewed me said they'd retrieved the audio file from my phone and that, together with El's drawing, the fragments of coffee cup (which should retain trace amounts of Denman's sedative), and the fact that Denman was caught red-handed attacking me, a conviction for rape and attempted murder is pretty much certain. When I heard this I knew I should feel elated, but all I could do was nod and thank him.

After we left the station my parents begged me to come home. I told them, very gently, that I wasn't ready yet. That

I might never be ready. My mum kissed my cheek and my dad said he understood.

And so here we are. After fussing around us and receiving a hundred reassurances that we're okay, Big Mike and Carol have gone to bed and we're alone.

Now it's just me and Mike, facing truths that neither us want to face.

"There are still things that don't fit," I say at last. "Like, why did the journal-sender leave that page until last? Okay, it was an abstract drawing, he probably didn't know what it meant, but it also hinted that something awful might have happened to El. Something worse than in any of the other drawings. So why not send this one first?"

I grip the creaking rope that holds my swing to the tree.

"Mike, when you called the police, what did you know?"

I turn to him. He has his head in his hands. His shoulders tremble. I reach for him and he pushes me away. When he finally looks at me, I know what he's going to say. We've always been like that, me and Mike.

"It was me, Dylan. I let Ellis drown. It was me."

I know it's true but still I try to resist it.

"You had chemo that day." I shake my head. "You were still at the hospital when I called you from the dance. You'd have been chucking your guts up, there's just no way."

"My chemo was cancelled," he says. "Something went

wrong with the hospital's IT and all their routine appointments were called off for the day."

Suddenly I remember the nurse who glued my head together. The gentle nurse complaining about the cyberattack and how all non-emergency treatments had been abandoned. And then that conversation with Mike in which he never actually said he'd been hooked up: *"Yeah, today was all kinds of mad… I'll tell you all about it later. Might make you smile or maybe burst a vessel."* And then Carol saying something about Mike not being as far on with his treatment as he should be, because the last cycle had to be rescheduled?

"After I spoke to you, I took Becks for a walk," he says, getting slowly to his feet. "We'd spent half the day in the chemo suite waiting for nothing. It was draining, you know? You build yourself up to face it and then some lonely little dweeb in a basement sends out a virus and you're back to square one. Waiting. Dreading. So we got home late and I just needed a bit of space away from my folks. The looks, the sympathy, the tiptoeing around me…it was like I couldn't breathe."

I can see him pulling on his hoodie, taking Becks's leash from the hook by the door…

Carol asks if he'd like some company, Big Mike tells him to remember his gloves. Then the driveway, and Becks straining at his collar. Mike takes them on a winding tour through the woods, Becks snuffling out their path, Mike crunching slowly behind. The fresh air feels good against his skin, raw and real, not like the clinical, filtered air of the hospital. The dog keeps up a frantic pace, never tiring, and that suits Mike just fine. He has a million thoughts racing around in his head – concern for his best friend, anger at the video someone posted of Dylan and El, frustration that he isn't another step along his road, and always the constant fear that that road might not be as long as everyone has promised.

He's tiring. His heart is full. He thinks back to the conversation with Dylan. He's not fooled by his best friend's upbeat vibe. He knows the McKees and doesn't believe that their acceptance of Dylan's relationship with Ellis will stand the test of time. He starts to stumble over the uneven forest floor and decides to take Becks off the leash. Let the mutt run free. Lost in his fears, he doesn't realize how far they've traipsed through the wood nor how close they are to the lake road.

Before he can call him back, Becks explodes through the trees.

A white blur, a dashing comet on the road.

He reaches the treeline just in time to see a car swerve across the tarmac. He stands frozen. All he can do is watch as the Nissan tumbles, smashing and reshaping itself as it hurtles down the incline towards Hunter's Lake. He knows the car. He wants to move. He can't. A frightened, whimpering Becks dashes back and twines around his legs, glimmering upturned *eyes full of guilt. It takes a small nip at his fingertips for Mike to come round.*

He starts to run.

"You know the rest," he says.

"No," I tell him quietly. "I don't."

"Are you going to make me say it?"

"I think you need to. For both of us."

"I got you out. I dragged you out of there and I tried to go back. I did, Dylan. I tried. But I couldn't." It's then that he breaks, roaring, slamming his palms against his chest. "Because I'm weak and I'm tired and I'm fucked! I wasn't strong enough to save him."

"Why didn't you just tell me?" I shout back at him. "I'd have understood."

"No. No, you wouldn't. Not then. Because you want to know the truth, Dylan? If El had been in the passenger seat and I'd saved him first, I would have found the strength from somewhere to get *you* out. I'd have killed myself trying anyway. But honestly? I didn't love him as much as I love you. I couldn't find that last bit of strength and courage and I wasn't willing to die for him. I just wasn't. And I knew that you would never forgive me for leaving him." He takes a breath, then plunges on. "And I thought maybe it'd be worse even than that."

"What do you mean?" I ask, not wanting to know, but needing to.

"Maybe you'd think I left him on purpose. Because he came along at the time I needed you most and he took you from me."

"Is that really what you felt?"

"No, Dylan. But it might have been what *you* thought, if you knew I hadn't saved him. And I just couldn't bear you thinking something like that."

He reaches into his coat and brings out your leather-bound journal.

"When I heard the sirens, I crawled back into the woods. I could hardly stand at that point, but I managed it. And then I saw this, caught in the bushes. I took it on impulse, something I could give you later to remember Ellis by. But then afterwards, I couldn't think how to do it without you getting suspicious. And then we had that moment after the funeral, in the memorial garden. I could see it in your eyes, Dylan. You wouldn't ever let it rest. You had to find these people who you held responsible for El's death."

He passes a hand over his face and casts a look at the starless sky. "I could feel this hatred coming off you. For your rescuer. For me. I was scared, Dylan. I couldn't lose you. Not now, when I need you most."

"So you decided to use the journal to implicate other people. I thought the journal-sender was a friend trying to help me, but you used those pages to keep me guessing.

And you what? Just pretended to see that mysterious person in the garden?"

He nods. "It all sounds so calculated, like it was some big plan, but it wasn't, I swear. All through this insane week, it was just me desperately improvising, clutching at any possibility to keep you from the truth. Me getting more scared and more stupid and more desperate every time you came close. At first, I tried to talk you out of the whole thing. Even tried to play up the idea of the survivor's guilt theory. But straight away I could see you'd never buy that. 'I'm not letting this go, Mike. I won't ever stop.' That's what you said. And so I used the journal. It made me sick, doing it, and with every page I sent, I hated myself more and more." He covers his face with his hands. "God, Dylan, I didn't know what to do."

"But you'd read the journal. You must have guessed from that last drawing that something bad had happened to El. Why didn't you send that page first?"

"I didn't know what it meant. Didn't even know if it represented anything real. But it was the most powerful image in the book and I just...I felt the darkness in it, Dylan. I didn't want to show you that darkness unless I had to." He shakes his head. "But then last night, what you said about us all being responsible. It's true. All of us, in our own way, are responsible. We rejected El or wished he was different or wanted to make him in our image. And that isn't me trying to get out of my responsibility. Me and Denman, we hurt him most. But last night you said again that you had to know. That it was killing you. And, Dylan, it was. I could see it. If there was some truth you could get out of that last picture, I didn't have the right to keep it from you. So I sent the page. Jesus, I'm so fucking stupid!"

"But you always knew." I nod. "When you said at Hinchcliffes that it wasn't me that caused Ellis to go off the rails at Christmas. You'd read the journal. You guessed something must have happened to him."

I get up from the swing and approach him. He flinches at my touch.

"I was so scared," he says. "So scared and so ashamed. And so I did these things, these *mad* things I'd never have thought I could ever do, all because I was terrified of losing my friend. My friend who sits with me in the hospital and makes me laugh. My friend who rubs my back when I'm puking my guts up. My friend who saves me every day and doesn't even know it. I couldn't lose him. And so I betrayed you, Dylan, and I'm…" His voice cracks. "I'm so sorry."

"I know you are."

"Dylan…" He's sobbing now, his face shining with tears, his poor body shaking. "Dylan, I can't love you like Ellis did, but I *do* love you. So much. You're my brother, my best friend. But I also know, after what I've done, things won't ever be the same between us. And I can accept that. I can.

I just hope…" He presses his hands together. "Dylan, please. Just *please* don't hate me."

"Mike?"

I wait until he turns to face me.

And then I don't hesitate.

I pull my best friend into the fiercest hug.

NOW: Wednesday 15th July

24

It's still Year One, Anno El, but three months since he died. I'm standing on the shingled shore, feeding mouldy bread to a very dysfunctional family of ducks. The father's strutting about and the big brother seems to be a crumb-stealing jerk but the mother still fusses over him. The youngest, meanwhile, is doing his own thing at the waterline. I wonder if he's into dude ducks, but I guess that would be stretching a ridiculous comparison too far.

Looking down, I brush the crumbs off Ellis's old yellow shirt. I talked to my therapist about vacuum-sealing it to keep the El smell alive, but I decided you can't hold onto things like that. Maybe I'll remember his smell forever, maybe it'll fade over time, and maybe I'll be pottering around in the library's large-print section sixty years from now and two kids will wander by, laughing and hugging, and I'll catch the ghost of it again. Who knows?

Another therapy decision: helping Julia pack up his room. She told me I could take whatever I wanted and I chose a drawing or two, and these I *will* preserve as best I can. Not just because they're memories, but because I will show them to the people I love and the people I'll come to love and I'll say, *This was who he was. This was my Ellis.*

The ducks scatter and I kneel down and unzip my backpack. This is the last time I'll talk to him, at least for a while. It's a deal I've made with Dr Rosenthal. So here goes:

I think you'd like her, El. She's quiet and listens and sits on the floor with me while we talk. We even share a packet of Starburst every now and then. But don't get big-headed, we don't just talk about you. We talk about how it's going at my rented place and how Mum and Dad pop round for a cup of tea and a chat every Thursday. We've kept it weekly because it's hard, rebuilding trust, and baby steps are best. Anyway, up until last month I was buried under catch-up essays and exam prep, so I didn't have time to see much of anyone.

Mr Morris has been amazing. I think he practically had a heart attack when I called the school and asked if I could at least try to get back on track with my A levels. Mr Robarts was wary, especially after the police officer/assembly showdown, but – get ready to piss your pants laughing – it was the Grand High Dementor herself who defended me. Yup, Miss Harper went into battle on my behalf, taking on all-comers, slaying every opponent with a single glare. I think she did it for you, El, but I'm grateful just the same.

So, yeah, university in September, *if* I've passed my exams. And I'm going into halls. I don't think I could afford a flat all by myself, and anyway, starting a new life as the weird Billy-no-mates is not a way to meet friends and influence people. And I want to meet new people, El. I really do. So I'm thinking of signing up for theatre club (I know, I'm bound to trip over a spear-carrier or whatever) and I'm going to enrol with the LGBTQ+ Society. I wonder if the spear-carrier will be cute and klutz-friendly, like you? A boy can dream, right?

Only one thing will interrupt my first term at uni. Sometime in October I'll be required to give evidence at Denman's trial. He hasn't confessed. I didn't think he would. It's not a monster's style to make things easy for its victims. Not that it matters – the police have more than enough evidence against him, and since his arrest, other students have come forward with their own stories. Kids from Ferrivale High and from a school where Denman taught previously. Their testimonies have added to the prosecution case, and maybe even more importantly, they're now getting help to deal with what happened to them.

Okay, El, I want you to know something: in all this moving on, I'm not leaving you behind. I don't think I'd be able to do that even if I tried, and Dr Rosenthal agrees. I'll always carry you with me. My first love, perhaps my best, maybe my only, who can say? All I know is that you sketched out a place in my heart and there you will stay, bold and strong and indelible. You changed me; you made me braver and better than I ever thought I could be. For that alone, I'll never forget you.

I squat beside you for a moment now, my head resting against you. It's almost time. But, oh yeah, one more thing to make you smile: Chris has come out as bi. Yep, seems you really were onto something with that infallible gaydar of yours. He's just started seeing his new boyfriend, Zac, the pedicurist from Mum's favourite beauty salon. Honestly, El, I hate to say it, but they're even a little bit adorable together. Anyway, I think that's pretty much all my news.

From behind me I can hear George Ezra singing "Pretty Shining People". I turn and smile up at Mike and Ollie, Mike carrying his dad's old boom box down to the shore. Ollie gives me this sheepish grin. I don't know. Yes, he did a shitty thing, but we're all human and we all do shitty things to each other all the time. Anyway, we've talked and, although we'll never be best buds, I can't carry around all this hate. And that's not Dr Rosenthal talking, that's just my own brilliant insight.

The same goes for Mike. He's doing okay, by the way. His chemo's finally finished and he's starting his final year again just before I head off to Bristol. He's already planning a couple of weekend visits and has made me promise to find him a LGBTQ+ Society Alliance straight girl who has a thing for footie boys with buzz cuts. I watch him bounce down the incline, chatting away to Ollie, and I send up a prayer, for what it's worth. There are no guarantees, I know that now, but there's hope, right? That's the one wildcard the universe lets us hold onto.

"Hey, Bumboy," he says, cuffing my head.

"Mike, I gotta say, that is a bit homophobic," says Ollie.

"Oh, get over yourself. Just because you're now all out and proud, it doesn't mean you get a say over my and Dylan's perfectly harmless nicknames."

He nudges Ollie with his hip and starts singing along with George. I squint. Mike's singing has this nails-on-a-blackboard quality. It really is something special. I bump fists with Ollie and ask if Mumzilla and Big Mike are in position.

"They're on the spot. I told Dad it was totally illegal and he's really excited. Mum said she's waiting in the car in case a quick getaway is required."

"And you're sure about this? Mike, it's all the money Gemma gave you from the Easter dance."

"Correction: the Dipshits Ball. And I can't think of a better way to spend it."

"Seconded," says Ollie.

"Okay then."

I lift your urn out of my bag and hand it to Ollie. He holds it like a sacred object, which I guess it is.

"I'll take care of him, Dylan."

Me and Mike watch him head back up the incline to where he's left his car.

"He's not a bad kid," Mike says.

"He's a spectacular moron." I smile. "But no, he's okay."

We don't discuss our next move, but the psychic link of the Incredible Twat Brothers holds true, and as one we sit cross-legged on the grass and wait. On the far side of the lake the last spears of sunlight are pricking the water. The McKee family ducks are gliding towards a fringe of trees, kid-brother duck a little apart, of course. It's quiet now. Families are packing up their picnics and heading home. Mike leans into me as I dig a yellow sheet from my pocket and unfold it, holding my image up to the sunset. I don't feel embarrassed or ashamed. This was how you saw me, El, a guardian to watch over you as you slept.

"He was pretty amazing, wasn't he?" Mike says.

"He was." I shift a little and put my arm around my best friend. "He said once that Art is a wonderful lie we tell ourselves so we can bear the truth. But El wasn't right all the time. He saw more truth than anyone I've ever known."

The sun vanishes.

I grab Mike's hand.

And in the next moment the sky's ablaze. You'd describe what we're seeing in a thousand beautiful ways, El, picking out every shade of every changing colour of every firework, and I can kind of hear you anyway, but it's not the same, because my imaginary El will never be a match for the real thing. So I just lean back on my hands and watch and wonder which fantastic, fabulous flare is yours. I told Julia what we planned and she said she'd be watching from her balcony at Mount Pleasant. I'm sure she's smiling and crying now as we turn your ashes into a starburst firework, a final roar and crack and dazzle from the boy I loved.

Mike stands and pats my shoulder, giving me a minute as the sky fades to black.

It's time to move on. Because that's what you'd want for me. And it's what I want for myself. But I've learned now there are no real goodbyes. I will always keep coming back to you and I will always be thankful for the truths you showed me.

I pick up my empty bag and walk with Mike into the trees.

THEN: Wednesday 1st April

(The night before the Easter Dance)

The Picnic

"So I was talking to Ollie Reynolds," I say, treating El to a mischievous grin, "and he says that most people think George Ezra is not even the slightest bit cool."

El throws his head back and takes a huge breath through his nose. His nostrils arch like he's been caught in the downdraught of one of Mr Robarts's epic accidental farts. Honestly, our headmaster seriously needs to get his bowels checked out.

"Ollie knows nothing." El tries to smile but his eyes cut away from me.

"Hey," I say, waddling forward on my knees. The gravel on the rooftop makes me wince. It still seems an odd place for a picnic, but I guess that's my boyfriend all over. "Something up?"

He grins and brushes my cheek. "Something's always up when you're around, Frecks. Anyway, that philistine

Reynolds is wrong. George is achingly cool because I say he is."

"And you're what? Her Majesty's Arbiter of Coolness?"

"Can you think of a better candidate?"

Truly, I can't, so I shut up.

"Coolness is in the eye of the beholder. George is cool. The calves of the England men's volleyball team are cool. Dylan McKee is *very* cool. So sayeth the Arbiter. Now shut up and help me unpack this thing."

I squat down beside him and we start taking supplies out of this huge wicker hamper. After the fourth suspiciously green package, I rock back onto the tartan blanket.

"Is there anything here that's not *not* heavily processed?"

"Sorry, Frecks, I was catering with the hope that I wouldn't have to roll you back down the stairs. We aren't really supposed to be up here, and I'm not sure I can stealthily evacuate you if you're chomping a burger mid-heart attack."

"Okay, but quinoa?" I stick out my tongue and El pinches it between his thumb and forefinger. "Wha h'even h'is kwweeen-wuh?"

He releases my tongue and kisses my nose. "Some things must remain a mystery. File quinoa away with the Loch Ness Monster and the popularity of the *Pirates of the Caribbean* movies." El sits cross-legged and prepares me this ridiculously horticultural sandwich, which he stuffs into my mouth before I can protest. I hate to admit it, but it actually tastes pretty good.

"So." He smiles. "The Easter dance."

"No way!" I glare at him. Then, in case I haven't been completely clear: "No *fucking* way."

El pouts. He loves to dance. I'd love to dance if I danced like him, but I don't, so I don't.

"What if…?"

I hold up my half-eaten plant burger. "Ellis, I swear, there is no bribe that you can invent that will persuade me to attend what Mike and I have long-dubbed the Dipshits Ball."

"What if I re-enacted our driving lesson from the supermarket car park?"

It's tempting, but… "No. I still have the gearstick bruise on my arse."

"Then what if I tickled you in that place you like? For an hour."

I open my mouth then shut it again. Crap. He's good at this. But…

"No deal. Anyway, I'm not ticklish down there any more."

"Then what if I…?"

He leans in and whispers in my ear.

I drop the sandwich.

"You are a very evil temptress, Ellis Maximillian Bell."

"I know."

Afterwards, El tells me I've cheated. I've allowed myself

to be pleasured by a master at the absolute pinnacle of his powers (and, seriously, I can't argue with that) but I still won't promise him we can go to the dance tomorrow. I tell him that he is a skilful lover but a poor negotiator. He ought to have secured my agreement before giving me a sample of his wares. If he wishes to present his case again for the Dipshits Ball, well, I will consider any new proposal he has to offer. He laughs and snuggles his head into the crook of my shoulder.

We stay like that for a while. At some point during El's magic-making I thought I'd heard the screech of the rooftop door, but it's quiet now. Anyway, no one's started shrieking about two sixth-formers up on the roof getting busy, so I'm assuming we got away with it. A few lazy blackbirds circle overhead, eyes on my weed burger. We ignore their caws and turn to our second favourite subject: plans for summer and uni.

We rehearse this same conversation every couple of hours. He tells me about the gigs he's excited to attend in July, I tell him about the comic-book convention in August. We then discuss his idea for a mural in our little living room in Bristol and he asks my opinion on the right colours for the bedroom. "The bedroom's your department," I tell him, and he grins. I try to act all nonchalant during these talks, but every time I think about our future together… yup, my stomach flips. So I just lie there on the prickly gravel and listen like an enchanted child to these amazing stories of times yet to come.

Suddenly I roll sideways and kiss him hard.

"Wow! What was that for?"

"For forever," I say.

His eyes cut away. "Forever's a long time, Frecks."

I take his chin and draw him back to me.

"Are you giving up on me already?"

"No way."

"So we'll be together forever then," I tell him, and start to spin my own future histories now. He snuggles in and listens. "There were once these two boys, Ellis and Frecks, and they fitted together so well no one could ever tear them apart. They lived and studied together, and after university they went and found a place for themselves in a huge city where they made new friends and partied hard. But they worked hard too. And after a few years they decided that, although they were totally happy just the two of them, they might have room for some little people." I look at him, because we've never talked about kids and stuff, but he smiles this contented, lazy smile, so I continue. "So one day Ellis and Frecks and their little people all decide that their love is so fucking huge and immense—"

"Shhh," he says. "No swearing in front of the kids."

"I'm sorry. But they all think, *We'd like to show the whole world how special our family is*. So they invite all their family and friends…"

"Aunt Julia," El sighs. "And we buy her an amazing dress."

"And maybe even Chris." I nod.

"If we must."

"But before the invites are sent out—"

"Designed by me, with the little guys's handprints on them, like butterflies."

"Ellis, who's telling this story?"

"I'm sorry, Prof. Please continue."

"That's better. So before these very cute invites are sent out, Dylan gets in his car, which isn't that great a car because he's only on a history teacher's salary—"

"But I'm a famous artist by then, exhibiting at The Prado and The Met, and so I buy you a Bentley and… I'm sorry, go on," he giggles.

"Okay. I get in my Bentley and drive all the way across the country to this perfect little village, where Mr Michael Berrington lives with his beautiful wife Anne-Marie and their kids, Little Mike and Even Littler Mike (because we know the Berringtons are pretty awful at thinking up non-Mike names for boys). I take Mike to the pub and, you know, he's absolutely fine. Healthiest he's ever been. In fact, he's now captain of the England footie team." El kisses me again and squeezes my hand. "And I ask him to be my best man."

"The *best* best man." El nods.

"And then it's our day. We're on this amazing beach somewhere abroad. And the vicar, who's Spanish or something, accidentally makes us laugh by gesturing at the sand and saying, 'Just look at dis beautiful beetch!' But he ends up pointing to Gemma Argyle, who's our bridesmaid."

"No fucking way!" El says.

"Shhh," I tell him, "the kids."

"Sorry, Little Frecks and Little Julia. But no way is Gemma there."

"Okay, no Gemma. Just us and all the people we love. And the vicar says to you, 'You may kiss the groom.' And he says to me, 'You may kiss the groom.' And we kiss and everyone applauds, and then, because you've been teaching me for the past ten years, we dance."

"What do we dance to?"

"What else?"

El hugs me tight. "George."

"And the years go by," I say, "and the kids grow up and become these amazing people who make us proud. And soon it's just us two again in our little house. I've got my study and you've got your studio, and at the end of every day we snuggle up on a tartan blanket and talk about all the things still ahead of us. And when there's more behind us than ahead, we talk about all our memories and laugh and cry together."

"Dylan?"

"Yeah?"

"You're crying now."

I waggle his chin. "So are you."

"I like our story. It's makes me happy. *You* make me happy, Frecks. But how does it end?"

"So," I say, "there were once these two old men. No one could remember the name of the sexier one, they just called him 'Frecks'. Ow! Don't pinch me. It's not my fault the story thinks you're marginally less sexy than me. Anyway, they lived together all their days and the neighbours said it was amazing that, in the distant past, when these two men were boys, one of them had been too scared to admit who he really was. 'Imagine a world like that,' they would say, and shake their heads. It took the brave, kind, brilliant, but slightly less sexy boy to show him the way. And Frecks never once forgot to thank his friend, his partner, his lover, for being that guiding light."

"And then?"

"And then… Who knows? One day the neighbours found the house empty and the two old men gone. And they were never seen again. They just wandered away together, hand in hand."

Ellis looks at me and I look at Ellis.

"That's not how real stories end, Dylan."

"But it should be," I tell him softly. "It should be."

"*Shallow understanding from people of good will is more frustrating than absolute misunderstanding from people of ill will. Lukewarm acceptance is much more bewildering than outright rejection.*"

Martin Luther King Jr.

IF YOU HAVE BEEN AFFECTED BY THE ISSUES RAISED IN THIS BOOK, THE FOLLOWING ORGANIZATIONS CAN HELP:

Samaritans are available round the clock, every single day of the year. You can talk to them any time you like, and in
your own way, about whatever's getting to you.
Call, free, any time, on 116 123 Or email jo@samaritans.org
Find your nearest branch on samaritans.org

The Mix is here to help under 25s get to grips with any challenge they face. Anywhere
and anytime, online, over the phone or via social media.
Helpline: 0808 808 4994   themix.org.uk

The Survivors Trust is the largest umbrella organisation for specialist rape and sexual abuse services in the UK.
The Survivors Trust will help you find support in your area
through their free, confidential helpline 08088 010818,
or you can message them through their website
www.thesurvivorstrust.org/contact

SurvivorsUK support
boys and men who

SURVIVORSUK

have experienced sexual abuse at any time in their lives.
They provide a national web/sms chat, one to one
counselling, telephone counselling, ISVA and groupwork in
London. The organization also supports their families and
carers through provision of helpline and counselling services
and signposts to other organizations nationally. They are an
inclusive service and welcome anyone who identifies as
male, trans, non-binary, has identified as male in the past, or
anyone who feels that SurvivorsUK are the right fit for them.
They support anyone 13+ who has experienced abuse either
as a child or as an adult.

Log on www.survivorsuk.org   Text: 020 3322 1860
Whatsapp: 074 9181 6064   Email: help@survivorsuk.org

Turn the page for a letter from Katherine Cox, clinical
supervisor, counsellor and groupwork co-ordinator
at SurvivorsUK. Katherine has previously worked as
a social worker, and as a therapist in a hospice, an
HIV support organisation, Terence Higgins Trust, Body
& Soul and in secondary schools in the UK.

Hi,

My name is Katherine and I am a counsellor who works with young people and adults who have experienced sexual abuse. I hope you loved **Hideous Beauty** but I also realise it can be a tough read. And it should be a tough read because sexual abuse is, as the title says, hideous.

I'm wondering what you might be feeling. Disbelief, anger, fear. Perhaps you feel weird, unsettled? All feelings are okay.

Has this happened to you or someone you know?

You might be asking yourself all sorts of questions:

Why do people sexually abuse?
How can I look out for myself?
How can I look out for my friends?

The first question is a very big one and, to be honest, I don't know the answers. I think it's very complicated and I guess it's important to remember that the world is full of kind and generous and warmly loving people you can trust as well as some people who you absolutely can't. It's because of that the two other questions become important:

How can I look out for myself?
How can I look out for my friends?

One of the things I hear a lot in the conversations I have with people is that worries, trauma, fears and experiences that we feel ashamed of and unable to talk about, can become bigger and bigger and more unmanageable later on. It can be hard to believe that you can share your worries, but think about everyone in your life and who it is that you feel you can most trust. That's probably the right person to talk to. If there is no one you feel you can trust, there are a number of organisations you can approach confidentially to share your concerns and feelings. You may feel better after you have spoken to a trusted person.

Reading about Ellis may have left you worrying or wondering about somebody you know. Thinking about the way Ellis changes after the sexual abuse might leave you wondering if this has happened to someone you know. Changes in behaviour, irritability, mood swings etc can of course be a result of all sorts of different things, not just sexual abuse, but if you are worried about a friend of yours, see if you can find a way of letting them know that they can talk to you if they want. If that feels too difficult or weird, just making sure you stick with being their friend will make an enormous difference. Dylan stuck with Ellis and that mattered to them both. Again, you can speak confidentially to one of the organisations listed previously if you want to discuss this more without feeling you're betraying your friend.

If you have been abused yourself, please, please remember: it was not your fault. This may sound odd because of course it wasn't, but there is something really hideous about sexual abuse which leaves the person who was abused thinking they encouraged it or they should have stopped it or that in some way it was their responsibility. Sexual abuse is the responsibility of the abuser. Always. If you have been abused yourself, please speak to someone. If you absolutely can't bear at this point for anyone else to know at all, you can call the Samaritans in complete confidence.

Everyone is different and you are unique, just as the people around you are unique, so think about what helps you to manage your life and what it brings. Here are some ideas, but think about what's on your own list:

Do something physically active
Listen to music
Dance
Watch sport
Play a computer game
Write stuff down
Draw or paint

Chat with a friend about something else

Have a long bath

Sing!

Do something practical which requires focus and concentration

And do please remember that speaking about sexual abuse can help destroy the power it can have over someone's life. There are some contact details of some organizations on the previous pages. However, as always,

If you feel you are in immediate danger, call the emergency services.

Remember: you matter, your feelings matter. Your life is important and valuable, and the lives of the people you care about are important too. Do what you need to take care of yourself.

Best wishes,

Katherine

For information about where to find confidential help near you, wherever you are in the world, visit www.helpnearme.info

A letter from the author

Dear Reader

I hope you enjoyed Dylan and El's story.

I know it contained some tear-jerking moments, but one of my reasons for writing this book was to say, despite all the ugliness life can throw at us, there is always hope, and that the people who matter to us – the Mikes and Els of this world – outshine any darkness that threatens to overwhelm us. We just have to hold onto them. Very tightly.

So when I first started writing *Hideous Beauty*, I knew it couldn't just be a (hopefully) cool love story wrapped up in a mystery: it had to say something. To mean something.

When I was a kid growing up in the 90s, you would face a beating or worse if you dared to come out as LGBTQ+. I remember once a kid calling me a "fag" and chasing me down the street after school. The experience terrified me. It kept me locked in the closet for many years. Just the memory of it was enough to keep me awake at night, my heart hammering, fearful that someone would look at me, just look at me, and know.

Although I knew, of course, that our community continued to face violence, I had hoped things had changed in the years since. I at least expected that the daily fear I went through to be a thing of the past. But as an author visiting schools and talking to LGBTQ+ groups about their experiences, I discovered that the old prejudices and their impact hadn't died. It was just that they now sometimes came with a mask of "acceptance". A phony mask and a dangerous one because, as Dylan says to Mike, acceptance can't be conditional. It must be absolute and on the terms of those asking for it or it's not acceptance at all. It must be complete and strong because, once it's tested (and it will be – almost every day) and it breaks then it leaves kids just as vulnerable and at risk as they were in the past.

Interviewing young LGBTQ+ people for the book, I heard many examples of this. Kids whose family and friends appeared to offer them love and acceptance only to withdraw it again when the reality of being LGBTQ+ became too much for them. Obviously, I don't want to go into real examples that were shared with me, but I'll give you two invented scenarios that fit the pattern I heard: a girl identifies as a lesbian until he begins to understand his true identity as a boy and the mother who was fine with her daughter being a lesbian draws the line at him being trans. This young man is thrown out of his home. Or the kid who comes out as gay and the dad who grudgingly accepts him, until Dad catches his son dressing "too flamboyantly". This ends with the kid absorbing his father's loathing so much he retreats away from the wonderful young person he was just starting to become.

You see, coming out is never a one-off thing for LGBTQ+ people. It is ongoing, sometimes even with the people who have already been told. And so, unless you're quite lucky, the original fear and trepidation of taking that immense first step is there on every occasion acceptance is required. It's part of the reason El can't speak about the rape he suffers at the hands of Denman; because sometimes having to unpeel yet another layer of yourself when that's all you've been doing for months – for years – is just too painful.

This fear and this danger are at the heart of *Hideous Beauty* and I want to thank all the brave, compassionate kids who shared their stories with me.

So this is really why I wrote this book; to speak for those teens, and to say that for acceptance to be worth anything it must be total and on the terms of the individual asking for it. I took this message seriously. When researching the book, I had the advice of John Neary, a brilliant psychiatric nurse from CAMHS (Child and Adolescent Mental Health Service) to guide me. Once the book was finished, it was read by Katherine Cox, clinical supervisor, counsellor and groupwork co-ordinator at Survivors UK, who has written a brilliant, insightful letter to you all. They helped to guide me and ensure I handled El's trauma in as sensitive and realistic a way as I could whilst also reflecting the concerns and confusion of the people who loved him.

But as you know, *Hideous Beauty* isn't all darkness. Not a bit! The light and love it contains comes not only from the Berringtons (I mean, who wouldn't want Carol and Big Mike as their surrogate parents?!) and Mike himself – a reflection of so many of my incredible friends (you know who you are, you adorable bunch!) – but also from the flawed and fleeting characters like Ollie Reynolds and Raj. Because none of us is perfect, and not every enlightened soul we encounter stays long in our lives – but just like Dylan with El, we carry them with us and hold their memory out against the darkness.

Lastly, I'd just like to address one other central aspect of the book. First love.

So often young people are told that their first love is unimportant. That it's meaningless. That it is so inconsequential that it barely deserves to be recognized. What do people say? Oh, it's just puppy love, they'll forget all about it by next week. Well, I say, don't ever listen to such unmitigated crap.

First love matters. It matters so much. And sometimes, just sometimes, it can change your life forever.

Acknowledgements

So many people helped me with this book, so please forgive what will probably sound like an Oscar acceptance speech!

As I've already said in my letter, when researching the story, I was lucky enough to speak to many LGBTQ+ school clubs. Particular thanks go to librarian Lorraine Gill at Dereham Neatherd High School and to Dawn Andrew at Lincoln Christ's Hospital School for facilitating conversations with some fabulous students. These kids' insights proved invaluable in creating the characters in *Hideous Beauty* and the dilemmas they face. I would also like to thank Levi Palmer and Bradley Wall for early conversations about their experiences of coming out, intolerance and prejudice.

My undying gratitude goes to three incredible writers and friends who read early drafts of the book – Michelle Harrison, Jo Cotterill and Alex Bell. Their support, encouragement and critiques gave me all the motivation I needed to complete the project (BTW, please buy and read all their books, you won't be sorry!). Apologies to Alex's husband, who found her weeping at the kitchen table one day and thought something awful had happened – she had in fact just reached El's funeral scene! Sorry (sort of not sorry!).

Two other early readers were my friends Dawn Andrew and Deborah Scarrow. Dawn I met through author visits to her school and many a jolly Pride event. Thank you, lovely! Debs, Eternal First Reader, what can I say? I wouldn't even be a published writer without you.

My fantastic agent Veronique Baxter and Laura West at David Higham Associates gave me heaps of encouragement early on. In fact, I only had to outline the idea to Laura and I remember her telling me: You MUST write this! Veronique, thank you, as ever, for supporting me when I'm doubtful and planting my feet firmly on the ground when required. Other fabulous David Higham people who deserve my thanks: Clare Israel, my tireless TV and film rights agent, and Allison Cole who handles my foreign rights. Thank you for all you do!

The most wonderful and surprising thing about the whole *Hideous Beauty* adventure has been the friend I've made along the way. Not only a wise, incisive and generous editor, but one of the warmest, kindest human beings I've ever met. Thank you so much, Stephanie King. I hope we work together on many more books but, most importantly, I'm just glad we've become mates! I've said it before, but editors should get a front page credit for all the work they put into a book. Never has this been more deserved than in Steph's case.

Huge thanks as well to all the amazing people at Usborne who have been so creative and generous with their time and talents: Will Steele – what a cover! You're a genius. Publicity and marketing wizards Kat Jovanovic, Stevie Hopwood and Jacob Dow. Editors Sarah Stewart, Rebecca Hill and Becky Walker and proof-readers Anne Finnis and Gareth Collinson (all errors are mine!) and typesetter Sarah Cronin. Best team in the biz!

Lastly, thank you as ever to my family: Dad, Georgia and Jon, Carly and Jamie, Johnny and Lyla, Jackson and Charly. If only Mum could have been here to read this one.

Next from
WILLIAM HUSSEY

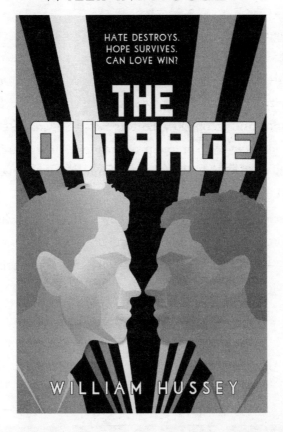

Welcome to England. Here, there are rules for everything.

What to say, what to think, who to hate, who to love.

Your safety is assured, so long as you follow the rules.

Gabriel is a natural born rule-breaker.

And his biggest crime of all? Being gay.

Page-turning and heartbreaking, this is
The Handmaid's Tale for LGBTQ+ YA.

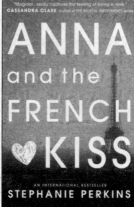
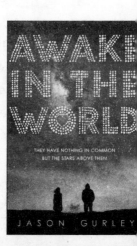